ALARM CRY

A Suspense Novel by

Phillips Huston

ISBN: 1-4107-3165-0 (e-book)
ISBN: 1-4107-3164-2 (Paperback)

Library of Congress Control Number: 2003091755

This book is printed on acid free paper.

Printed in the United States of America
Bloomington, IN

1stBooks - rev. 08/04/03

ACKNOWLEDGMENTS: Many persons made helpful suggestions as the project moved forward. I especially want to thank Thomas Huston, Sarah Truly, and Anne Taussig, for their thoughtful feedback; Don and Barbara Metcalf, for their shrewd suggestions concerning the birding and other nature references; Steven Nguyen and Dale Dibble for invaluable production help; and my editor, Ruthann, for many "catches" and felicitous suggestions over various rewrites and revisions.

Cover art by Norman Small

For Charlie Huston
He good-naturedly tolerated his little brother's
tagging along when he pursued bird study merit badge.
This set the stage for the younger boy's lifelong
interest in the worthwhile activity of watching birds.

Part One

Disappearance

~~ PROLOGUE ~~

With no obtruding hills or towns, with no more than 15 feet variation in elevation for 100 miles, the sun shoots up quickly over the saw grass prairies and tropical forests of interior south Florida. Even where cypress trees tower 120 feet or more, full light soon makes its way through their feathery branches.

A man rejoices at this quick transformation from dove-colored predawn light to full sun. He sets up a tripod and trains a spotting telescope westward on an enormous eagle's nest near the top of a lofty cypress in a dome-shaped cluster of trees, or hammock, 40 yards away. The trees, which rise abruptly from a wet prairie of pinkish, spiky grass and black marsh, increase in size toward the tallest at the center. The nest is near the top of one of the trees that flank the tallest, perhaps 80 feet up.

As he swings his scope upward, the man is temporarily distracted by the petulant whistles of an osprey in rapid, low flight. "Hmmm. A competitor for fish." He is thinking how the raptors might vie for catches in a wild unnamed pond that lies on the other side of the hammock. He makes a mental note to look for the osprey's nest later.

But now that mammoth eagle nest, four or five feet across, consumes his interest. Some of its boughs appear an inch or more thick and splay out at bizarre angles. He adjusts his focus on its owners, two adult bald eagles perched on a branch above their home.

He has recently heard about this nest in a hard-to-reach area, and has wanted to view it even though eagles themselves are no longer rare in south Florida. The bad old days of DDT damage are thankfully history now in 1991, and he can't suppress a moment of pride in remembering how he had lobbied against use of the deforming pesticide back in the 1960s.

Although the man is a well-known birder with upwards of 500 species on his American life list, this isn't part of a listing effort. This is simply the joy of a bird-watcher watching birds. Amidst the orchestra of a dozen songbirds and marsh birds tuning up with an alligator's bellow serving as percussion, he is aware of a human footfall approaching. This doesn't surprise him; he had breakfast a half hour earlier with several other birders, as he regularly did. Their custom is to eat an early breakfast at a remote cafe, then go off singly or in pairs to pursue their separate ornithologic interests. Often they encounter one another in the field before returning to the cafe to talk about the morning's sightings over coffee.

The increasing sunlight is intensifying the brightness of the eagles' white hoods and yellow beaks, so he continues to study the birds, thinking the footsteps probably belong to one of his friends. Or maybe they belong to a couple of somewhat bedraggled but friendly Indian youngsters he had greeted earlier. "Looks like they've been out all night," he had thought.

Finally, the man turned around to acknowledge whoever it was. "Oh, hello…" He recognized the other person.

Hello. That universal greeting may also have been his farewell.

Miss Jean McKay's internal alarm clock awakened her, as it nearly always did, at about quarter to six. As usual it was *carpe diem* for her, so she bounced out of her trailer's narrow built-in bunk a moment or two later. She made her morning ablutions but didn't bother to comb her wispy, dishwater-colored hair. She put a tired house-coat over her thin little body, all 98 1/2 pounds of it, turned on the coffee in the tiny kitchen, and went to check her tape recorder. Bad news; the reels weren't turning although the timer was set to run another 15 minutes.

As part of a research project on bird communication, she was recording the ambient "dawn music," as she called the bird songs and other natural sounds of the awakening day in the remote Florida cypress and pine wetlands that surround the Airstream trailer. Her research centered on communication among different species of birds. She gave an example to her biology students at Oak City Central High before she left for sabbatical in Florida:

"Suppose a hawk swoops into a woodland where songbirds have staked out nesting territories. A resident blue jay decides to play Paul Revere and shrieks his alarm call (and she really shrieked a high-pitched imitative cry, much to the delight of some of her students, to the embarrassment of others). I want to know what are the reactions of other birds as well as the other jays. And how does 'Paul Revere' pitch his warning so as not to give away his own location?"

She was also researching other ways the songs of one species might affect another. If the cardinals tuned up, did that inspire the mockingbirds? Did the first notes of the various species appear in the same sequence every morning? Additionally, she also was comparing slight differences in songs, "Southern accents" she called them, among Florida versions of such familiar northern singers as song sparrows, house wrens, and orioles. Some mornings she ranged out to the shores, waterways, and swamps to record the notes of various species of waterfowl as they partook of avian conversations.

As the project advanced she used her considerable editing skills on the tapes, juxtaposing comparative songs, notes, squawks, warbles, and whistles. She had enlisted her friend Tom Russo, head of the computer sciences department at the high school, in her project. He converted Jean's high-resolution tapes into computer images—sonograms—whose patterns offered visual pictures of frequencies and intervals that even reveal the distinctive voices of individual birds.

The dawn music had sounded more lively than usual when she awakened on this particular morning, and she had looked forward to listening to the tape as she dawdled over her toast and coffee. So the mechanical failure, whatever it was, was especially disappointing. She did what people usually do when an electronic device fails. She flicked the red on/off button several times. She checked the wall plug, took the cord out and reinserted it upside down. Nothing restarted the machine. She looked around to see if other appliances were working; they were. Her electric clock was on time; there'd been no outages during the night.

She concluded that the cause of the malfunction must be outside, perhaps at her parabolic dish receiver or somewhere along the 70 feet of wire that linked the dish and the tape recorder in the trailer. She recalled another mid-recording interruption a few weeks back, and that time she'd found the connecting wire shredded and frayed. She had concluded that a raccoon's curiosity had gotten the better of him and that he had chomped the wire. After that, she had concealed the replacement wire under fallen palmetto fronds.

She grabbed a flashlight and went outside where already the air outside was leaden with humidity. It was spring, and the predawn sun was rapidly spreading a diffuse light through the tall pines and cypresses, but she still needed the torch beam to help locate the wire and to place her footing over the pathless undergrowth. First she examined the exposed stretch of wire where it entered the trailer. Intact. Then she tramped out to the dish and lifted the cover that protected its on/off switch. Of course, it was "on"; otherwise she wouldn't have had the partial recording. Besides, she never turns it off. But she checked it anyway.

Next she began to kick aside the fronds covering the wire in order to follow it back toward her trailer. Sure enough, within a few feet of the dish, probably 60 feet from the Airstream, there was a break. A raccoon again? She looked closer. This time there were no signs of an animal's chewing—no shredding, no fraying. This was a clean, precise snip. This had been done by a wire cutter, not an animal's teeth. This had been done deliberately by a human.

Why had someone committed such a bizarre act in the near blackness of the awakening day? Her first reaction was to play detective and look around for clues with her flashlight: signs of a human thrashing through the brush, footprints, items left behind. But as she did that rather haphazardly, other ideas crowded into her mind... maybe the tape held a clue... she would figure out the time of the intruder's visit by measuring the time from 4:30, when the timer activated it, until it stopped... she would call her new friend, chief deputy sheriff Rusty Torrance, whose responsibilities included the remote parts of the county, as soon as she thought he was up... she would look for tire tracks in the crude two-rutted road that lead to the Airstream from Orville Wilson's double-wide combined office and mobile home a quarter of a mile back. He was the owner of the trailer camp and the source of her power and water. She would ask Orville and his wife Dot if they'd heard anything, but she knew the Wilsons were sound sleepers, long inured to sounds of the night.

Sounds of the night. Now she dimly remembered that some kind of unfamiliar noise—more than a noise, a shriek—had momentarily disturbed her deepest sleep. She would concentrate on trying to bring back that brief awakening. "Think, Jean, think!" Normally, if she had awakened she might have heard the rhythmic hoots of the resident great-horned owl. But they were so familiar they would have comforted her, not disturbed her. Then instinct took over. The owl! She remembered that the great-horned owl also rarely emitted a terrifying blood-curdling scream, sounding more like a bobcat than an owl. She had heard it once before, years ago. Her memory searched for that sound. She tried to match it with the dim echo of the scream she'd heard during the night. Yes, the sound that awakened her for a moment must have been the ghastly alarm cry of the big owl.

Straining to recall images made fuzzy by the curtain of sleep, she seemed to remember that she switched on her bedside light for a moment. Perhaps the combination of the bird's eerie alarm cry—she was convinced now that was what it was—and the light had frightened off whoever it was.

All these thoughts were hazily focused and frantically tumbled one on another. Increasingly, another idea was relentlessly pushing itself into her mind as she, just as relentlessly, tried to push it back out.

It was the realization that the snipped wire was no weird act of vandalism. Nor had she a professional rival who would want to sabotage her work. No, the snipped wire could mean—surely <u>did</u> mean—that someone had come that night to harm her and wanted to leave no auditory trace. Worse, that someone was almost surely one of five people, five friends and fellow birders, who knew about her recording set-up. One of them, maybe more than one, must have concluded that Jean had learned too much about the disappearance of a well known ornithologist two years before.

But she couldn't guess which of her five companions had committed the strange, sinister act.

~~ 2 ~~

The events that swept Jean McKay from her peaceful schoolroom in the frozen Midwest 1,200 miles away to a threat on her life in a steamy South Florida swampland began in her vice principal's office three months earlier. She was bidden there, purpose unknown, by the vice principal of Oak City Central High School, Ross Emmet, and Arnold Benson, head of the science department, who was Jean's superior.

Jean arrived first. She stared at a few photos of Emmet with school board big shots, a family picture, and a couple of diplomas on the institutional green walls while waiting for the men.

They arrived together, directed disarming smiles at Jean and apologized for being late (they weren't; she was early).

Benson was a fiftyish man of medium height, with neatly-trimmed gray hair, rimless glasses, and a kindly face that became especially so where Jean McKay was concerned. The two had a strong mutual respect. Emmet was tall, rail-thin, erect. He had slits for eyes, almost no lips at all, and slicked-back hair. He had the stern mien of the school's chief disciplinarian; some of the boys called him "Dracula" behind his back.

Even Emmet's severe visage softened for Jean. He too liked her. The adjective that so many people apply to Jean when first meeting her—"mousy"—had long since passed from the minds of both men. They no longer noticed her baggy, nondescript clothes, her unkempt hair, skinny body, and broad face; they saw only a skilled, popular teacher, one of the most respected on the staff.

Emmet disdained his leather swivel chair behind the huge mahogany desk that dominated his office (it seemed like a fortress to many a frightened student) and took a seat in a simple Windsor chair beside Jean and Benson. The day was cold and gray, spitting flurries. It was early in January, just after the return from the Christmas Holidays. Although Jean was usually at ease in the familiar office, she was a little antsy waiting for them to come to the point.

They soon did. They wanted her to take a six-months paid leave of absence. They and others were concerned about her recent involvement in bringing the kidnappers of a girl from a prominent local family, Georgina Pearson, to trial and conviction. Surely, Jean would appreciate a period of calm.

She said a firm no thanks to the proposition, but Benson urged her to reconsider. He called her Jean. First names were seldom used among faculty on school premises, especially in front of Emmet. Benson reminded her of her recent ordeal that began when she came up with the concept that solved the kidnapping of six-year-old Georgina and her uncle. Then came her long hours on the witness stand. Benson and Emmet didn't mention what Jean knew they were thinking about—possible reprisals against her.

The little teacher held her ground. "I understand and appreciate what you are trying to do. But I'd like just to settle down right here and teach my students biology again." She didn't bother to add that she felt perfectly safe with the kidnappers in prison. She simply said, "A sabbatical at this time would just waste the school board's money."

The two men gave up temporarily, but two days later Benson telephoned asking to come to see her at home about a revised proposition. She didn't want to be tempted further, but of course she couldn't refuse a visit from her department head. Besides, indifferent as she was about her own appearance, she kept a neat, interesting little house that she enjoyed showing. It stood on a four-lot parcel right in town at the end of a dirt lane and was surrounded by fairly thick woods. A brook trickled through a corner of the property; she had diverted it to feed a lily pond that was now the residence of a green heron.

The house was ramshackle when she bought it, but over the years she had transformed it, mostly by her own hands, into a picturesque little cottage, which she described as "Scottish" in style, a nod to her roots (she pronounces her name "McEye"). She named the little house "Warblercroft," after her favorite birds.

She had the teakettle on for Benson and a cheery fire in the fireplace she'd rebuilt herself. He took an interest in her active bird feeders. After a little biology banter, Benson came to the point. He was offering essentially the same proposition, but wrapped in a more attractive package. "I've talked with Arthur Pearson about our disappointment that you wouldn't accept a leave, and he came up with a great idea. He has authorized the Pearson Family Trust to entertain a proposal for a six-months research grant for $30,000 to further your bird recording projects. You'd have to write a grant proposal, of course, but it's just a formality. And you wouldn't cost the school district a nickel. We'd discontinue your salary."

"Well, it's certainly generous, but I'd still rather be teaching my students." Nevertheless, she'd been thinking a lot about the original offer. She thought of Orville Wilson's trailer camp on the edges of Big Cypress National Preserve and Everglades National Park areas of south Florida. She'd anchored her Airstream trailer there a couple of times before, but only for brief stays on summer vacations.

Wilson's camp was the most remote place she knew about where she could hook up her trailer into power and water. She thought about ospreys, eagles, kites, and herons, and all the other birds that she could watch and whose cries she could record when she ventured deeper into the swamps and everglades from the camp.

It was an easy drive from the camp to such bird-rich environments as the Gulf beaches where even such common sights as the sanderlings darting in little clusters to tippy-toe into the waves and darting back again were a novelty for a Midwesterner.

She thought of the willets, the drabbest birds of the beaches until they reveal their spectacular wing patterns in flight. It didn't occur to her that the transformation of this bird was a metaphor for what happens when the plain little woman's teaching skills and personality give her wings and sweep at least some of her students along on the flight with her. It was then that her students would forget her unprepossessing appearance.

Or she could drive to Corkscrew Swamp Sanctuary to observe wood storks nesting in the world's oldest stand of bald cypress trees with their flared trunks, or to Ding Darling Refuge on Sanibel Island and run up single-day counts of close to 100 species, or to several other preserved wildlife habitats within a 50-mile radius from Wilson's camp. The various ecosystems were so different from the rolling green fields and leafy woodlands of the Midwest that she loved so much; yet she recalled being just as struck by the beauty of remote South Florida as she was by the familiar, beloved surroundings of the Heartland.

This opportunity to extend her studies of bird language in a totally different setting, not the chance to escape from an Oak City winter, brought Jean around. After she had made her little protest that she'd "still rather be teaching my students," she eagerly filled out the grant application. Within a week the details were buttoned up, and she telephoned Orville Wilson that she'd like her favorite spot for six months. Wilson was fond of her and jockeyed space assignments to accommodate her.

So she hooked her Airstream to her locally famous 1975 Pontiac Bonneville convertible, a gas guzzler that seemed inconsistent with her fervent support of the environment in other matters. She was grateful for its power to tug the trailer around the country.

She packed her modest personal things and extensive recording equipment and nature library, and pointed south. Her students considered the huge bright red car with its immaculate white top the class of the faculty lot. When the boys learned that the tiny woman did her own minor tune-ups, their esteem for her soared. That helped protect her from adolescent shenanigans that her unstylish appearance might otherwise have provoked. As it was, despite her reputation as a no-nonsense tough grader, she was one of the best-liked teachers in the big highly rated school.

For the next six months she would trade the cozy cocoons of Warblercroft and Oak City High School, where she was so comfortable and useful, for a remote subtropical environment where she barely knew two other people, the operators of an isolated trailer camp. It didn't bother her in the least to do so.

~~ 3 ~~

Jean arrived at Wilson's camp in the late afternoon of the fourth day (she couldn't resist detours to Great Smoky Mountain National Park and Okefenokee Swamp on the way down). As she moseyed along the county road, she spotted the familiar crude log sign proclaiming Wilson's Mobile Home Camp. The proprietor had nailed wooden letters fashioned from small branches to a large weathered board. The o's were diamond-shaped and the s's resembled lightning streaks. Some of the letters and support poles looked newer than others, suggesting that Hurricane Andrew last September had caused the need for some replacements. The entire contraption included a non-functional wooden gate and a flimsy log framework that suspended the sign over the dirt road that led 200 yards back to Orville and Dot Wilson's combination home-office trailer. The effect would not inspire tourist confidence, and Jean was glad it didn't.

Orville greeted her warmly as an old friend even though she'd been there only twice before for 10-day stays. "Lookee who's here, Mama," he called back into the trailer, and Dot came out, leaned across the door of the open convertible, and hugged the little teacher.

"Got your favorite spot for you, number 8, although it took a little doing," said Wilson genially in his soft rural Florida accent while humanly seeking a little credit for accommodating her. Jean properly thanked him. "'Member how to get back there?" Wilson asked. Jean thought she did.

16

It wasn't easy to maneuver her huge car and the Airstream down the two ruts that stood for a road, but with Orville's help she got set up. The trailer was almost concealed by low-growing saw palmettos and sabal palms. It was more than a quarter mile east of Wilson's trailer and almost out of sight of the nearest other trailer, that of a more or less permanent resident, Annie Crews, whom Jean remembered warmly.

Wilson was a big good-natured man in his mid-fifties with a sun-lined face. He had suggested that Jean take a less remote site.

But when she insisted, he yielded. What worried him, but not her, was that it was possible to get back to her site without going past his office. An abandoned road veered off about half way along the access that linked the county highway and Wilson's double-wide. It swung around a patch of swamp on the south side toward Annie Crews' and Jean's trailers; the lane regularly used by the campers bordered the north edge. The abandoned road was drivable unless the swamp spilled over on it, which was not the case this dry winter. Of course it was also walkable. Wilson advised Jean not to use it. He wanted to make sure she would pass the office so they'd know when she was and was not at home.

She didn't want a phone, so she made arrangements with Wilson to hold her mail and take phone calls. She began to unpack a few essentials, but was more eager to set up her recording equipment. She connected the microphone on her small dish to a tape recorder in her trailer. Eventually she would radiate the mike in various directions from her trailer to capture the sounds of several distinctive environments—dark

17

swampland, or a cluster of ancient cypress trees heavily laden with Spanish moss, or an open wet prairie dotted with a few hardwood trees. She thrilled at the acoustical possibilities if the birds were there.

To help ensure their presence she put out half dozen feeders of different shapes, sizes, and colors and hung them in contrasting surroundings. Then she stocked them with several kinds of seed mixtures, some of her own concoction. She had the birder's equivalent of a green thumb; magically she enticed interesting birds wherever she went. Straightaway some tiny yellow-rumped warblers, cardinals, and other bold creatures that are at home with human habitation scouted the feeders and declared them fit for avian dining. By the second morning, the recorder was picking up a variety of notes and calls amidst the mockingbirds' free lance repertoire.

So she was quickly, eagerly engaged in what she was down there to do: recording, editing, splicing, writing, observing, photographing. She went to the Gulf beaches a couple of times to observe shore birds and record their squawks and whistles. Once she sauntered into Everglades National Park. Although she was at the western and northern sections of the park, where Andrew had been less ferocious, she was aghast at the devastation that remained. Even on a humid morning the stripped mahogany and scrub oak trees recalled Shakespeare's mournful description of winter trees: "bare, ruined choirs where late the sweet birds sang." She wondered what the storm had done to the sweet birds.

* * *

These side trips to beaches and the park were work missions. Soon she longed for a recreational break. A local newspaper reported that a park ranger was going to conduct a bird walk on the next Saturday morning, open to all, and she decided to take it in. It was still birds, but recreational birds.

Driving to the assembly point, she did a little introspection and acknowledged a flaw in her character: She embodied "the absorbing snobbery of birds" as Angela Thirkell has written. She really didn't like public bird walks where she'd have to endure little old ladies and men who call cardinals "redbirds" and starlings "blackbirds" or who get all atwitter over a mourning dove. You were either an accurate, committed birder or you were something else.

Aware of her snobbery, she lectured herself to be tolerant when she joined the public walk. During an earlier stay at Wilson's camp, she had visited the little field station that would be the starting and finishing point of the stroll. Her warm recollection of the ranger was one reason she decided to take part. She recalled him as an amiable bird-knowledgeable young man.

She was pleased to find him still in charge when she entered the cement block station that chilly Saturday morning. She was aware that he gave her a second look, but no voice recognition.

She put the worst face on that; she assumed that he didn't remember her and was put off by her skinny appearance. As her fellow hikers gathered, Jean examined some excellent specimens of area birds and mammals in the display cases and a well thought out diorama depicting the early life of the Seminoles in that area.

She gave high marks to the displays; she was less enthusiastic about the eight or ten people whom she sized up as walk-mates.

The ranger introduced himself to the group as Don Purvis. Jean related to his flat, pleasing Midwestern accent. He was an inch or two over six feet, with close cropped red hair over dark blue eyes and a surprisingly unfreckled face. His uniform covered a spare frame. His impression said "Eagle Scout" to Jean.

After a few minutes on the walk, it was clear to Jean that, with one exception, her misgivings about being amidst "amateurs" were fulfilled. The exception was a fortyish woman whom Purvis called Doris. She was a big-boned person, with large hips propelling a long-striding walk. Blonde hair, helped along by a bottle of something, was heaped on top of her head, making her seem taller than she probably was. Her features were a bit too sharp to be pretty, but her good skin and erect carriage contributed to an overall attractive, athletic appearance.

Jean noticed that Doris carried an expensive Zeiss spotting scope, an indication that she was very serious about her hobby. So did her knowledgeable chatter, which was plentiful but only at appropriate times. Somehow she reminded Jean of an enthusiastic tour bus guide.

Doris stuck to Purvis stride for stride and seemed to be his self-appointed aide-de-camp. Jean herself was a bit of a bird show-off, and soon she positioned herself near Purvis and Doris, impressing them with her ability to spot and differentiate winter warblers. It didn't take Don and Doris long to perceive that Jean wasn't just another little old lady bird watcher in tennis shoes.

She dazzled them with her ability to recognize distant calls and songs. They also appreciated her unwillingness to settle on an identification unless it was verified. "Boy, you know your calls," the ranger said. "Let's see, you introduced yourself as Miss McCoy, didn't you?"

"Miss McKay."

"Sorry. Miss McKay. Don't I remember that you came to the station once before?"

"Yes, two-and-a-half years ago. But we didn't go out in the field. It was in August."

"Well, we're glad to have you along today."

"Gosh yes," agreed Doris.

After the walk, she had coffee and doughnut holes with the other hikers and did her best to put up with what she considered their inanities. At one point she was aware that Purvis and Doris were giving her the once-over and probably talking about her. That made her uncomfortable, but as she was leaving they approached her, expressed their pleasure at her being there, and urged her to join them again next week. "Please come," implored Doris, whose last name she learned was Groot.

Despite her problem with dilettante bird walkers, Jean approved of the leaders and agreed to come. After that the two women chatted for ten minutes or so mostly about how their interest in ornithology developed. Jean learned that Doris was a legal secretary in Fort Myers, and she deduced that she was overly self-conscious about being unmarried at 43.

On the next walk, a week later, she quite naturally gravitated to the front with Don and Doris and became a sort of second assistant. At the post-walk coffee and doughnut holes session, she found out why Don and Doris had been talking about her the previous week. Doris took her aside and said, "We were wondering if you'd like to join Mr. Purvis and I and several other birders on one of our informal Sunday morning hikes." The grammar jarred Jean, who was upset when anyone used the pronoun "I" or "we" after a verb or preposition. Normally such a blunder might have set back any attempt at friendship, but her appreciation of a competent birder won out. She recovered sufficiently to say, "Sounds interesting. Tell me more."

That Doris did, offering flattering thumbnail profiles of the other three "regulars," whom she identified as Bill Long, Bob Sanderson ("We usually call him Sandy"), and a woman named Con Smith. "Everyone of us except me has been published in prominent ornithology journals," she gushed, "and that of course includes Don...Mr. Purvis." She paused to gaze at the ranger.

She explained the format: They meet for a 5:30 breakfast every other Sunday morning at a remote place called Big Cypress Cafe. Its location offered a variety of birding environments fairly close by: saw grass marshes, ponds, sloughs, subtropical cypress forests, hardwood hammocks, wet prairie, dry pinelands; even farms, citrus groves, Gulf beaches and estuarine mangroves were within easy driving distance from the cafe. After breakfast, "members" usually went out alone or in pairs to pursue individual interests. They returned to the cafe at about 8:30 to share experiences over coffee.

Jean correctly surmised that Don and Doris had chatted about adding her to the group. Doris had drawn her out about her education (B.S. and M.S. in biology from Ball State University—she didn't mention her impressive scholarships—and a summer fellowship at the Cornell Ornithology Laboratory). She had described the satisfactions she derived from teaching biology and talked a little about her research. She carefully avoided mentioning the Georgina Pearson kidnapping (just as she hadn't mentioned it to Orville and Dot Wilson). Don and Doris had no doubt informed others in the group of her credentials, and she had passed the test to join "our funny little impromptu group," as Doris called it.

So Jean asked directions to Big Cypress Cafe and said she'd be there at 5:30 next Sunday. She was pleased at the time. She had no foreboding of the mysterious events that her innocent decision to join in with a few competent bird watchers would bring.

~~4~~

Jean McKay wasn't very comfortable entering new social situations. To ensure that she didn't embarrass herself by being late Sunday morning, she practice-drove the 24 miles from Wilson's Camp to Big Cypress Cafe on the Friday before. The part of the drive that was on Route 29 was easy, but leaving the highway for the cafe involved hard-to-find roads. She clocked her test drive at 41 minutes. So, on Sunday she started out at 4:40 to get to the cafe a little before the 5:30 breakfast.

She made the proper turns and found the parking lot without delay. She was full of anticipation as she got out of her monster car, but her excitement flagged a bit as she negotiated the cracks and places where tree roots pushed up the asphalt like mole tracks in the neglected parking lot. Fortunately, two out of four floodlights were working, allowing her to pick her way in the early dawn. The walkway to the building was no more inviting than the lot. It was crisscrossed with creeping weeds and led to a frame building with flaking gray paint and a badly patched screen door with sagging hinges. Many old wooden South Florida buildings have a rustic charm, but this one missed.

She hoped Doris or Don would be there to introduce her, and both were. So was Sandy Sanderson. Doris introduced him to Jean, and he responded warmly. Ever self-conscious, she was pleased that he betrayed no reaction to her appearance. He looked to be about 50, bald in front with a full black fringe, a stocky frame, about 5'11". He could

24

easily weigh 220. He tried to compensate for his high hairline with an ample, iron gray mustache. Even under the red and black checked wool shirt he wore in the chilly early morning air, his thick forearms suggested physical strength. Yet Doris had called him a pussycat, a description suggested by his cordial face with its pleasant brown eyes, an unremarkable nose, and ready smile. Jean guessed that the flashy new white Mustang convertible she had admired on the parking lot probably belonged to him rather than to Don or Doris.

A large plastic camera bag lay on the bench beside him. Apparently he'd been showing a lens to Don when Jean approached. Don explained, "Sandy's the group's champion photographer. He can tell you more than you'd ever want to know about lenses, filters, film, and the rest of it. You've seen his pictures in most of the birding journals as well as Natural History and Audubon."

"And National Wildlife," put in Doris.

Jean was impressed and said, "I'm sure I've seen your pictures because I see all those publications and love the bird photography in them. But I'm afraid I'm unaware of any specific shots that were yours."

"Well, they don't exactly put the photographer's credit line in large bold type," Sandy said good-naturedly.

"Now I'll be sure to look for your work," Jean said. She was doing well. She wondered how such a burly fellow would have the agility and stealth of movement she imagined it would take to be a successful nature photographer.

They were seated at a long table against the wall of a barn-like rustic room adorned with fishnets, lobster pots, and fading autographed photographs of local dignitaries—town councilmen and proprietors of fishing camps and general stores. There was also a signed picture of Dwight Eisenhower. When Jean asked about it, Don said the former President sometimes retreated to a fishing camp down in Everglades City. As valuable as the picture might have been as an interest-getter for the cafe, it had been allowed to yellow and become dusty. Somehow Ike's broad grin couldn't overcome the oppressive effect the grey, dank place had on Jean.

At first, the red-checked tablecloths helped brighten the atmosphere, but when she sat down, she saw food and coffee stains and crinkles on the cloth instead of the checks.

So her first impression of Big Cypress Cafe itself wasn't very favorable, but she felt so warm about her companions, she decided it would be petty to let the atmosphere depress her. Clearly they chose the place for its proximity to good birding sights, not its neatness and charm.

As first arrivals Doris, Don, and Sandy had seated themselves, left to right, on a bench along the wall, and Jean, at Doris's beckoning, took the chair facing her. Jean was eager to meet the other two "members" that Doris had described. She could see out an unwashed window to the crumbly parking lot where two contrasting cars were being parked. One she guessed was a new high-styled Jaguar, the other small, Japanese, old and in the need of paint and body work. A tall man got out of the Jag, a woman from the other car. He waited for her, and they walked toward the cafe together.

They proved to be the other two. Don introduced them as Bill Long and Con Smith, adding helpfully that Con and Jean would have a lot in common since they were both science teachers. Both newcomers greeted Jean cordially but not effusively.

Con Smith made a striking appearance. She had clear olive skin, black eyes, and black hair with a contrasting white streak, pulled back in a bun. Her smile when she met Jean revealed gorgeous teeth, straight and white and encircled by bright red lipstick. Jean detected a slight Hispanic accent. She suspected a lovely figure was obscured by the baggy slacks and shirt she wore for the outdoors. Up close, there were signs of creases in her otherwise blemishless skin, suggesting she might be older than she seemed on first impression; but few would guess her actual age of 52. Most men between 30 and 70 would probably think her sexy although nothing in her careful, subdued demeanor would give them hope. She was tall and had the assured walk of an athlete. With all her beauty and grace, still the most remarkable thing about Con Smith to Jean was her name. It just didn't fit a Latin beauty.

Bill Long was about 6'3" and spare. Wet, bulging grey eyes looked intently at Jean through black-rimmed glasses and from beneath heavy, nearly black brows, making Jean a little nervous.

His pink cheeks were somewhat sunken, and tiny red eruptions wandered erratically over his face. He'd had several skin cancers removed from his face and head and protected himself with a white fishing hat, brim down all around. Jean guessed his age at 65 (she found out later he actually was 71) and reckoned it that high only because of a liberal sprinkling of aging spots on his hands and pate, which he exposed when he courteously removed his hat on meeting her. Overall the man appeared remarkably fit.

He also appeared to be remarkably prosperous. The Jaguar wasn't the only sign. Even dressed for a hike, his shoes, slacks, and shirt were top-of-the-line Eddie Bauer, and a Rolex adorned his wrist. After Don's straightforward introduction, the eager Doris chimed in, "Bill's our member of the 600 Club!" Jean knew that this meant that Bill Long was someone who had the time, money, and perseverance to identify 600 American species in a single year, and she offered appropriate congratulations.

"Thanks, but I haven't done it in recent years," Bill said modestly but with a tone of regret. Jean guessed the reason later when she found out about his wife's poor health.

All five were big people. Among them little Jean was like a coxswain on a heavyweight crew.

A jolly Native American woman waited on them. Two sparkling round black eyes penetrated her huge bronze dish of a face, but the effect was spoiled by her cigarette-stained, crooked teeth, which she displayed constantly. She was dressed in a bright blue Mexican-style dress. They called her Marie, and she had flippant nicknames for some of them—Ranger Don, Shutterbug Bob or Shutterbob, and Senora for Con. Jean speculated that if she ever "belonged" to the group— and she was already hoping she would—her nickname would no doubt relate to her small size.

She examined the poorly typed, stained menu, then decided to follow the lead of Doris, who looked as if she had good nutritional habits, and ordered waffles with strawberries. The berries were wonderful, but the waffles probably had been put frozen into a pop-up toaster. Oh well, she wasn't there primarily to eat.

Since Doris and Don apparently had filled the others in on Jean's background, they didn't press her with many questions at breakfast, and the few there were concerned her portable recording equipment. Jean was relieved that none of them had connected her name with the Pearson kidnapping.

Don gave a little history of the Sunday breakfast group, as they called themselves: They had originally sprung as a rump group from one of Don's public hikes about five years ago. The current timing, location, and personnel, they said, evolved gradually. Doris asked no one in particular, "Other than Max, there was Susan Waymire, but was there ever anyone else?"

"There was that unfortunate Moss fellow," grumbled Bill Long. "He was a mistake," Don added, looking at Jean, "but was with us only a couple of times." These were certified bird snobs, and they were letting Jean know she should be thankful to be with them. She was. Doris said that Susan Waymire had married and moved to the Boston suburbs where she was active in the Massachusetts Audubon Society. Whoever Max was, wasn't explained.

They described for Jean the terrain for a mile or two in all directions surrounding the cafe. On an enlarged map of the area, Don traced trails and roads leading to desirable sights reachable on foot. "But," he added, "we wouldn't let you go out by yourself the first time." Jean detected Don catching Con's eye, and she picked it up. "Of course, not." Con said. "You'll come with me."

Jean protested mildly that thanks to the good map, she didn't need to take Con away from her own interests, but she didn't mean it.

Ornithologically, the walk with Con was a success. She showed Jean several of her favorite spotting areas, and Jean was able to make some nice recordings of a white-eyed vireo and the cries of an osprey. But on a personal level, the walk was less satisfying. Jean had a healthy curiosity about people, but there was no satisfying it where her exotic companion was concerned. About all Jean could find out about her on a two-hour tramp was that Con was short for Consuela and that she taught science at a rural junior high school where many of her pupils were from families of immigrant farm workers. There was no explanation of the inappropriate "Smith," which Jean conjectured was a married name although no wedding ring graced her finger.

The handsome woman did volunteer one glimpse into a noble purpose to her life. She said that her "only hope in any semester is to open the eyes of one or two kids to the wonders of natural science. And that it stays with them, living in this environment so rich in nature." Jean found her cultured Spanish accent charming, something she just didn't hear in Oak City.

Back at the cafe, Jean entered easily into the conversation and played the white-eyed vireo recording to the plaudits of her new friends. She was thrilled to listen to the knowledgeable give-and-take of five expert birders. She also enjoyed their clever talk, filled with puns and wordplay. Bill Long asked if anyone had spotted any of the black-backed gulls reported on nearby beaches. No one had, and with that Sandy Sanderson burst into "The Sweetheart of Sigma Chi," to wit, "The gull of my dreams was the sweetest gull of all the gulls I know," and the others, including Marie, joined in. It was a good morning.

The next session, two weeks later, was even more satisfying.

She walked most of it on her own. The only moment to mar her morning was a bit of a contretemps with Bill Long over the territory of the rare mangrove cuckoo. Long had found it necessary to point out that they didn't need people from up north to tell them about southern birds.

But Bill's good nature quickly returned, and at the time Jean wasn't bothered very much by his little scolding. By now she'd eased comfortably into the group and was aware that well meant disputation was part of the dynamic that made it work.

~~5~~

Yes, Jean really felt as if she belonged at that successful breakfast. That's why she was so hurt when she perceived that she was being eased out. It came about when she walked out with Doris and said cheerfully, "See you in two weeks, Doris."

Doris hesitated. "Not in two weeks."

"Won't you be able to make it?"

"Uh, it's not that. We just won't be getting together at all," Doris said uncertainly. She sucked in her breath as if to amplify that remark, but thought better of it.

About all that Jean could say was, "Oh, I see." But she didn't.

Doris seemed preoccupied about something, but finally sensed Jean's distress. She smiled at her and said, "I'll leave word at Wilson's Camp when we plan to get together again. I'll be in touch."

Jean didn't believe it, but gave her Wilson's number and said. "Look forward to it. Bye."

Suddenly it seemed oppressively humid on that neglected parking lot. The weeds forcing their way up through the wiggly cracks and holes looked uglier than usual. The drive back to Wilson's seemed long and depressing. Hurricane Andrew's devastation to stretches of wetlands never looked more sickening to Jean. "Bare ruined choirs" again.

Once, on a brief westward stretch of the route, the glare of the morning sun off the windshield of an oncoming car flashed in her eyes. She had a moment of panic and her right wheels veered off on the shoulder, which was fortunately broad and firm. She regained control and drove on. But Jean was normally a skillful driver. Had she not been disconcerted, she would have anticipated the glare, averted her eyes, and stayed on the road.

As she drove, she reflected. The breakfast group comprised the most accomplished birders, collectively, that she'd ever associated with. But more than that, she liked them all, even corny Doris, patrician Bill, and remote Con. She thought she'd been welcomed by them as a peer, and that pleased the modest little teacher. Now she saw herself as another "Moss," the "mistake" that Bill Long and Don Purvis had alluded to.

Bill Long, of course, was the key. Jean had sized him up as the unofficial leader, and she had made the mistake of challenging him the second time she met him. It was the mangrove cuckoo incident. When they had regathered, Bill had wondered if anyone else had heard what he had perceived to be the "kow-kow-kow" of the rare bird. Nobody had, but Jean, to her present regret, had added rather brashly, in what she thought was the give-and-take spirit of the group, "Are you sure it wasn't the yellow-billed? As I understand it, the mangrove's note is pretty much like the yellow-billed's." By her tone, Jean had let it be known that when there's a choice of two identifications, she always opted for the more common one.

"'As you understand it,'" Bill had mocked. "By that do I infer that you've never seen a mangrove cuckoo? Well, I have. Several times. And by the way, little lady from up north, if you imply that I might confuse the mangrove with the yellow-billed, it might interest you to know that the yellow-bills haven't

33

returned from wintering in South America. They won't show up for a couple of months." He had craned his long neck so he could see around Con who was seated between them.

Jean had tried to scramble out of it. "I envy you. I'd love to see and hear a mangrove cuckoo. Perhaps you could guide me to where you think they are around here. I guess I thought they were most likely in the keys."

"I don't need anyone from the Midwest to tell me about the birds in the keys. I make birding trips down there every year and have for a long time. Other than Max, I probably have seen more rare birds down there than anyone."

There was that name "Max" again.

Jean was embarrassed and the redness at the tips of her ears had shown it. Don had caught a look of distress on Doris's face as Bill picked away at her little friend and quickly jumped in. "Speaking of cuckoos, did any of you see the article on nest parasitology in the recent issue of the <u>Journal</u> <u>of</u> <u>Ornithology?</u>"

"I not only didn't see it, but I don't know what you are talking about," Sandy had said. Of course, the good-natured photographer did know, but he wanted to join the mission to rescue Jean. Sandy also was famous for bringing esoteric discussions back to earth.

"Sorry, Sandy," Don had apologized, going along, "It's the cowbird bit. Some cuckoos also lay their eggs in smaller birds' nests and let them bring up their young."

"Well, whatever bird does it, it sure is an unlovely trait," Bill had remarked, adding with still a trace of sarcasm, "Do you know about shiny cowbirds, Jean?"

She did, but now, quite intimidated, she shook her head. "They are showing up in Florida for the first time. I saw a couple at the Briggs Nature Center the other day. It was a thrill to see them, but I sure don't admire any bird that lets others do the work and then takes the credit. Most unlovely. By the way, Sandy," he added, "We won't talk about obscure ornithology if you won't talk about obscure photography stuff."

That brought a chuckle, and it put an end to Bill's little tiff with Jean. Before long, he was smiling at her, or as near to her as possible with Jean shriveled up on the other side of Con. He showed genuine interest in her successful efforts to record the songs of a couple of other inhabitants of the mangrove swamps that day. At the time Jean wished she'd kept her mouth shut about the cuckoos. But she hadn't dwelled on it, thanks to Bill's quick return to graciousness.

* * *

Now, driving back to her trailer, she concluded that her challenge to Bill was why she was destined to be the next "Moss." She speculated that the others met quickly when she was putting away her recording equipment and decided they didn't want someone from "up north" to tell them about local birds.

Her blues were still with her on the following Tuesday when, as she passed Wilson's trailer on her way back from getting supplies, Orville signaled her to stop. "A gal named Doris something called and would like to come by this evening after work. About 5:30. She left a number. Want to call her, or want me to?"

"Oh, you do it, Mr. Wilson, please," Jean implored. "And tell her fine. I'll be here. Can you give her directions?"

This would be it, she thought. They've sent nice old Doris to tell me they don't want me. She felt sorry for her friend and thought of her warmly despite those "between you and I's."

A little before 5:30 Jean went out to stock her feeders, and soon she saw the long-striding Doris walking toward her. Jean had not seen her before in anything but outdoor tramping clothes and was surprised to see her in a rather severe dark blue suit while negotiating the ruts in the road in pumps. Jean imagined that her face was that of someone who faced a difficult task.

They greeted each other. Jean had made herbal sun tea and invited Doris to partake. She did and complimented Jean on it. They both forced some talk about kinds of teas as they sat on lawn chairs on Jean's makeshift patio. When they got up, she took her friend out to the dish and showed her the details of how it was hooked up to the recorder in the trailer. Doris reacted with the expected oohs and ahs. Then more small talk. A pair of indigo buntings lit on a feeder, and they talked about them and almost anything else that would stall serious discussion.

Finally, Doris blurted out, "Jean, I'm here on a rather strange mission."

"I can guess what it is."

"I doubt that." Doris looked at her, surprised and puzzled. "Have you ever heard of Max Wein?"

Now they both were puzzled. Jean had heard of him. She knew he was a well known birder and remembered that she'd read scholarly articles by him some years ago. She also was vaguely aware that some sort of tragedy was attached to his name. All she said, however, was, "Yes, I think so."

"Ah, you are wondering what he's got to do with anything. Well, before I get into that let me apologize for being rather noncommittal after our last breakfast. I realized, and so did Don, that we owe you an explanation. That's why I'm here."

"I know why you are here. What's it got to do with Max Wein?"

Doris gave her a perplexed glance. "Max was part of our Sunday group." Jean remembered an unidentified Max was in the little list of alumni along with the pariah, Moss, shortly to be joined by herself. Bill Long had mentioned him too. Doris couldn't have known what Jean was thinking, however, and went on, assuming a dark tone, her eyes widening. "Two years ago he vanished into thin air. Last year at about the anniversary of his disappearance, we had dinner in his honor and vowed to do so every year to, well, sort of to pay our respects until we know what happened— although I guess some of us think we probably do know.

"The second anniversary dinner will be Saturday," she went on, "so we decided to skip getting together the next morning. It wasn't until you said goodbye on the parking lot that I realized we hadn't filled you in. At the time, I just didn't want to take it on myself to invite you, or not invite you, to our dinner. I didn't even know whether the next breakfast would be the week after the dinner or two weeks. We're pretty private about this, and I didn't think I could even get into an explanation at the time. I'm afraid I left you hanging. Understand, dear?"

Doris was a blusher, and she reddened as she explained. But Jean's wide mouth widened farther into a grin. "Of course, Doris."

"Well, there's a little more. I talked to the others, and we decided that it really wasn't appropriate to ask you to the dinner. Max was our special friend, and it might just embarrass you to be there. We just don't like to speculate about what happened to Max outside of our group. But we also decided we owed you an explanation of why we were skipping a breakfast.

"You do understand, don't you, dear?" she repeated.

Jean didn't exactly, but reassured Doris, "Of course, I've told you I do." Frankly, she was mystified as to why it all had to be such a secret.

"Well, you are a good sport. And I know you'll keep anything I've said about Max to yourself. Now then you said you knew why I was here, but I bet you didn't."

"No, I was wrong. Foolish as usual."

"What was it then?" Doris teased.

Jean shifted in her chair. "It's not worth mentioning," she said. "I was all wet."

"C'mon, tell me," urged Doris. "I let you in on <u>our</u> secret."

Jean guessed she might as well own up. "Well, I thought that I was the next 'Moss' and that you'd come to drum me out of the group because of the way I sassed Mr. Long."

Doris' voice became quite emotional. "Kick you out of the group? You, our famous song recording person?" Doris was as genuine as could be, and Jean was glad of it. Doris added in her more normal tone, "But between you and I, it wasn't a good idea to take on Bill Long the way you did." Jean tried not to visibly gasp at the grammar and acknowledged her mistake.

By this time, they'd moved inside the trailer. Doris inappropriately gushed how "cute and cozy" it was, which it wasn't and Jean knew it wasn't. The furniture that wasn't built in consisted of hand-me-downs from her parents years ago. The shellacked plywood walls and ceiling had taken on an orangey hue over the years. Sometimes she wondered if Doris was a phony with her stream of overdone compliments. She decided, however, that it was just part of the acutely self-conscious woman's trying too hard in social situations. She concluded that Doris was a worthy friend. She watched the large woman adjust herself in the "darling" little chair, something else on her mind.

"Back to Bill Long," she said seriously, looking right at Jean. She seemed to be setting aside her gosh, gee-whiz manner. "We are a little careful about how we talk to him. At 71 he's earned the right to be a little crotchety."

"Seventy one? I would have thought 61," said Jean.

"He'd love that! He's very fit and takes pride in it. No, he admits to 71. We had a 70th birthday party for him last year."

Doris went on to say that he's used to having his own way. He is extremely wealthy, and once or twice a year he'd have the group over to his home in the Port Royal section of Naples. "It was like entering another world for us," Doris said, but this time as a statement of fact, not in her gushy style.

She offered an admiring thumbnail profile. He was from a small town in Pennsylvania, won college scholarships, and put himself through law school. He plugged steadily upward until he became a senior partner in one of the elite law firms in New York, and Doris understood that he still was a director of three or four multinational companies and banks. Her boss at the law firm where she works in Fort Myers knew Long's name immediately and described him as "one powerful guy." He was said to have known Nixon quite well and Carter a little.

Jean asked if he had a family, and Doris replied a wife, Alma, and a daughter, Wilma, who was out west somewhere. The wife was a burden now. Bill had taken her to The Mayo Clinic in Jacksonville, then to New York, to try to find a cause for her forgetful and inappropriate behavior. Sadly, early Alzheimer's was the diagnosis.

"He's loyal to her, and that's why he no longer has time to qualify for the 600 club," said Doris. "Of course, she has the best custodial care, so he still can get together with us Sundays and occasionally go down to the Keys and over to the East coast."

It was humid, and Doris paused to slide her glasses higher on her nose, then resumed looking straight at Jean. "Please don't misconstrue what I'm saying about Bill. It's just that you should know about his background and his wife's illness. He never consciously lords his stature over us. He's one of us on Sunday mornings. And at other times too," she added. "He even takes a genuine interest in the cases of our little firm of six partners in Fort Myers," Doris said, proud that this friend of presidents took notice of the small firm she worked for. "Still, we don't give him the needle like we do each other."

As interested as Jean was in this profile of this distinguished birding colleague—and she wished for similar backgrounders on the others—she really wanted to know about Max Wein and his disappearance. There, when she broached the subject both indirectly and directly, Doris was not nearly so forthcoming.

Jean tried the oblique approach first, hoping to elicit a general discussion of the events of two years ago. "Why is the name Max Wein familiar to me?" she asked.

"You've probably read his articles. He was widely published in both scholarly journals and in general birding magazines."

End of discussion. Doris moved forward in her chair as if to get up to leave. Jean tried again.

"That must be it. What did he publish about?"

"Max was—or maybe is—an all around bird man, but he was best known as an authority on casuals and accidentals, any bird that was out of place geographically. He was on a Rare Bird Alert team and was generally a person that people turned to when someone claimed to sight something in the Miami area or the Keys that was not where it was supposed to be. He was very tough about confirming such sightings."

"Miami?"

"Yes, he lived there."

"But came over here for Sunday mornings?"

"Yes. He'd come over on Saturdays. I think maybe he stayed some Saturday nights with Sandy Sanderson.

Anyway he'd always show up at 5:30 ready to go on Sunday mornings.

"So he disappeared from the Miami area?"

"No, from here."

Now Jean really was interested and sought some elaboration.

"From here?"

"Uh huh."

These staccato answers certainly weren't typical of the usually voluble Doris Groot. Nor was her unsmiling, unanimated face. She seemed uneasy as she sat primly in the upright wooden chair. Jean decided that the indirect approach was getting her nowhere, so she fired a direct shot.

"What happened?"

She didn't land a direct hit.

"No one knows. He just didn't come back one Sunday morning, that's all. We don't talk about it much any more. I for one like to think he might be happy and well some place. But Max was known to have a sizeable sum of money on him, so the sheriff concluded robbery was the motive. He thought some Indian kids had something to do with it. They'd supposedly been on an overnight binge and were seen in the area. He singled out one boy in particular, but he couldn't prove anything. I think the others accept the sheriff's version; I know Don does."

Jean drew in her breath to say something, but Doris got out of the chair and headed toward the door, talking as she did, not giving Jean a chance for another question. "Look, Jean, I've said too much and I've got to go, or I'll be late for choir practice. I'm really sorry I didn't tell you about the dinner before this, but I

42

thought it should be a group decision on whether to ask you to come. Please understand that you are a solid member of our group. Forgive me?"

She squeezed Jean's hand warmly, and Jean assured her there was nothing to forgive. "Gosh, that's great," said Doris, her gushy personality returning. "Remember, there is nearly two weeks before we meet." "Are two weeks," Jean thought, wishing that Doris could marry the good grammar of her laconic personality with the flow of information from her gushy one.

After Doris left, Jean couldn't get the Max Wein disappearance out of her mind. She reviewed what she had learned from Doris, which wasn't very much. He'd disappeared two years ago. He lived in Miami. He didn't return while birding with the group. He was a bird scholar whose expertise included rare strays. The sheriff thought robbery was the motive and tried to connect one or more rowdy Indians with his disappearance.

Simple story. So why was Doris defensive when she talked about it? Was she speaking for all five of them when she said they don't like to talk about the disappearance? And why would that be?

She admitted to herself that perhaps she was a little inflated by her role in the Georgina Pearson kidnapping. She realized that every time she encountered something in life that was not fully explained it didn't mean that she was in the middle of some great mystery crying out for her to solve it—just because it had happened to her once. After all, adults have the right to just take off so long as they don't commit a crime in doing so. Maybe that's what Max

Wein did. Rationally, she said to herself that it was none of her business anyway. Doris, a very polite person, had almost said as much.

Yet she also knew she usually had good instincts, and they were practically screaming at her that there was something here that she ought to find out more about—whether her new friends wanted her to or not.

Jean mapped a strategy to try to find out more about the Max Wein puzzle. From the way Doris talked, she thought it better not to meet the issue head on at their next breakfast. But certainly she could inquire about the memorial dinner generally, and perhaps a revealing discussion would ensue. If that failed, she would see what she could learn from one of the other birders one-on-one in the field.

She was thwarted in her effort to initiate a general conversation about the missing man. Despite her early start, Don Purvis was already there when she arrived at the cafe. He greeted her and said sincerely, "I'm sorry about the misunderstanding, Jean. Believe me, it wasn't anything personal." Jean assured him that she understood. It was almost mandatory to follow up with an inquiry about the occasion, which she did. Don replied, "It was very nice. Sad, but nice. Max was a fine guy; still hard to believe he's gone. Wish you could have known him."

That effectively preempted her ploy to draw the group collectively into conversation about the dinner. Don would be suspicious if she asked them the question he had just answered. She even wondered if Don had staged it that way to quash broader questioning. No, not the clean-cut ranger. She admitted to herself that her imagination was getting a little overactive.

So it was left to her to try to draw out an individual. She selected Sandy Sanderson as her target for several reasons. He was the most amiable member of the group. He was easy to attach to; she merely had to be interested in whatever he was photographing that day. And, finally, Doris suggested that Max sometimes stayed with him when he came over from Miami. Perhaps he was Max Wein's connection to the group.

Jean wasn't above a little guile to advance her purpose. There was no set seating arrangement at breakfast, but they were like a church congregation; most of them unofficially sat in the same seat every time: Doris, Don, and Sandy against the wall on the bench, left to right, and herself, Con, and Bill on the chairs opposite. That made Sandy and Bill the most difficult for her to talk with. This particular Sunday, she made sure she arrived early enough to slide into the chair opposite Sandy before Bill did. Then she locked Sandy into a conversation about his craft. When Bill approached the table, Jean offered to give him his usual seat, but he replied, as Jean hoped he would, "Don't be silly, Jean. We don't have assigned seats in this classroom."

Jean recalled Sandy talking about some glossy ibises he wanted to photograph, and she used this as the springboard to engage him. She asked a couple of mildly technical questions about his technique and he took the bait. He showed her some fancy new photographic gadgetry he had purchased, then added, "Why don't you come along with me, and I'll show you how I do it. You gotta promise to be quiet though," he said with mock sternness. Jean accepted, and her tactic was working.

Before they left, Sandy gathered his equipment together and removed a manila envelope from a briefcase. He explained, "I often take some Polaroids ahead of time when I'm working on an important series of shots, looking at angles, lighting, backgrounds. I took these last time." He showed her some grainy blowups. Interleaved among them she saw a picture of the breakfast group laughing. He snatched the print away from her, too quickly she thought, and jammed it back into the envelope. "How'd that get in there?" he muttered to himself. But since it was clear that Jean had a brief look, he answered himself, "Oh, I took that to our dinner for Max the other night. I had tested my camera the last morning Max was with us and took that picture of our motley gang. Thought the others would like to see it."

Even Sandy wants to shut me out, she thought. But in the few seconds that she viewed the picture, she easily identified Max Wein. And she noted a couple things about him she hadn't expected to see. He wore a yarmulke and used two canes.

Sandy clumsily put the envelope in his brief case and returned to the morning's subject as he did so. He explained that they would be tramping about a mile and a quarter southward along "the Ditch," the group's name for a straight slough about 12 feet wide that flowed about 50 feet west of the cafe. He added that they would come to an abandoned platform that would enable them to get out over the water and have a broad view of the marsh and a saw grass prairie dotted by hardwood trees. Jean looked forward to that. She hadn't been there before.

Jean imagined that they probably made a comical pair as they trudged along, he nearly a foot taller and more than twice as heavy as she, both laden with their specialty equipment plus scopes and tripods. There was a faint path, or at least a place where the grasses had been matted down by previous walkers. It was March now, before the heavy summer rains, so there were only a few places where they had to slosh through a little mud. Ospreys, egrets, and kingfishers all but ignored them as they slogged along chatting amicably. Once they stopped to marvel at the striking black and white coloration and the deeply forked tail of a swallow-tailed kite soaring gracefully overhead. The bird uttered some shrill but pleasant notes that Jean attempted to record.

Suddenly Sandy cut off his chatter. They were coming to the dilapidated platform out over the widening ditch. He whispered, "Here's where I go to work." The big man was as quiet and agile as a cat as he set up his equipment and used his light meter. His first target was a glossy ibis, whose iridescent bronze back glistened in unspeakable beauty in the early morning sun. The bird dabbled in the mud at the ditch's edge not 12 feet from the platform. Click, click, click of the shutter in quick succession was the only sound.

A moment later, stabbing its huge, downward curved, slate blue bill into the shallow water, the bird lifted its head with a small water snake struggling in its beak, hanging from it like a Fu Manchu mustache. More clicks. Sandy whispered, "Oh boy. I got it," while continuing to track the ibis through the viewer.

Jean heard the unusual gurgling song of a marsh wren, and her tape reels whirred quietly. Then she saw the male playfully swinging down and up on a cattail at the marsh's edge, tail upright and almost over its back in classic wren fashion. She touched Sandy's arm, calling his attention to the secretive little fellow. He focused his camera and photographed the bird in perfect light before the second click caused it to invade the marsh and disappear, still gurgling its unusual trills, in the labyrinth of cattails and reeds.

And so it went. They worked at their respective skills for three quarters of an hour before Sandy first used his nonwhisper voice to announce, "I've lost my best light. Willing to stay as long as you'd like but I'm going to be packing my stuff." Jean said she was just as happy to begin to amble back, and in a few minutes they were heading northward alongside the Ditch chatting, both newly respectful of the other's craft. In less than an hour two people who had been essentially strangers had forged a bond of friendship, almost without words, that was as firm as that of yearlong roommates. Jean's spontaneous, entirely natural act of tugging on his arm to call his attention to the marsh wren testified to her comfort level with her new friend.

Sandy remarked that he thought he had made a few "saleables" that morning—pictures for which he could find a market. He was sure the glossy ibis with the snake and the marsh wren swinging on the reed could be sold, and he thanked Jean warmly for alerting him to the latter.

She asked him what else he did beside sell bird photographs. He replied, "Nothing. I've tried a lot of other things, but now I've resolved to try to eke out a living from bird photography, which is what I do best and like best. Of course I'm church mouse poor. It doesn't help that I'm disgustingly conscientious about support payments for my ex and kid in Atlanta. At least I've got some pictures in a gallery on Marco

Island, and that's pulling a few sales. I'd like for you to see them." Jean assured him she'd get over to the gallery.

As interesting as it was to hear about himself and his craft, Jean at first looked for an opportunity to broach "the subject" as she had planned. Then she had second thoughts. "Maybe it's better this way. This is fun. What right do I have to link a bunch of birders, of all people, to somebody's disappearance that I don't know anything about in the first place?" As she was mulling that idea, Sandy also was occupied with his own thoughts. The two walked for maybe ten minutes in silence absorbing their surroundings. Then Jean heard an unfamiliar cuckoo-like call nearby. She switched on her recorder and suddenly, not 15 feet away, a tiny heron was flushed from the marsh, flew feebly for a short distance while flashing handsome buff-colored wings, then disappeared into another hiding place in the marsh. It was a least bittern. Although it didn't repeat its call for her recorder, the sight was conclusive: She'd forget the Max Wein thing and concentrate on her research project.

Sandy even gave her an opportunity to engage the subject. "Sorry that we messed you up about the dinner for Max. Doris had the guilties about it, but it was all our faults. Dumb communication. We didn't have a hidden agenda or anything like that."

"No apology needed. I understand perfectly. I hear it was a fitting occasion," remarked Jean, wondering why she didn't close the subject. Maybe it was his unneeded reference to a "hidden agenda."

"Fitting? Yes, I guess so. The dinner was marvelous, and Max liked good food. Don the Sunday

School teacher said a nice Presbyterian prayer and Con added a Catholic one while we did the hand-holding bit. Don't know if it would have meant much to Max, who was Jewish, but it all was very nice. Of course, for me especially so."

Jean wasn't surprised that Max was Jewish; she had noted his yarmulke in the group picture. But "for me especially so" was a surprise, and for once the conversation flagged. Then Sandy figured it out. "You are wondering why for me especially. Max was my cousin."

Again Jean was at a loss. Sandy chuckled. "Well, the cousinship wasn't very close, but in tiny families you sometimes cling to a rather remote cousin. Max's father was a first cousin of my grandmother. That lady flabbergasted her friends by marrying a man with the fine Scottish name of Gordon Sanderson. Technically I guess I'm one-fourth Jew, three-fourths WASP, but I don't think of myself as anything. Still Max was my cousin all right."

"You say, 'Max was...'" ventured Jean. As she said it, she knew she again was being untrue to her new vow to nib out.

"Well, I don't mean there's a corpus delicti, but I think most of us accept the case against the Indian kid." Echoes of Doris, thought Jean, and not very convincing. Why did he assume I'd know what he meant by "the case against the Indian kid"? Doris must have talked to the others about me, she concluded.

Sandy resumed, "Actually, we just don't talk about it in terms of what happened any more, not even at the dinner. Frankly, Jean, I'm uncomfortable talking to you about it now. As a family member I wish there was some kind of closure, of course, but we all just prefer to remember the good times with our friend."

When they got back for their "post-game wrap up," as Don called it, Jean was grateful that she'd decided to stop worrying about something that didn't concern her. Everyone was in a good mood, and it was a relief not to listen for clues to a mystery that probably didn't exist. She and Sandy were the last ones in, and even Bill Long teased them about that, punctuating his jibes with his black eyebrows archly raised. This pleased Jean because she wasn't very often teased about anything remotely involving man-woman relationships.

As they were having their coffee, she played her tape, and the marsh wren song was absolutely clear and unblemished. They complimented her, and she felt as if she belonged again. So before they broke up, she spontaneously invited them all to an informal barbecue at the trailer. "Bring your families" she said, adding with unpracticed coyness, "Or your significant other." Each of her new friends thanked her, took down the directions to the trailer and noted the time, 5:30 next Friday.

So the morning turned out quite differently than she had planned. Instead of advancing her knowledge of the disappearance of Max Wein she decided to chuck the whole thing.

When Jean returned to her trailer, she was happy with her decision. She had her work to occupy herself. She was on schedule, and she even played one of her favorite Mahler symphonies, the fourth, instead of transcribing bird recordings.

She slept well that night, yet before she dropped off she couldn't help pondering, "If Sandy is 'church mouse poor,' what's he doing with all that expensive new photography paraphernalia and that new Mustang convertible on top of alimony?"

~~ 7 ~~

Over the next few days Jean had the barbecue to plan. When she thought of Max Wein's disappearance at all, she imagined that perhaps someday Doris would write to tell her that his remains had been found or that he turned up in Antigua with a pretty lady on his arm. Or maybe Jean would read his obituary in one of the bird journals or nature magazines. However she found it out, there'd be a logical explanation that hadn't required her help.

That's how matters might have stood forever if it hadn't been for something that Jean stumbled on the next time the group met.

Meanwhile, her little party was a success. That added to her relief that she'd dropped the "case," as she now jokingly called it to herself. Everyone came except Doris, who begged off with a rather flimsy excuse having to do with the law partner she worked for, a litigator. Supposedly, he was going to work most of the night before going to court. It didn't occur to Jean at the time that this was rather surprising on a Friday night. Jean also saw the party as an opportunity to repay her elderly neighbor, Annie Crews, for her welcoming courtesies. Mrs. Crews accepted the invitation and fit in nicely.

Don Purvis brought his pretty little wife, Susan, and their stair-step sons, 11, 9, and 7. Susan had nice features, but her solemn demeanor didn't show them off to best advantage. She clung to her husband and was not very relaxed in conversation. She was unduly

54

nervous about the deportment of the boys, which on the whole couldn't have been much better.

Con brought her son, whom none of the others seem to know. The young man, Pete (no last name was introduced), captivated everyone. He was tall and slender, about 21, with a mop of dark hair over his ears and flopping across his forehead. His handsome features favored his mother, whom he was visiting for a few days while on spring break from the University of South Florida, but he didn't share her verbal reserve. He had a million-dollar smile that he flashed regularly. He was especially nice to the Purvis boys and pegged a Frisbee around with them in a way that made them look good with fancy catches. They loved that.

Another of Pete's conquests was Alma Long. Bill surprised the others by bringing her, and Jean was flattered that he did.

She was abnormally thin and overdressed in a white suit. Her sparse hair looked as if it had been colored and set for the occasion. She diffidently met Jean, Annie, and Pete, and remet the others, none of whom did she seem to recognize. Otherwise, she sat there smiling and not saying anything other than "Yes, I think so," when someone would ask her a question. She took no more than a couple of bites of the barbecue, beans, and taco salad that Bill tried to get her to eat. She did show a little sign of life when young Pete brought her some ice cream. She told him it was good and asked him if it was vanilla, which the young man assured her it was. Jean wondered if the frail 70-year-old woman enjoyed herself at all. She deduced from Alma's perpetually benign smile that perhaps she did. Jean also wondered if the reason Bill brought her was, in part, to show his friends her deterioration and the difficult time he was having.

Pete took a lot of interest in Jean's recording equipment. When they tramped out to inspect the receiving dish, other guests traipsed along. After she showed them her setup out there, she led Pete and some of the others back to the trailer to show them the recording end. She concluded her little show by playing some of her better tapes for them. Jean soon declared, "This isn't what we are here for. Everybody out!" Obviously, she was enjoying her own cook-out.

So was Sandy Sanderson, who came alone. He was the life of the party. At the urging of the others, he sang all 14 verses of "Abdul Abulbul Amir" in a stylish tenor that Jean thought might have had professional training at some point. He was the last to leave and helped Jean clean up.

As the other guests prepared to depart, they swapped stories about taking wrong turns on the way in and hoped to do better on the return trip. Pete remarked that they never did see the Wilsons' office trailer that Jean had mentioned in her directions.

Somehow they had veered off on the old abandoned road that swung around the south side of the marsh past Annie's trailer and thence to Jean's. Everyone joined in some good-natured teasing about Boy Scouts getting lost (although Pete wasn't exactly the Boy Scout type).

* * *

The mood of the cook-out was still with her when she arrived at the cafe for the next breakfast nine days later. She was fully at peace with her friends—no suspicions, no longer serious concerns about the disappearance. Nevertheless, she resolved to strike out on her tramp alone to remove any lagging temptation to bring up the subject of Max Wein.

She had decided to seek out a huge eagles' nest that she'd heard the others talk about from time to time. Con had given her directions on how to reach it, which she'd scribbled in her ever-present notebook. According to Con, the nest was a fair distance away, and there were two ways to reach it.

The one that Con had suggested involved driving up West Road #2, a nearby lane that can accommodate a car safely for about three miles where it ends in a clearing wide enough to turn the car around. After that, one had to slog on foot another half mile along a crude path at the edge of a dark cypress swamp to an opening where one could see the nest. At that point, however, the viewer was looking east, getting an eyeful of morning sun. For the best viewing, one had to circle through the saw grass around the top of the hammock, slashing through the sabal palms and mangrove tangles where they'd overgrown the path. The ground was still relatively dry; later, heavy late spring rains might make the way almost impenetrable.

Con said the other way involved a longer drive on a crude road that roughly parallels West Road #2 on the other side of the swamp, then loops around the north side of the prairie and hammocks. It brings the viewer closer to the nest by car, but that didn't matter to Jean; she'd enjoy exploring new terrain on the first route. Seeing bald eagles was still a thrill to this Midwesterner. Down here she had already seen them in a residential neighborhood in Naples and on Marco

Island, but that didn't diminish the excitement of seeking out another aerie.

Rather than driving to the turnaround she decided to walk the whole way, roughly an eight-mile round trip. She didn't tell anyone of her plan because she knew they'd try to talk her out of hoofing it or might want to accompany her. She wanted to ensure that she had this morning to herself.

She plodded up West #2 for the better part of an hour, stopping occasionally to look at a bird or snake or butterfly or water animal. She watched a quartet of gorgeous pink and white roseate spoonbills sloshing the water by swinging their huge flat bills from side to side in their quest for edible crustaceans, to the consternation of water striders and other creatures who depend on the water's surface tension for their habitat. Jean was thankful that these spectacular birds had not been totally wiped out by the hurricane and other severe unnamed storms.

The track of a car, perhaps made that morning, helped her footing on the crude road. Finally, she arrived at the turnaround clearing and found the car parked there. It was Don Purvis's Escort wagon. Maybe she would encounter his pleasant company.

Jean plowed on through some of the most difficult terrain she'd seen, with the dark cypress forest on her left made darker by thick hanks of Spanish moss. She saw evidence of deer and quieted her step hoping to encounter them. She heard a rustling sound in the undergrowth over to her left that could have been made by the beautiful animals. A thick growth of palmettos blocked her view. Silently, she parted the branches, training her eyes in the direction she guessed the sounds came from.

There she saw, instead, Doris Groot backed against the soft moss on a live oak, locked in an embrace with Don. The sight was so unexpected that it wasn't until Jean saw the motion of Doris's bare, white thigh that she realized what she was seeing and what she had heard. Not that she was so sheltered; she'd counseled pregnant high school girls, and her graphic descriptions of the mating processes of various mammals had been known to make worldly seniors on the football team squirm.

But the lovers were her friends, the first she had made down here. She had met Don's attractive family; she knew now why Doris hadn't come to her party. Her disappointment and disgust were almost physical. The fact that she saw them but they didn't see her only intensified her revulsion, as if she herself were part of the deception.

The last thing Jean wanted was to be a voyeur. Quickly but silently she closed the palmetto-frond curtain and carefully withdrew. At first she headed back toward the turnaround and West Road #2. But on second thought she realized there would be a strong chance that they'd encounter her as she plodded back down the road. That would lead to awkward explanations. So she turned back around and proceeded as silently as possible past the trysters in her original direction. She had all but forgotten about the eagle nest; she just wanted to hide herself in the opposite direction from the one they'd take back to the car. Then, when she would hear the Escort start, she would reverse her direction again and hurry back down the road. She would be noticeably late, but there'd be time to concoct a believable explanation.

In her haste, she penetrated farther around the prairie than she had realized. The path became a little less primitive. At that point, she instinctively looked up and beheld a magnificent view of an eaglet and its parent perched on an exposed limb alongside a huge nest, waiting for the male to bring back a meal. She tried to interest herself in them to blot out what she'd just seen. The shock she'd experienced couldn't entirely quash the curiosity of a scientist.

When she looked down to place her footing, she noticed something else to divert her: a small fragment of wool cloth, about the size of a pocket watch face. It was strikingly out of place in this remote swampland, which was the wildest she'd seen so far. She picked it up, and when she scraped off some dirt, the black and white heavy strands suggested that it was woven in a lovely design. A bit of Indian garb? Possibly, but then her mind took her back to the brief glimpse of Max Wein she had seen in the picture Sandy Sanderson didn't mean for her to see. Could this be a fragment from Max Wein's yarmulke? Control your imagination, Jean, she lectured herself. That idea didn't make sense because she had seen also that Max Wein was seriously deformed, perhaps by polio, and was leaning on two canes for support. How could he have struggled along the uncertain path to this desolate spot, a mile beyond the clearing where he could have parked his car?

She thought the cloth worth saving, however, and stuck it in her pocket. Then, looking up for another view of the eagles, she observed an osprey, and she recalled that those big fellows have been known to use all kinds cloth in their nests, up to and including full-sized towels. The osprey could easily tear whatever the piece of cloth was with its talons when he grabbed it for his nest.

She heard the Escort start. That was her signal to head back to the cafe. She hurried, but by the time she reached it, the group was breaking up. Don had already left in order to get back in time to teach his Sunday School class. Her heart ached for the adoring, uninteresting little wife and the appealing sons. She couldn't bring herself to look at Doris or say a warm good-bye to her. She hoped her disapproval didn't show.

She wondered if anyone else had ever seen the lovers. She wondered if Max Wein had.

~~ 8 ~~

Not for a moment did Jean think that Max Wein was blackmailing Don or Doris or that either of them was capable of being the agent of Max's disappearance or death. Nevertheless, stumbling on them was a defining moment for Jean. She was an admitted bird snob. It is not much of an exaggeration to say that, up until then, her world was divided into two groups, birders and non-birders. Birders wear the white hat. When she beheld Don and Doris together, she came to grips with the realization that birders are capable of infidelity, crime, meanness, murder, anything, just as athletes, politicians, entertainers, business tycoons, and biology teachers are. God had given birders free choice along with everyone else, and they too could make horrible ethical and moral botches of this privilege.

This revelation reawakened Jean's sense of duty to act on her suspicion that one or more of her friends had some unreported knowledge of the disappearance or death of Max Wein. She would resume her quest for more details although she knew she would risk incurring her friends' hostility.

She would begin innocently enough by searching out the newspaper accounts of the disappearance as it was reported two years before. She hadn't done this earlier because her original interest was not much more than curiosity, call it nosiness, but now she was serious. She allotted a day to drive to the Fort Myers central library to see how the Fort Myers and Naples newspapers and the Miami <u>Herald</u> reported the event.

She checked out the microfilm for the three papers and began to advance the Fort Myers <u>News Sentinel</u> film of two-year-old issues through the reader. She stopped at the Monday in March that most closely corresponded with the date of the anniversary dinner of the current year. Nothing there. She scrolled forward to the next Monday, and there was this first page headline:

Noted Birdman missing

She took careful notes of the facts reported and the slant of the article. She would put the related information from the three papers in parallel columns. On the first day all three put the story on page one. The Fort Myers and Naples articles featured it as a local story; the Miami paper played up the fact that Wein was a Miami citizen. Only that paper ran his picture and a respectful biographical sidebar about how he juggled his vocation as a successful jeweler with his avocation as a respected ornithologist.

Each paper reported that Bill Long called the sheriff's office about 11 a.m. Jean had thought that Don Purvis would have made the call, but then remembered that he had probably left to fetch his family for Sunday school before the group was alarmed by Max's failure to return. That only made her more bitter toward Don. Both Long and Sanderson were quoted in the stories, the women only named. The <u>Herald</u> identified Con Smith as Consuela Martinez-Smith, a former resident of Miami, and the daughter and onetime protege of the late Dr. Hector Alphonso

Martinez, a militant leader of the Cuban community in Miami.

Long was identified as "G. Williamson Long, Jr." The papers made much of the fact that he was a resident of the "exclusive" Port Royal section of Naples and was a retired senior partner of a prestigious New York law firm. They also apparently quizzed Sanderson at some length. The journalists were interested in him primarily because he was identified as the missing man's cousin and presumably knew him the best.

In piecing together the three accounts, Jean learned that Bill Long said that by about 9:30 the others were getting quite concerned; Wein was usually back by about 8:30. His car was not on the parking lot, so they checked with Big Cypress cafe personnel (unnamed) to make sure he hadn't left before the others came back. The waitress hadn't seen him. Long suggested that Wein might have gone to a large hammock about two miles south that was a popular site for smaller songbirds, many of which were now migrating through Florida to their northern nesting sites. It had the local name of Panther Hammock although no Florida panther had been seen there for years. Jean knew the place and recalled that it was easily accessible by car.

According to the newspapers, Long and Sanderson drove to the hammock and found Wein's car there, locked. Seriously concerned by this time, the two men decided not to touch the car. They spent 15 minutes calling and searching for their companion. Then they agreed that Long should hurry back to the cafe and call the sheriff if Max hadn't shown up in the meantime. Sanderson would stay near the car, continuing to search for his cousin. (He was identified that way in all three papers.)

The articles reported that the hikers complimented the officers on their quick response. At Long's suggestion on the phone, they sent one car to meet Sanderson at Max's car and another to the cafe to meet Bill and the two women. Bill Long forthrightly shouldered some blame in the newspaper accounts. "I feel terrible about this," he was quoted as telling the officers. "I had told Max I thought I'd seen a pair of migrating Kirtland's warblers at the hammock, and I wondered if he could verify them for me some time. We often verify each other's sightings. I have no doubt that's why he was there." One of the reporters added that Kirtland's are rare warblers that nest in a restricted area of Michigan and winter in the Bahamas and are seen in Florida only rarely when migrating between their two limited territories.

Chief deputy sheriff Ed Beggs was leading the investigation. He made a point of the fact that he left the 16th green on a Sunday to take the call when summoned by his pager. "That's how important I think this is," he told the Naples reporter. His group admitted that they found no important clues at the site of the car, a Ford Taurus station wagon with special hand controls for handicapped drivers. After dusting for prints, they forced open a locked door, the glove compartment, and a valuables compartment in the rear of the wagon, but reported nothing of suspicious nature. They confiscated what items they did find. The other birders stated that Wein always had some elaborate bird spotting equipment and a camera or two with him, but nothing of that nature was in the car, pointing to robbery as a motive if indeed there was foul play. Sanderson said he didn't know whether his cousin normally carried much money or other valuables with him, but he doubted it.

Beggs sent for a Sergeant Fred Billie, a Seminole Indian and skilled investigator of the natural surroundings, to examine the area. Unfortunately, there had been a brief but moderately heavy shower around 9:45 in the hammock area. That plus the tramping that Long and Sanderson had done on the long grass and white morning glory ground cover conspired against any definitive tracking clues. The two men had radiated off in several directions from the car looking for their friend, but in doing so, they were stomping over any tracks or other clues Wein or someone else might have left.

Two of the papers reported that Sheriff Beggs already was seeking to identify and find three Indians that he said were known to be "raising Hell in an all night party" in the area that night. Without naming names, he said he was "pretty sure" he knew who one of them was, and "it is a guy who's given us trouble before." He promised that they would quickly round up the three Indians. Jean wondered on what grounds he would bring them in.

She was already beginning to dislike Beggs just from the two-year-old newspaper accounts. Nevertheless, she gave him credit for efficiency. He had set up a separate phone line for anyone who had information. He was regularly on the local television and radio stations and was accessible to reporters. He didn't discount kidnapping but said they'd found no ransom note. Sandy Sanderson was quoted in the

Miami paper as saying that Wein had no close relatives in the area other than himself and supposed that if there were a note it would be directed to him. A question about possible suicide also was unproductive. His relative said he had no known problems other than his congenital disability, and he'd come to grips with that as a child. Besides, there was no note, and the action of locking the car and then disappearing wasn't thought to be indicative of suicidal behavior.

The follow-up articles on Tuesday and Wednesday were of the "still-no-news-of-missing-birdwatcher" variety. On Tuesday the authorities hauled some dragging equipment out to a slough near the hammock where the car was found, but it yielded nothing but a fishing rod, some animal carcasses, and the inevitable shoe.

Beggs had interviewed Don Purvis, and the Naples paper also had sent a reporter out to talk to him. Purvis said he was "broken up by Max's disappearance. He was a super guy and probably one of the two or three sharpest birders I've ever known. I'm sure he'll show up. No way anyone would want to do him harm." In other words, he like the other friends added very little of substance. Jean noted that only Bill Long had been of any help. He'd accurately guessed where Max had gone, and he even assumed some responsibility for his being there. She was glad to see some compassion issuing from this sometimes imperious personality.

Meanwhile the chief deputy was still holding court and making unsubstantiated promises. His "operatives" had been out interviewing people in a nearby migrant community while he himself interviewed Purvis. The sycophantic Beggs added that the Purvis interview was a matter of routine, assuring the reporters that neither Purvis nor any of the other birders—"a high class group of people"—were suspects. He said he just wanted to make sure that every stone was turned. "Maybe some shred of conversation they had with Dr. Wein might not have meant anything at the time, but could offer a glimmer of light to we in law enforcement." Beggs had anointed Max Wein with a phantom doctorate because he'd heard that he taught some classes at a community college. And of course, you can guess what Jean thought about his grammar, although she wondered why the reporter didn't correct it.

At one of his press conferences Beggs had distributed glossies of Max Wein that Sandy Sanderson had taken. The papers ran the pictures prominently with instructions as to how to phone information. He added that the pictures were going out "over the wires" and being shown on Florida television stations.

The <u>Herald</u> had a story investigating the Sanderson-Wein connection and printed an unconfirmed report that Beggs had interviewed Sanderson at length. The story, in a veiled way, suggested that Sanderson could be a beneficiary of Wein's estate because of the lack of other relatives. It accurately traced the cousinship of the two men. This was the first suggestion of a possible motive for one of the breakfast group.

On Friday the story found its way back on page one. There was a suspect and a clearer motive, at least to Beggs. He brought in Robert "Bobo" Jumper, 22, for questioning and was understood to have grilled him for several hours. Like so many Seminoles, the suspect bore the proud name of a tribal hero, in this case that of the trailblazer for the legendary martyr, Osceola. But unlike most of his huge extended family, Bobo had found it difficult to stay out of trouble. He'd had several arrests for minor infractions and two for car theft, according to Beggs. The deputy had "witnesses" (unnamed) that Bobo had partied all night on Saturday and on Sunday was seen near where Wein's car was found.

Apparently, this was evidence enough for Beggs to hold Bobo, who admitted to having been to a couple of roadhouses in the vicinity that Saturday night, but claimed he'd returned home early and otherwise asserted he knew nothing about the man's disappearance.

"If I'd known he [Beggs] was hunting for me, I would have come in. I got nothing to hide," declared Bobo to the press, adding that "getting home at one o'clock ain't partying all night."

Bobo's public defender, Patricia Guzman, made a big fuss, and Beggs released him that evening. "But believe me that lady lawyer can't stop me from keeping an eye on him, and that's what I aim to do," Beggs said to the press.

At the time when Bobo was being questioned, a man named Herman Robinson came forward with information that fueled the robbery motive angle. Robinson, like Max Wein, was a jeweler. His store was in Fort Myers. According to the newspapers, the two men were close business friends. Frequently on his biweekly trips across the state Max called on Robinson. Sometimes they did business. According to Robinson, if he had a customer for certain items that he didn't presently have in stock, he would call Max. If Max had it, they'd arrange a deal, and Max would bring it with him when he came over to meet with the bird group.

They negotiated these deals several times a year, and last Saturday was one of the times, according to Robinson. "Max brought over several gemstones that I needed, and I went to the safe and paid him $4,500 for them in 45 hundred dollar bills. I've got the receipt right here." He was asked what Wein did with the money. "What he always does. Stuck it in a money belt."

Robinson explained that he usually had a substantial amount of cash in his safe on the Saturday afternoons that Wein was coming over. He added that he'd been to the bank that Friday after the two jewelers arranged the exchange on the phone.

One reporter asked why Robinson had waited until the following Thursday before coming forward. The jeweler said he'd been out of town the early part of the week. Another reporter recalled that Sandy Sanderson had said that as far as he knew Max didn't carry much money with him. She got back to Sanderson, and he said, "You quoted me correctly. 'As far as I know he doesn't carry much money' and that's as far as I know. I don't know Mr. Robinson, although now that you mention it I've heard Max mention seeing him sometimes when he comes over here. I just assumed they were social friends." Sanderson also stated he didn't know Max wore a money belt.

When Sanderson's remark about the money belt was relayed to Beggs, he said, "Somebody knew about it, and I think it was that troublemaker Bobo." Clearly,

Jean thought, Beggs had made up his mind that there'd been foul play and robbery was the motive. The newspapers seemed to buy that line, too.

When the story petered out on the microfilms, as it soon did, Jean went to the indexes and checked out several key words, but found nothing for "Wein" or "Sanderson" or other birders for nearly a year, except for one squib in the Naples paper that reported that the ranger, Donald Purvis, had been questioned about the disappearance in response to an anonymous tip. Both the sheriff's office and Purvis dismissed it as a "routine matter." The searches for references to "Jumper" were concerned with Indian ceremonials in which people of that name were active.

The Fort Myers and Miami papers had one-year-later follow-up stories to say that the case was still open and then reviewed it. The Miami story concentrated on Wein and his good citizenship and demanded action. Apparently, it caused little stir, because the story soon died out again.

That night Jean reviewed her notes and began sorting out her ideas and questions. The robbery motive was logical; she accepted that. But how would Bobo Jumper or anyone else know that $4,500 was in the money belt? Presumably only Herman Robinson knew that.

<u>Robinson</u>. She supposed an unlikely case could be made that Robinson assaulted Max to get his money back or that Max had given him fake stones. Both very doubtful. So far as Jean could tell no one had checked out Robinson's story that he'd been out of town early in the week of the disappearance and therefore waited until Thursday to come forward. Well, wherever he

had been, thought Jean, his appearance certainly helped Beggs' theory that robbery was the motive and Bobo the culprit.

<u>Bobo</u>. Even if Bobo found the money accidentally while assaulting Max, had there been any change of pattern in his spending or banking behavior? Had he paid for anything with a $100 bill? None of the follow-up stories addressed this question. Could that be checked now—two years later?

<u>Beggs</u>. She didn't like him. He was, she thought, too quick to jump the conclusion that either an Indian youth or a migrant worker was responsible. In fact, he was too quick to rule in foul play. There was nothing to disprove that Max had simply locked up his car and disappeared with his own $4,500 to start a new life somewhere. People had done that before, and that explanation had some appeal for Jean, as it did for Doris. She also found the sheriff's toadying to the ornithologists a little cloying. He even did so to the one person in the group who might, so far, have a motive, Sandy Sanderson.

<u>Sanderson</u>. Forget that I like him, she said to herself, he does have a motive. He'd told her that he was having a tough time financially. She couldn't bring herself to believe that he'd harm his cousin for $4,500, but the stakes possibly were a lot higher.

Max was a successful jeweler and had no close relatives other than Sandy. Still, she conjectured it would take several years to declare him dead (She'd look up the Florida law later if it became important). Sandy would derive no immediate benefit from his disappearance unless a body was found and none had been in two years.

It had been a productive day, but it stirred up new questions and answered few.

9

After reading the newspaper accounts, Jean pondered her next step. She considered a bold one—approaching Ed Beggs, which would involve her completely, but she decided that was premature.

Perhaps it was better to try to learn more about Max Wein's disappearance from members of the breakfast group despite their seeming reluctance to talk about it. Her friendships with Doris Groot and Sandy Sanderson had survived such discussions. Why not the others?

But which one? She found Consuela so guarded in anything she said that she doubted a conversation with her about Max Wein would be productive. She felt intimidated by Bill Long, and she was so angry with Don Purvis that she questioned whether she could sustain a rational conversation with him. However, her intuition that the story of Max Wein was incomplete had grown stronger. If she didn't want it to molder, she'd have to stop finding excuses not to talk to people.

Thus she decided that it was foolish to be intimidated by Bill; besides, he was extremely intelligent, analytical, and experienced. If she could inveigle him into a chat, he was likely to have something interesting to say.

She approached him at the next breakfast group. "What are you up to today, Bill?" she inquired. "Oh, my darned gout is acting up a bit, so I thought I'd lay off heavy walking for a day or two. Maybe drive over to a patch of shore between Goodland and Everglades

City where I've seen some pretty good stuff. Care to accompany an old man with gout?"

Exactly what she wanted. "Love to," was Jean's quick reply.

He pointed out that he didn't think it was much of an environment for making recordings, but Jean assured him that was OK. Soon she found herself for the first time in her life enveloped in the genteel luxury of a Jaguar Vanden Plas automobile.

On the way over, Bill was all birds. He identified species on telephone wires, flying overhead, in roadside ditches. Two or three times they stopped to investigate interesting sightings more thoroughly. An inveterate lister, he asked Jean to keep a tally of everything they were seeing. She knew it would be folly to interrupt this mood with a question about Max Wein. She decided to bide her time until the return trip.

At the beach Bill was still wound up. So she settled in to enjoy the early morning on the wide strand. There were no spectacular sightings by Florida standards: sanderlings, gulls, terns, turnstones, pelicans, red knots, a few assorted "peeps." But these were enough for a Midwesterner. The black-bellied plovers were beginning to show signs of their spectacular summer plumage. She was enough of a landlocked hinterlander to thrill at the sight of dolphins leaping out of the surf just a few yards out at high tide. For the first time she watched a black skimmer scoop up a small fish with its huge, brilliant red mandible while flying at terrific speed. But her greatest excitement came when magnificent frigatebirds soared at low altitudes overhead. She wished they'd utter some sort of cry that she could record. They didn't oblige.

All the time Bill was good company. She updated the daily list as they both spotted additions to it. It was a cool, bright morning. The clouds hanging low over the Gulf horizon were narrow white stripes with blue-grey bottom edges. They were all that marred a clear sky. Once Jean took off on a quarter-mile walk up the beach. She dabbled in the water and was surprised at how warm it seemed. "I'll bet it's at least 75," Jean remarked. Then Bill reminded her she was stepping in at water's edge. "You get that little body of yours all the way in, and you won't think it 75," he joked.

She brought back a few pretty shells and showed them to Bill. One was a sand dollar, or about two-thirds of one. "A dollar is worth less even on the beach," he smiled. Of the other shells, he said, "Pretty, but nothing special. You're looking at the molluscan equivalent of cardinals, mockers, and mourning doves."

Bill looked at his Rolex. "About time to get back, but before we go, I'm going to try to show you something special." They walked about 200 yards up the beach to where a little estuary emptied into the gulf among some thick red mangroves. "There," whispered Bill. "See it on the other side?" Jean didn't at first, then with the help of a silent gesture she saw her first reddish egret. Just then the bird began to ply his unique style of fishing by erratically chasing his quarry and acting quite tipsy.

Bill's thoughtfulness in showing her this sight made her feel their friction was well behind her. On the drive back to the cafe, Bill was much less hyper about bird counting, so Jean was emboldened to broach "the subject."

"Did you know Max Wein very well?" she opened.

"Very well."

"More than just at the breakfast group?"

Bill took his eye off Route 29 in front of him just a second to look at Jean. He made her feel that he didn't like being pressed, but he responded helpfully.

"Yes, I was at his condo in Miami many times, and he stayed with us over here sometimes. Perhaps you didn't know it, but he knew as much about casual, accidental, and occasional visits by exotic birds to Florida, in fact to the entire East coast, as any man alive. That's an interest of mine, too, and I looked on him as a mentor in that field." Bill went on to tell about a trip the two had made to Newburyport, Massachusetts, to see a Ross' gull, a handsome Arctic rarity that had inexplicably made its way to the Cape Ann area of Massachusetts in 1974.

"I'd heard of his expertise," said Jean. "What do you think happened to him?"

Uh-oh, she thought. Too sudden a transition. She was right.

Again the quick, perhaps disapproving glance. But again the helpful response.

"Conventional wisdom has it that he was robbed. He was known to be carrying a large sum of cash in his money belt. Maybe he foolishly resisted. I don't know, but I have no reason to doubt the conventional wisdom. It's a logical explanation."

"But couldn't he have just pulled up stakes and decided to start life somewhere else? No body was found, was it?"

"How do you know no body was found?" There was a note of antagonism in his voice.

"Somebody, Sandy or Doris or somebody, said so, I think."

"Well, that's right. As to your question about a voluntary disappearance, that possibility used to fascinate me. But nobody else, least of all the boob that investigated it, would have any part of that idea except maybe good old Doris."

"So Beggs was a boob."

"How did you know his name?" This time the antagonism was real.

"Somebody mentioned it when they filled me in on the dinner for Max Wein," Jean lied, realizing she'd made a careless mistake that would probably shut things off.

"I shouldn't have called him a boob, I guess," said Bill, apparently satisfied by Jean's explanation. "He did the right investigatory things, I suppose. I just didn't like him. He was a crude redneck, in my opinion. When I told him that Max was going through a tough emotional patch, he wasn't interested because it didn't implicate an Indian or a Hispanic whose name ended in `e-z'."

The words "tough emotional patch" interested Jean, and she wondered why Sandy Sanderson hadn't mentioned anything like that to her or to the press. But instead of following up, she took another tack—an unfortunate one.

"Was Max well off financially?" she asked.

"That question is out of bounds, little lady. Way out of bounds. And if it implies that Sandy might profit from his death, it's way, way, way out of bounds." Then, simmering down a bit, he reverted to party line.

"Look, Jean, drop it. We all buy the robbery motive. Probably Bobo Jumper. Nothing else makes sense.

"We loved Max, and we don't want to go through again what we went through two years ago. Forget that I said Beggs was a boob. Forget that I suggested Max had an emotional flair-up. Forget everything. It doesn't concern you or anyone else any more."

Jean had tried to interrupt him several times, but Bill talked right through her. Finally, she stumbled through a sorry apology. "Please, Bill, I didn't mean to imply anything at all about Sandy. I was aware that they were cousins, Sandy told me that, but as I understood it, the relationship was pretty remote. I wasn't suggesting that he'd receive anything if Max died. I feel awful if you think I implied that. I just wondered whether money could have been connected with the emotional problem."

"No, but just forget it. The emotional thing had to do with a disabled lady he'd met at temple. Forget that too. Everybody is satisfied, and it doesn't concern you, dear," he said again, this time softly.

Bill sounded conciliatory, but the rest of the drive was painfully monosyllabic. Back at the cafe, however, the mercurial gentleman was very talkative about the day. It was "Jean and I" did this and "Jean and I" did that. He made an outrageous pun about "Miss Otis egrets," and winked at Jean when apparently she was the only other one familiar with the sophisticated Cole Porter lyrics.

Nevertheless, Jean felt thoroughly rebuked. Bill Long wasn't exactly a father figure, but he assumed leadership, and as far as Jean could tell, the others willingly granted it to him. The rebuke from him swung a lot more weight than the sincere little cautions from Doris a few weeks earlier or even than Sandy's reasonable pleadings. So for a second time, Jean thought she might give it up although her feeling that something was hidden was getting stronger.

* * *

But she didn't know what to do about it. Don Purvis, of all people, solved that problem for her at the next breakfast. He got her aside and said, "I was over at Panther Hammock a couple days ago, and the sounds there are spectacular. I'll bet you could really do some good with your recorder. If you don't have any other plans, I'm driving over there right now, and maybe you could show me how you do it."

Jean was taken aback by his friendliness. Since her dismaying discovery of Doris and him together, Jean had limited her conversation with Purvis to one-word sentences and then only when spoken to. Did Don's cordial overture mean that he hadn't noticed her coolness? Or perhaps he had noticed, and he would probe to find out why. Or could this be a peace offering?

Don's next remark pulled her back to reality. "I'm afraid you'd have to walk back. I can stay at the hammock only 45 minutes or so." "Of course," Jean assured him and added to herself, "And I know why." She experienced a pang of regret for the way her friend Doris was being used. She'd forgiven Doris, but not Don. Her ethic didn't permit a husband with a sweet little wife and three young sons to behave that way. Nevertheless, she managed some sort of a smile.

They piled into the familiar Escort and in a few minutes were at the hammock. Jean took advantage of an easy opening.

"Isn't this where they found Max Wein's car?"

"So I'm told," said Don. "Actually, I never saw it. I had already left to take the family to Sunday school before anybody became alarmed." Don obviously was distancing himself from the event. Jean didn't like the answer, but as long as the man seemed talkative, she pushed ahead.

"But they never found his body?"

"No, and they dragged all the water around the hammock."

"So what do you think happened?"

"What everybody else does. Someone, probably Bobo Jumper, knew about the money belt and also found his cameras and binocs. It was robbery, pure and simple. And what a shame that whatever went wrong during the course of it, went wrong. I'd give anything to have Max back."

"Could the money be identified?" Jean supposed that someone had checked with the bank, but it wasn't reported in the newspapers. The question seemed to make Don a little edgy for the first time.

"How could it be?" Then he reflected a moment, looking at Jean as if trying to decide how much to let her know. "Oh, come to think of it, I think some bank person had a record of the serial numbers."

"Did any of the bills show up?" Jean asked.

"Not around here that I know of. But Bobo has family all over. He could have mailed or taken the dough to some relative in exchange for small bills or a check." Then Don added thoughtfully. "But that's just hypothetical. The Jumpers that I know are good people. It's hard to think they were in cahoots with Bobo."

"So maybe it wasn't Bobo."

"Oh, it was Bobo all right. At least, the sheriff sure thought it was. And Beggs knew more about it than anyone else."

"How do you suppose Bobo, or whoever, knew Max would be here?"

"Beats me."

"Maybe it was where he went every time, and the robbers had followed him knowing that he sometimes carried large sums," Jean surmised, trying to draw the naturalist out.

"Maybe, but I doubt it. I don't think he'd normally come here if Bill hadn't suggested it that morning."

"Where did Max usually go?" Jean prompted him by naming three or four popular places with the birders, ending with the eagle's nest.

With that Don shot her quick glance. "I doubt if he went there. In fact, he couldn't have. He was disabled," he said with finality. "Listen to that singing! What say we start recording."

End of conversation.

The recording went well, and Don was an interested partner.

But when his Timex dinged 7:00, he said he had to be off, and after getting Jean's assurance that she'd have no trouble getting back, off he went.

Her thoughts on her walk back centered on the fact that Don, too, accepted the verdict and didn't want to push it further.

He'd even worked out a way that Bobo could have laundered the money. And he squirmed when the eagle's nest was mentioned.

Jean was more puzzled than ever and didn't have her heart in recording bird calls the rest of the morning. She shambled back to the cafe earlier than usual and found Con sipping coffee alone.

The latter beckoned Jean to join her. She was the only one Jean hadn't asked about Max, so she thought she might as well do that if she could work into the topic gracefully.

"I've been to Panther Hammock," she said.

"Interesting place," Con said laconically.

"I guess Max Wein must have thought so. I understand it was one of his favorite haunts."

"I don't know about that, but I don't think so."

Jean pressed. "But isn't that where his car was found?"

"Yes. That day he went there at Bill's suggestion. Or so Bill says." Con just wasn't going to elaborate.

"Where else did he like to go?"

"He was like the rest of us, lots of places. They had to be accessible by car. He talked about wanting to go to the eagle's nest."

"But he couldn't have made it down there, could he?"

"Not the way you went," Con said. "But I think he knew the other way that I think I mentioned. Supposedly, it's reachable by car. Anyway, he wanted to go there somehow."

"Just the opposite of what Don just said," Jean thought.

Jean hoped her eyes didn't light up to betray her interest, so she changed the subject.

"Tell me something, Con," said Jean. "If he was somehow the victim of foul play, how did you people have the nerve to go out again in the early dark mornings?"

"We didn't at first," Con remembered. "We decided, or rather Bill decided, that we should not let the tragedy put a stop to something that was very positive in all our lives. We all agreed; I'm sure I did. For the next few times we went out en masse, but gradually one by one we began to saunter off for short solo side trips. We'd tell each other exactly where we intended to go at first, but after a while we drifted back into our old routines. By then we were sure that there wasn't some maniac out there, that it was a robbery that somehow went awry."

"You say 'we were sure' of that. Does that include you?"

"Of course. And I'd advise you to be sure of it too," tempering her advice with a faint smile. She drew in her breath to add something, but just as she was about to say whatever it was, Sandy Sanderson came toward them and Con clammed up as if she were a child whose mother caught her talking in church.

Still it was by far the most Con had ever chatted with Jean on anything other than the nature observations at hand. She was disappointed that she joined in the "it was probably Bobo" chorus with the others, which was beginning to sound about as convincing to Jean as the "my dog ate my homework" excuses of her students.

Still the cumulative effect of the morning's conversations charted Jean's next step for her: to visit Ed Beggs. The others came back just as Jean was leaving, and she noted that Don and Doris had arranged not to come in together. She hated herself for doing it, but she sneaked a peak at the back of Doris' denim jacket and saw bits of debris on it. She really didn't want to talk with Bill and Don, so she bade them all a quick farewell and went to her car.

10

Jean was a churchgoer but not a church member. She attended services nearly every Sunday, spreading herself over as many as a dozen different congregations in Oak City and had already visited half a dozen this year in Florida. Wherever she was, she always folded a $20 bill into a tight little square and left it in the plate, then recorded the date, place, and amount in a running tally of tax deductible expenses she kept. She observed the church manners of the various traditions where she worshipped; she didn't want to call attention to herself by not doing so.

She especially loved church music and always joined in hymns in her thin but accurate soprano. This morning she chose a church in Naples with the reputation of having excellent music—just right for composing herself and reflecting on what she'd learned from Bill, Don, and Con.

It worked, and when she got back to her trailer she booted up her computer and began a letter to Lt. Francis Sheehan of the Oak City Police Department. She and the policeman became very close during her involvement with the Georgina Pearson kidnapping. He was the first person to listen to her ideas seriously and stood up for her against those who pooh-poohed them, including the FBI agents and even Georgina's father. She had a head start in her relations with Sheehan because two of his five daughters had been her students, and they had praised her warmly.

After a warm greeting and brief reference to her project and the weather, she wrote:

April 22

...I'm writing to ask a favor, Francis. I've run into something rather strange. A famous bird watcher named Max Wein disappeared down here about two years ago. He simply didn't return to rejoin his colleagues after a short bird walk. His car was found but no clues of the man. The nearby waterways were dragged without result. He could have simply walked away to start a new life somewhere, but most people are convinced there was foul play. He was known to be carrying $4,500 in $100 bills, and the only serious suspect was an Indian youngster who was supposedly a bit of a troublemaker and who was reported in the area in the early morning that Wein disappeared. But apparently the law people couldn't make anything stick.

What does this have to do with me? Well, without knowing about the connection to Max Wein, I was asked to join the same group of five birders that Wein had been part of. I didn't know about the disappearance until I'd been with the group a couple of times, and when it came out, they were collectively quite close-mouthed about it.

They said they went through a pretty dreadful time when their honored friend disappeared and simply don't want to relive it. That's understandable, but what little bits I've gleaned aren't always consistent. Each one of the five, in his or her own way, has told me in effect to butt out when I ask questions. They profess to believe that the young Indian has something to do with it and that robbery was the motive. Still there's nothing tangible to connect him to the disappearance.

It seems peculiar to me that five educated, very sociable people, who are very prominent in birding have so little interest in finding out what happened to their colleague.

Frankly, I have very little working for me other than instinct; still I'd bet the farm that one or more of the five knows something about the disappearance that hasn't come out. So I've decided to probe a bit—on the q.t.

To help me penetrate what if anything is going on here, I'd like to talk to chief deputy sheriff, Ed Beggs, who was in charge and if possible peek into his file. One of our group describes him as an "insufferable redneck," so it might help a little woman without a Southern accent if you'd write a note of introduction. I've included his address and a suggested letter for you.

She closed by thanking him for the favor and extended warm greetings to his family. Although it was a long letter, she'd been thinking about it so much that she wrote it straight through on her word processor almost without correction or hesitation. And when she scrolled back to take a second read, about the only change she made, other than correcting typos, was to delete "likeable" when she described the group as well educated, sociable, and prominent. She thought about "likeable" a good deal. Certainly Don, especially, and Doris were less likeable than they'd been when she first met them. Bill was more so, and Con and Sandy continued to be very likeable. But as a group, not a collection of individuals, they were no longer likeable.

Joan Sheeehan, Francis' wife, had mentioned the arrival of the letter as a newsworthy tidbit when she had phoned him on a household matter, and he looked forward to reading what his little friend had to say. He accorded it the honored position of the last read piece of mail after he'd splashed a couple of ounces of bourbon over a few ice cubes and tipped the recliner in his den to look at the mail. The bills, the opportunity to request a Visa for about the 15th time, and all the other mail were out of the way when he opened the envelope from Jean.

"Pretty thick," he said of the letter.

His broad ruddy face, with its handsome Irish features, displayed a pleasant smile as he began to read. His clear blue eyes crinkled as he got into it. Once he interrupted himself to ask Joan, "What the hell is a `hibernal blast'? H-i-b-e-r-n-a-l."

"Beats me," Joan replied. She got up and went to the small desk in the den and opened the dictionary on top of it.

Sheehan read on and began to chuckle softly. Once his brow furrowed a bit, but mostly he appeared to enjoy the letter thoroughly. After he reread part of it, he handed it over to Joan.

"It looks as if our little friend has stumbled into another rather interesting situation," he said.

"Hibernal means 'winter'…winter blasts," she said before she began to read.

"Trust Jean. Who else in the world, given several months in Florida to escape the winter we had, would complain about not having snow and ice?" He chuckled at the idea.

Joan agreed, and like her husband she smiled as she read the letter and, like him, reread parts of it.

"What are you going to do?" she asked.

"I'm going to try to get her in to see that sheriff."

Joan hesitated. "I don't like thinking this, but do you think Jean may be a little full of herself after having her triumph here? There doesn't seem to be much to go on."

Francis didn't argue the point. "I guess the same thing is in the back of my mind. But I'm still going to go ahead. Her instincts are awfully good, and she's about the most modest person I've ever known. I just can't see her reading something into a situation just for the glamor of it."

"Good," said the realistic Joan. "I just felt I should bring it up. I'm glad you are going ahead."

"Tell you what I'm <u>not</u> going to do. I'm not going to use that namby-pamby little letter of introduction she suggested. If he's an incorrigible redneck, or whatever the word was, that would never get a little Yankee woman in the door. Especially if the sheriff has his mind made up, as I suspect he has."

He asked his wife to hand him the yellow legal pad on the desk. He sipped the bourbon, took a handful of unsalted peanuts, and with Jean's letter alongside, began to pencil out a note to Beggs. After several scratch outs and erasures, he handed the product to Joan who made a couple of suggestions he accepted graciously. Over the years, he'd found the calm, better educated Joan an awfully good sounding board.

The next morning he handed his secretary this note for word processing:

Dear Sheriff Beggs:

This is a letter of introduction for Jean McKay. I would be very grateful if you could show her the courtesies of your office. You would be doing a fellow law officer (myself) and I think yourself a big favor if you could receive her for a brief visit.

Jean is not in police work. Actually, she's a school teacher, and a very fine one. But I can tell you from personal experience that she has an excellent analytical mind and a determination that can be extremely useful in baffling cases. Perhaps you recall the Georgina and Robert Pearson kidnapping and murder, which was solved last year. Despite the solid police work of our department and of several FBI agents, that case lay unsolved for 10 years until Jean came up with the concepts that eventually led to the arrest and conviction of the gang that was responsible. Agent George Hillman of the FBI, who initially opposed Miss

McKay, is on record as saying the crime could not have been solved without her. As for me, I'll be frank to say that I owe her the nice citation I got for helping solve the case.

To get to the point: Jean is down there in your area and purely accidentally has learned about the disappearance of the ornithologist Max Wein two years ago. She would like to talk to you about it and look at the case files to confirm some ideas she is developing.

If she's on to something, and I think she is, it could result in nice things happening for you, just as it did for me in the kidnapping case.

One more thing, sheriff. Don't be put off by her appearance. I can't imagine anyone who looks <u>less</u> like a person who can help solve baffling and even dangerous crimes. She's a tiny woman and doesn't dress conventionally. But she's as smart as anyone I know.

If you'd like to talk over any of this before she calls, please call me collect. Use 555-8126 instead of the numbers

```
on   the   letterhead.   It's   my
direct  line  and  is  used  only
for confidential matters.
I  do  hope  you  can  give  her  a
little  time.  If  you  can,  I'll
owe  you  one.  If  you're  ever  up
here  in  the  Midwest,  sometimes
I  have  access  to  tickets  to
some  of  our  best  sports  events:
Kentucky   Derby,   Indianapolis
500, Notre Dame football, etc.

Sincerely,
```

The policeman didn't like to put the offer of tickets or the business about his citation in the letter, but suspected that's the only way to get the attention of someone like Beggs. Of course, Jean's suggested model letter had nothing as crass as that in it. Sheehan didn't send Jean a copy, partly because of his frank description of her (which he considered essential) and partly because he didn't want her to see how nervy he could be.

Instead, he wrote her a short note outlining what he'd written and suggesting she wait ten days or so before calling him. "If you call him before he gets the letter, it could blow the whole thing," he warned. He added to himself, "Not that I'm very hopeful no matter how well timed the call is. I don't think I'd let a plain little lady who dresses funny in to see any of the case files in _our_ office." He didn't like that thought, so he promptly dismissed it.

Jean received his note on Thursday. She was grateful not only for his prompt action, but also for his advice about timing.

So she went about her recording, splicing, editing, and writing without being overly preoccupied about Max Wein. She'd fixed on the next Thursday as the date on which she'd try to reach Sheriff Beggs.

But on Wednesday she spotted Orville Wilson trudging up the crude road toward her trailer. She greeted him, and he said someone had called her a little while ago.

"Thank you, Mr. Wilson, but you don't have to walk back here when I get a call. Remember our agreement. You save them until I come by to pick them up," she said, knowing full well that's what always happens and wondering with a twinge of apprehension why he chose to make an exception this time.

"Needed the exercise." Wilson reached in the pocket of a tattered green tee shirt and pulled out a scrap of paper. "The name sounded like Francis Sheen, or something like that, and he said to call him on the 8126 number." Wilson was more perceptive than some might give him credit for; he thought he noted a change in Jean's expression, so he added, "I'll walk you back to the office so's you can make the call. It's a good time for it. We ain't expecting any calls."

"Oh that's not necessary, Mr. Wilson. I was planning to come by the office in the morning," said Jean wondering why she said it and why she felt the need to put on an air of forced casualness.

"Look, Miss Jean, the operator who put the call through from there said somethin' about a police department, I think. There ain't any trouble, is they?"

"No, no. Francis Sheehan is an old friend who happens to be a policeman, that's all." Nevertheless, Jean had checked the time and realized if she put the call in the next half hour, she'd have a good chance of reaching Francis at the station. "But since you're not busy in the office, I'll call him now," and she fell in step with her thoughtful landlord.

The call from the camp went through smoothly, and the connection was clear, which was not always the case from the camp phone. Sheehan always picked up the 8126 line himself.

"Hello, Francis, it's Jean." After a couple of how-are-you's and responses, the police lieutenant came to the point. "We have a funny development here, Jean. I'd marked the envelope to Beggs 'personal,' and today it came back stamped, 'addressee no longer at address. Not forwardable. Return to sender.' You'd think if a sheriff's office got a letter from a police department they'd make an effort to send it on if the guy's been transferred."

"You'd certainly think so," Jean agreed. She was choosing her words carefully, conscious of Orville's presence across the room. Not that she didn't trust the likeable fellow completely, but still it was a touchy, private matter. She asked neutrally, "Can we try it again?"

"Sure, if we had the new guy's name," he said. "The letter's still on the floppy. It'd take Marion all of 20 seconds to delete Beggs' name and put in another," he said, then paused.

"You're getting me to do the talking. Do I get the feeling that someone's in earshot of you?"

"Exactly," said Jean.

"You'd probably like to tell me that you'll get the new sheriff's name as soon as you can."

"Right," Jean agreed.

"And you'd probably like to say to me that you can't understand why none of your friends had told you that Beggs was no longer about."

"I was wondering about that among other things."

"You'd probably also say that you can't ask any of the bird watchers about what happened to Beggs or the name of his successor because it might get you in trouble with them." The lieutenant was having a lot of fun with his little game.

"More than I already am," said Jean. "But I'll find a way and let you know soon."

"It does make the mystery a little more interesting from this end," said Francis. Then with concern, "You be careful now, lassie." He liked to contrast their Scottish and Irish backgrounds. After hanging up he said to himself, "I can't think of any group less dangerous than a bunch of bird watchers." But he wasn't scoffing; he took Jean seriously.

Jean was disappointed. This was going to delay her quest by several days. More than that, though, was her disappointment in her friends. None of them mentioned that Ed Beggs was apparently out of the picture, another little piece of evidence that there was a conspiracy of silence, or at least so it seemed.

Before heading back to the trailer she sat in one of the maple office chairs to ponder her next move. She looked up at Orville behind his maple desk, thumbing through a beat-up issue of <u>Field and Stream</u> probably for the 20th time. Suddenly she saw him as a possible source of information.

She was not above the creative fib. "Mr. Wilson." She paused for recognition, which she got. "My friend, Francis Sheehan, thinks he's met one of the sheriffs or chief deputies down here but can't remember his name. Who's our sheriff or chief deputy?"

"Arthur Garcia. Good guy. I know him a little."

"Is he new to the office?"

"Not hardly," Wilson chuckled. "They had a 20th anniversary bash for him last year. Me and Dot went."

Then Jean realized she might be in the wrong jurisdiction. The Big Cypress Cafe is some distance away. She got more creative.

"Well, I know it wasn't Garcia. Francis thought it was something like Biggs or Boggs."

Wilson was obliging. "That might be Ed Beggs who used to be at a post down the road, but I hope not."

"Why not?"

"Because I'd hate to think of your friend being a friend of Ed Beggs. In my opinion he is, or was, a numero uno jerko."

"'Was'?"

"He upped and quit, oh, maybe a year-and-a-half, two years ago. My friends there say it wasn't a moment too soon."

"Was he pushed out?" Jean was trying to keep the developing conversation moving.

"No. He played his politics too careful for that. He just quit. Sold his house in about two days and took off for some Caribbean island with his girl friend. She wasn't no bargain either."

"Well, he doesn't sound like the kind of person Francis would know. Maybe he just wanted some information from him. Do you know who took his place?"

"They had a temporary guy for quite a while, but they've recently put in a new guy. I met him couple weeks ago. Nice young guy, nothin' like Beggs. They call him Rusty Something. Rusty…Rusty…I just can't remember his last name. Rusty…If I think of it I'll let you know. Your copper friend'd like him."

Jean said she'd appreciate it, thanked him, and settled up for the call.

The next day as she drove by the office, Dot hailed her, "Orville said to tell you the name is Rusty Torrance. He even dug out his card. You got your eye on him, dearie?"

Jean smiled. She'd already launched another creative fib. She'd called the sheriff's office on the pretext of updating her church's mailing list. "I know you have a new chief deputy there, and we would like to update our mailing list. I think they call him 'Rusty' but we like to use real names on our list."

"It's William B. Torrance," said the phone voice. That was the name on the card. It was the name she telephoned to Francis Sheehan as soon as she could get to a phone booth.

~~ 11 ~~

The redirecting of Francis Sheehan's letter to William Torrance cost Jean another ten day wait before she could put her plan into action. During the nearly three weeks travel time of the two letters, she'd had no contacts with the birders other than one Sunday meeting. That was as neutral as she could make it—no mentions of Max Wein, Ed Beggs, or anything else to connect Jean with past events. She made sure of that.

When she thought enough time had finally elapsed to call Torrance, Jean was a little nervous when she entered a phone booth and lifted the receiver. She was trying to make an appointment with a chief deputy sheriff she had never seen. She gave her name and asked to speak to Sheriff Torrance, adding quickly before the receptionist could block her, "I believe Lt. Francis Sheehan of Oak City has written a letter of introduction."

"Hang on, a minute." Then Jean could hear, "Paula. Is Rusty expecting somebody called Jean McKay to call?" Paula's reply was muffled, but apparently was affirmative, for the receptionist came back on and said, "Yes, he's expecting your call, Jean. He's on another line, but if you'll hold I'll put you through next."

"Thank you." Remembering the formal environment fostered by her superiors at the high school, she thought, "Rusty," "Jean," it was a pretty informal office. But she was making progress, and the receptionist's easy manner helped quiet her nervousness. Soon the nervousness left her altogether.

The receptionist said, "I can put you through," and a genial, rich voice said, "Jean McKay? Boy, you really have a fan in that Lieutenant Sheehan. Got his letter a couple of days ago. When can we get together?" Friendly, direct, just like that. He mispronounced "McKay" but she'd take care of that later or else just ignore it. She'd done that before.

This was a Tuesday. She and Rusty agreed to meet at his office Thursday at "0930" as he put it.

With her usual precaution against being late, she test-drove to the station on Wednesday and that paid off on the morning of her appointment. She drove onto the lot about 9:20 on a bright, warm day. The district station had a good-looking stone facing; it had clean lines and appeared to be perhaps ten years old. A lofty antenna towered over the building. Two or three people were outside vacuously smoking.

Inside, the place was bustling. Uniformed deputies were answering phones, perusing files, discussing cases. A couple of young lawyers with their brief cases and seedy, sad-looking male clients were holding impromptu conferences. Two well-groomed young women hurried back and forth with files. There was a parade to and from the coffee machine.

But amid all the activity the reception area was orderly. Somebody's a good manager, Jean thought. The receptionist herself was behind a glass enclosure to the right as she entered. Jean identified herself. The attractive young blonde said, "Ah yes, Jean…" then looked up and unfortunately betrayed her surprise at the plain little woman's appearance. It was just a moment, but Jean saw it and was used to it. Still it hurt. "Miss First Names" as Jean dubbed her added, "You're

101

early. Good. I think you'll have to wait a bit, but you can wait outside Rusty's office rather than in this madhouse."

Then she called to Paula over a partition, "Paula. Jean's here. I'm sending her back." Paula materialized from some other cubicle, smiled warmly, and held out her hand. Jean doesn't follow fashion, but she correctly speculated that the black-and-white dress that looked so stunning on this slender young black woman might have come from one of Naples' upscale specialty shops. They went down a hall a short way where Paula pointed to a wooden bench.

"I hope you don't mind waiting here. Gets you out of the hurly-burly of the main waiting area. Can I get you a cup of coffee?" "No thank you." "Well, here's an old Cosmo. I hope you haven't seen it." She produced the magazine from an end table. Jean had not only not seen that issue, but hadn't ever seen any issue of Cosmopolitan. She thanked her and made a pretense of scanning it.

Before long Paula reappeared and said, "The sheriff can see you now. I'll take you in and introduce you," which she did after opening a door from the corridor into a small but neat office.

William B. (Rusty) Torrance looked exactly like what he was, a young Southern sheriff. He was about six feet one, 195 pounds, which was about his weight when he played tight end in high school in North Florida fifteen years earlier. He had dark red-brown hair that a lot of women would have killed for, but it was trimmed just short of a crew cut, barely partable. He had wide-apart brown eyes and freckles liberally spread over his tanned face. His hands were large and powerful looking. A gold wedding band graced his third left. His uniform looked as if it came straight from the ironing board and fit perfectly.

He rose to greet Jean, betrayed no surprise at her tiny size, egg beater hair, or drab clothes, but he must have noticed quite a contrast to the fashionable, handsome Paula. Even when Jean is in an office, a library, or a store, she looks as if she were dressed to go out and tramp after birds. (A stylish cousin once asked her why she habitually chose drab earth tones, and Jean replied that they made her inconspicuous in the field when she was pursuing nature. "But when you are not in the field?" asked the cousin. Jean said, "It's the same thing," meaning the self-conscious little woman always desired to be inconspicuous.)

She and the sheriff shook hands and he offered her a chair alongside his steel desk. A pull-out work surface was all that separated them.

"I guess I said it on the phone, but I'll say it again. You've got a real fan in Lt. Sheehan."

"Well, I'm a fan of his, too. We worked together on something once, and he was a big help to me when other people wouldn't listen."

"Worked on 'something'? I'd hardly call the Pearson murder and kidnapping just 'something.'" Jean was surprised and opened her mouth to ask how he knew, but Rusty went on. "He mentioned it in his letter to me, and I read up on it. I even called him up to find out more."

Jean blushed. "Oh that wasn't necessary."

The sheriff waved his large hand in a dismissive gesture then got down to business. "Now then, what have you got for me? I don't mind telling you, I'd sure like to get that case moving again. It has just sat there for a year and a half or more, and I'm not proud of that." Jean was aware that the young man needn't shoulder the blame for the inactivity, but she liked him for it. In preparing for the interview she had confirmed what Orville had suggested: For more than a year after Beggs left, the branch was run by interim leadership out of the central office. Torrance had been on the job only a few months.

Rusty's eagerness was wonderful to Jean. Here at last was someone who felt as she did: That whatever happened was too important to just let sit there idly. Even if Max Wein took off for his own reasons, it should be investigated.

But she said, "I'm afraid I don't have anything. Anything tangible. Nothing that would warrant opening the case up." She was groping how to say what she wanted to say. "But I do have a couple of feelings that I'd like to share with you. And I thought originally if I could talk to Sheriff Beggs we might be able to pool our ideas constructively. Or… (here she hesitated)…or perhaps peek into the files."

"Well, I'm afraid you can't talk to Beggs. He's out of law enforcement and is unreachable down in the Caribbean somewheres. I don't even know what island he's on, although I guess someone here in the office who worked with him probably does. As to the files, they can't leave the office or even be Xeroxed for you, but I can dig them out and find a cubbyhole where you can read them and make notes. First, though, I'd like to know all about how you got interested in the disappearance. Square one, if you don't mind. Take your time. We've got half an hour if no emergency comes up."

So Jean told him how she happened to be down there, how she got acquainted with the group, how she belatedly heard about Max. She told about the group's guarded answers to her questions, and she briefed him on her newspaper research.

Once he interrupted her to ask, "Do your friends know about your connection with the Pearson case?" Jean was quite sure they didn't. "Maybe you ought to..." then Rusty interrupted himself. "No, of course not. Keep it to yourself. You'd be putting yourself in all kinds of jeopardy if one of them is a killer and knew you were..."

"A <u>killer</u>? Oh, no, I'm not saying that!" Jean's voice became almost shrill and a look of terrible concern crossed her face.

"Aren't you? Isn't that one of the possibilities?" He was speaking gently but looking straight at her with a half smile.

Jean didn't know how to answer. The question introduced a possibility that she'd shut out all these weeks. Whenever the distant glimmer of a thought that one her friends might have a direct hand in any violence connected with the disappearance, she had always managed to arrest it and switch it off before it was fully formed. But she couldn't stop someone else from uttering the awful word "killer." Hearing it chilled her.

Rusty didn't force an answer. "I see that possibility troubles you, and I concede that lots of things could have happened. But do me a favor. Don't let those people know you have a background in helping solve a mystery. And don't let them catch you probing any more. Now tell me a little more about them."

Jean reluctantly did that. Up to this point in her account, she hadn't used names. She was made uncomfortable by the thought of spilling the names of her friends in the absence of any evidence whatsoever that would connect them to an event that might not be a crime at all. But Rusty was quietly persuasive, and he wore a uniform of authority. So she backed into her story. Her voice was even softer than usual as she gave each of the five, even Don Purvis, as generous a reading as she could. Yet she was true enough to her task not to minimize their reluctance to talk about the disappearance and to point out some inconsistencies among what little she'd learned from them. As she did this, she looked at objects on his desk rather than into his face. Had she been looking at him, she almost surely would have noticed a passing frown, a tightening of the muscles over his eyes, on hearing the description of Con Smith.

As Jean wound down, Rusty said, "If one or more of these people were somehow involved—and you've done me a big service already by opening up that possibility—can you think of a motive, no matter how far-fetched?"

"None at all." They talked briefly about Sandy Sanderson as a possible legatee in Max's will, but agreed that was hardly a motive when there's no proof the man was dead.

"Anything else?" Rusty asked.

"No," said Jean. "I'm sorry I've taken up your time. It all seems so insubstantial when I go over it this way. There's nothing here. My imagination got away from me. I want to forget about the whole thing." Jean was getting emotional.

"That's your choice, Jean," the young sheriff said kindly. "But before you bow out, if you do, do me one favor."

"Of course. What is it?"

"Do what you'd planned to do when you came here. Go through the Max Wein file and give me your thoughts. I'm impressed at what a keen observer you are...the way you pick up on details. I want to give the disappearance of Mr. Wein a lot of attention. Someone can't just disappear from my jurisdiction, even if I wasn't here at the time. I want to take advantage of any help you can give me, today at least. So go to it, Jean."

She didn't have a choice. The sheriff called Paula and asked her to dig out the Max Wein file and set Jean up with a legal pad and pencil in "the little room." As Paula was leading Jean out, Rusty said. "Take your time, Jean. But be sure to stop by when you are finished. If I'm not here, call me this afternoon between two and four. I'll make sure the call gets to me."

The manila file tabbed "Wein" was not well kept. There was a nearly complete circle of a coffee cup stain on the outside along with a couple of telephone numbers, which Jean took down, the words "Jumper" and "Sanderson," and a couple of meaningless doodles. A few of the papers inside stuck out and their edges were crinkled. The notes, which were clamped to the inside back of the folder, weren't much better. Many of them were scrawled in longhand; those that had been typed were scarcely any neater. There were lots of crossouts, strikeovers, and other marks of an indifferent typist. Certainly not Paula's work, Jean thought, although she had no basis for thinking so other than that she already liked Paula and was impressed with her personal neatness.

But Bill Long was right in saying that Beggs seemed to have done "the right investigatory things," and for the most part they jibed with what she'd learned from the newspaper accounts. There were a few new things. For instance, she noted that the idea of calling in the tracking specialist, Fred Billie, to look for footprints and other visual clues was pushed by a deputy, Joe Bob Carey, not Beggs. She also learned that the bank clerk who gave the jeweler Robinson the 45 $100 bills could pinpoint the probable serial numbers, which were broadcast to other police and sheriff offices. A description of Max Wein also was broadcast, and a picture Sanderson supplied was sent by fax to the media.

Jean didn't pretend to be a judge of good police work, but she did think that Beggs had been fairly methodical although she'd check with Rusty to see if he agreed. So that part was OK. What wasn't OK, in her mind, was the kind of man who emerged between the lines in the files. As she flipped through the notes she increasingly disliked their author.

A little of this arose from the sloppy, hastily written notes themselves. But mainly it was his leaping ahead to conclusions about suspects and ill-disguised mean feelings toward persons whom he had no reason to link to the disappearance. He was playing Claude Rains in Casablanca and exclaiming, "Round up the usual suspects." And the usual suspects were any local Indian or Hispanic boy in the area who had ever been in the least bit of trouble in his jurisdiction or any neighboring counties. For instance, the notes revealed that he sent out his men to track down and interview 23 migrant workers whom he classified as "known troublemakers." As far as Jean could tell, most of them had been guilty of no more than a Saturday night spree or driving with a suspended license, but he went after them all. The notes even referred to the "e - z people," referring to the last two letters of their surnames. She recalled that Bill Long had picked up on this unattractive trait in Beggs and used the same phrase to characterize Beggs' bogus suspects. "Bill's a shrewd one," Jean thought.

She perceived not only ethnic prejudice but also a giant ego in Beggs. He called daily press conferences and his notes commented on his own star quality. "Was in total charge. Put girl reporter from Ft. Myers paper in her place," one jotting said.

She was eager to read what the notes had to say about the witnesses who placed Bobo in the area. They didn't reveal anything about how Beggs was put on to the idea. But on Tuesday, he scratched, "IMPORTANT!! Learned that Robert Jumper, 21 year old Indian (see numerous other files), Darryl Barlette, white about 21, and a girl, Patrice Lopez, possibly under age, was drinking at two nearby establishments Saturday night and Sunday morning." The notes went on to say that Jumper "is well known to this office because of car thefts and several drunkenness, fighting, and vagrancy charges." Jean noted that there was no mention of previous convictions. Barlette had been cited twice for motor vehicle violations and once for fighting and drunkeness. Lopez had been cited once for loitering.

One of the "establishments" was the Big Cypress Cafe itself. The witness who identified the trio was LaWanda Carter, 34, who said she checked their IDs and served them three rounds and an extra one to Bobo. She said she refused him a fifth drink "because I didn't want the kid to hurt anyone with his pick-up. You know how Indians are with the booze."

The bartender, Billy Case, said he was aware of the three at a table but was busy filling drink orders and couldn't keep track of who was drinking how much of what. He promised Beggs he would check the order stubs from LaWanda to see if he could estimate how much the trio drank. A follow-up a couple of days later quoted Billy as saying "They was drinking pretty heavy, especially the one they called Bobo."

The other place was called The Spoonbill. There, the notes said, both a waitress and the bartender identified the threesome plus a second young woman who they said was called Carol. Other Indians sometimes joined them at their table.

Beggs and his colleagues had wasted no time getting out to see Jumper, Lopez, and Barlette. He assigned himself Jumper and simultaneously sent two deputies to see the other two so that the three wouldn't have time to coordinate stories. The notes recorded that all three admitted being to the two bars but say they returned to their respective homes between one and two in the morning. Jumper said he took Carol—Carol Musgrave—home at about 11 and rejoined the others at Big Cypress afterward. The notes referred to Jumper as "the suspect." After seeing Bobo, the sheriff noted, "Decided not to bring him in <u>yet</u>."

Later in the week when the jeweler Robinson turned up with the motive and Beggs brought in Bobo, the notes turned angry and personal. "Bobo acts like he's never heard of the disappearance of Dr. Wein, but we can see through him."

Nevertheless, he could dig up no specific evidence ("his family claims he got home by about 1:00 Sunday a.m. and slept til noon"). After Bobo was released, the notes trailed out for three or four more weeks, the last one being five weeks after the disappearance was reported, and Jean noted it was not in Beggs' handwriting. The broadcast of Max's picture produced only one lead worth following up and that was from the Chicago police department. But although the man had deformities similar to Max's and was at first vague as to who he was, he had old tattoos that quickly set him apart from Max. Once he sobered up, he was able to prove he was in Detroit the Sunday Max disappeared.

None of the things Jean found in the file that were new to her were particularly puzzling or startling. Nor was there anything that linked her fellow birders, even remotely, to the disappearance. She, however, had made several pages of notes. Several of them she put into question form, such as "Did any of the $100 bills turn up? Where?" "Why did Ed Beggs leave office?" "Where is LaWanda Carter?"

Next she turned to the description of the car, a light blue Ford Taurus, and the items found in it. The car's license marker checked out as being registered to Max Wein of Miami. The car was described as clean inside

111

and out although the tires were muddy. The team got only one fingerprint, on the left rear door handle. It proved to be Wein's. The car was fitted with a hand throttle and brake for disabled people.

The inventory of items found in the car was listed on a preprinted form with an identification of the car, date, and ownership. It was typed so sloppily that Jean wondered if she could trust the information:

<u>Passenger compartment</u> Locked. Opened with special tool.

Sweat shirt that said "Museum of Natural History" on it.

75c in quarters in coin holder.

Umbrella

Small red multiblade knife that had slipped behind seat on driver's side.

Special built cushion to raise driver's heighth [sic]

One VISA receipt for stay previous night in Holiday Inn.

Small cheap camera (under front seat).

<u>Glove box</u> Locked. Opened with special tool.

Valid registration

Insurance card. Hartford Insurance Co.

Tool to open windows if power fails.

Feild [sic] Guide to Birds.

American Orthological [sic] Union bird list.

Small blue-covered spiral notebook with bird notes.

Yellow pencil.

Crumpled paper with a 407 area code telephone number and the word "Owens" on it.

<u>Tailgate area</u> Also locked.

Beach towel spread over the area.

<u>Locked compartment</u> of valubles (sic) underneath towel

Spare tire, never used

Jack

Copy of July/August 1991 "Journal of Ornithology"

The last item was to Jean another proof of the sloppy work. The date was July/August but Max had disappeared in March of the same year! What, she wondered, was the real date?

Jean of course was familiar with the highly respected academic journal. Along with the note about the erroneous date, she made a couple of more pages of notes and questions. "Did anyone follow up on the 407 phone number?" "Who is Owens?" "The only prints on any of these items were Max's. Why no prints on steering wheel and inside driver-side door handle?"

After she had spent about 45 minutes reading and digesting the file, she felt it was time to give it back. She took it to Paula and asked if Sheriff Torrance were still in. "He's about to leave, I think. Poke your head in the door there, and you may be able to catch him."

Jean found him latching his inexpensive attache case. He looked up at her and smiled, but not with the warmth he had when he greeted her just an hour before. "Find anything?"

"Quite a few little things. Some questions, but nothing monumental. I'd like to digest my notes and think about some questions I have, and maybe we could meet again in a few days if it isn't an imposition."

"Of course not, Jean. I've got to move out of here now, but you can schedule something through Paula. Can we walk out to the parking lot together?"

"Sure," said Jean somewhat flattered.

They exited a door on the back wall of his office, went through a narrow hall with bare concrete block walls and a cold uncovered cement floor. It was lit by low-wattage bulbs. They came to a heavy steel door that Rusty unlocked by punching code numbers on a remote opener he carried in his breast pocket. Clearly this wasn't a public passageway, and Jean enjoyed the feeling of being on the "inside" of a crime facility.

They emerged into bright sunlight, right by the pool of official cars. Rusty approached the nearest white Chevy Caprice, paused and looked at Jean earnestly. "Jean, I'm afraid I've done something that isn't going to make your job easier."

His sincerity brought out the worry lines in Jean. She had already sensed that his demeanor was more subdued than when she first met him. She tried to ease his discomfort.

"Oh, I doubt that," she said, trying to hide her concern.

"No I'm serious. I may have spilled the beans." He was having a hard time saying what he needed to say. "You see, we know someone we call Consuela Martinez who I'm afraid is the same woman you call Con Smith. We saw her at Mass Sunday, and I foolishly said I was going to meet with a well known birder this week, knowing that Consuela is a serious bird watcher. I've been searching my mind trying to replay the conversation, and I called my wife to see what she remembered. We're pretty sure I didn't mention your name, but if she put two and two together she'd have to get Jean McKay. Why would a cop meet an ornithologist unless it was about the Wein case?

"No excuse, Jean, but when I took over here the Wein case was dormant. I had no way of linking Consuela to it. I checked the files, and she is barely mentioned in them, and then only as Con Smith."

"Maybe they are two different women," Jean said trying to be encouraging but knowing full well that they were one and the same because of the way the Miami paper had identified her.

"No, Jean. She teaches Hispanic kids, is a serious bird watcher, is so good-looking that Dawn, my wife, is a bit jealous. She has a white streak through her hair. Same woman all right. I think maybe you'd better pull out of this little game."

"Oh no, not yet," said Jean emphatically. "At least I'll learn how quickly the news that I've seen you spreads among the group. I suspect that they have a tight network in matters where I'm concerned." Rusty opened the patrol car door. "Well, be careful, Jean. Be sure to make a date to meet again through Paula. Again, I'm sorry."

"No problem," said Jean. But of course it would be.

Jean found it impossible to be upset with Rusty because of his gaffe. There was no way he could have connected Con Smith to Jean's forthcoming visit unless he'd suspected everyone in South Florida who had ever lifted binoculars to eyes.

Nevertheless, she was upset with the situation. As he requested, she telephoned him a couple of days later to arrange to discuss her impressions of the file. She was somewhat relieved when he begged off. His excuse was that he was up to his ears with a rash of car thefts. Jean accepted that; she was aware of newspaper stories of the thefts and their implications that the sheriff's office was lagging in breaking up the ring. Rusty assured her, "Don't think I'm any less anxious about the Max Wein file and your insights into it. Let's postpone our get together until next week after you see what kind of reception you get Sunday. That'll give us more information on which to make plans."

Jean agreed, but begged to ask one question. "Of course," said Rusty. "Shoot."

"Why didn't you interrupt me when I described Con? You just let me go ahead."

Jean heard him chuckle into the phone. "I didn't minor in psychology at Gainesville for nothing, Jean. I wanted you to be able to go through those files with as clear a head as possible. If we'd made the connection when you were describing the breakfast crew, you'd have been too upset to concentrate, and believe me, I need you at your best if we're going to accomplish what I hope we can. Fortunately, you weren't looking at me when you started talking about Consuela. If you had been, I doubt that you could have missed me blushing or twitching or something else to give myself away. I don't have a very good poker face."

"Thanks, I guess, for sparing me for an hour at least," Jean said, her broad mouth forming a half smile. "But I don't think it'll do you much good. I'm not excited about what I learned from the files."

"We'll see about that next week," Rusty assured her. "Call me Monday morning or even Sunday afternoon at home if you wish." He gave her his home phone number and wished her good-bye with his usual warning to be careful.

Jean hadn't looked forward to that Sunday with any kind of pleasure. The days were long now, and normally the sun would be up by the time she arrived at Big Cypress Cafe. But on this day a cloud cover produced a humid, leaden atmosphere. The ramshackle building seemed more ominous than ever when it loomed up in front of her as she bumped along its neglected driveway.

She had left her trailer earlier than usual to ensure not being the last to arrive. In her more anxious moments, she had envisioned the others lined up as a sort of tribunal as she entered the room. She even had had an anxiety dream a couple of nights earlier in which she was sitting for an oral examination for an unspecified degree. The professors judging her allowed her to use notes. They would ask a question, but Jean could never find the applicable notes even though she knew the answer. They would ridicule her, ask the same question again, and again ridiculed her for not being able to find the answer. Finally, in a sort of weird chorus they burst into cacophonous chant, "Give it up, Jean, give it up." It didn't matter that the professors weren't her five breakfast mates but rather an assortment of friends from Oak City and college days, nor that the questions were inconsequential. Jean had no trouble recollecting the dream and getting the message.

She reasoned that if she arrived first, she could occupy her friends in one-on-one conversations before they could organize themselves into the "tribunal" she dreaded. She brought along some of her best recordings and would ask them to critique them. She was ready with a series of responses to the kinds of comments she anticipated about her chumminess with the chief deputy. None of the answers satisfied her very much, but at least she would be prepared enough not to fumble. She even anticipated about how far things would go before she would step in and say, "Look, I think it's better if I stopped coming to these breakfasts." That would be her Rubicon. Once she said that, neither Doris's importuning nor Sandy's friendly arm around the shoulder would deter her unless one or more of them said in effect that they thought it was a good idea for her to pursue the solution to the disappearance. And that was very doubtful.

With all that buzzing in her mind when she drove up, she at least was relieved that her timing was right; hers was the first car. She went inside and tried to chat a bit with the waitress, Marie, who by now was a good friend. She was setting up her recorder when the others came up to the table more or less in a group. She suffered a wave of panic, speculating that they had met to confer about her beforehand.

She needn't have worried. They were all cordial and attentive to her new tapes. The usual good-natured banter prevailed during breakfast. They sat in their usual formation. Jean wished she had been across the table from Con where she could have detected any hints that she was any more approving or disapproving than at any other time. Once Jean initiated a conversation with her about Peter, her son, and Con did turn her head and talked directly to Jean. Again, though, she saw nothing in that lovely face other than pride in her son.

Jean concluded that either Con hadn't made the connection the sheriff had or, for reasons of her own, she hadn't rung the alarm bell. Well, she admitted, there was still another possibility: Maybe she had misread the situation. Maybe she was being overdramatic, imagining that the others were more close-lipped about the disappearance of Max than they really were. There was a certain plausibility to their collective reasoning that they just didn't want to go through the trauma of dealing with their friend's disappearance again.

Whatever the reason, Jean was off the hook for now. When they returned from their separate missions for a final cup of coffee, everyone was as friendly as they'd ever been. Doris and Sandy even asked for encores on some of the recordings she'd brought along. She felt light and free as she drove home. Even the dank, heavy feeling of the morning seemed to lift although not in actuality as much as Jean in her relief thought it did.

Under the circumstances, Jean saw no reason to act on Rusty's invitation to call him at home, but she did try him early Monday at the office. Miss First Names put her straight through, and there was noticeable anxiety in Rusty's voice when he picked up. "Jean? How did it go?"

"Amazingly enough, nothing out of the ordinary happened. I'm still a member in good standing," she replied.

They speculated on the reason, and Rusty naturally concluded that Consuela hadn't made the connection. That helped expunge his guilt feelings. He then asked her if she had an hour the next afternoon to discuss the file. They decided she would come to the office at "1400."

At the appointed hour, Miss First Names told "Jean" that "Rusty" was expecting her and reminded her where his door was. He greeted Jean with exceptional warmth, offered her the same seat as before, and asked Jean for her ideas.

"Oh, I wish you wouldn't put it that way. I don't have ideas, just hunches. And I've got to tell you straight off that I haven't found anything that links one or more of our breakfast group with Max's disappearance at all." Jean's little voice sounded plaintive, and she frowned as she looked at Rusty.

"'One or more' you say. That's interesting. They do seem to be conspiring to keep anything they might know to themselves. A conspiracy of silence just like doctors and lawyers when one of their own is under the gun," Rusty said eagerly.

"I'll admit I've thought about that." Jean hesitated. Then she decided to tell him about Don and Doris, which she'd omitted from their previous conversation and found difficult to talk about now. When she got to the sex part, the poor woman got stuck on how to describe it, so Rusty helped her. "I presume they were having intercourse," he said as matter-of-factly as he could and without looking at Jean. She didn't even have to respond. Rusty, who often showed a lot of maturity for a young man of 33, made it clear he wasn't interested in any prurience, but he was interested in facts. He made a note of it and concluded, "So we could possibly have a conspiracy of two."

"No, no, no," Jean exclaimed. "These people are my friends. I feel like a rotten old gossip. I can't think like that about them without any evidence whatsoever."

"Well, then how do you explain their unwillingness to open up with you?"

Jean took a while to answer. "I think about that every day, and so far this is about all I can come up with. Suppose for some reason we don't know about that Doris suspects Don of having something to do with the disappearance—or Don suspects Doris. Mightn't the other one protect his or her...lover if I came onto the scene asking a bunch of questions? Might the person doing the protecting go a step further and say to the others, 'Do you think it's a good idea for Jean to be nosing around about Max Wein? We went through enough a couple of years ago, and I'm not going to discuss it with her.' Conceivably that might carry some weight with the others, especially if it were Don. It's not much, but it's the only explanation for their collective behavior I've been able to come up with so far. It's awfully weak."

"I don't think so. I'm going to keep it as a live theory."

"Of course, we don't even know Don and Doris saw each other two years ago," Jean said. "Their romance, if that's what it is, could have started recently."

Rusty granted that she had a point, but added, "You know, you don't need a pair. Just one person could subtly manipulate the group in the way you describe. You've said how influential Long is and how popular Sanderson is."

He decided to change the subject. "Do you think it's possible the man just disappeared on his own hook? That he's alive and enjoying himself somewhere?"

"Yes, I do."

That surprised Rusty. "No kidding? He's never been seen, and he's pretty darned recognizable."

"I know. But there's no body, no clue to any other explanation. I'm just saying he could have disappeared on purpose. He was a very smart man, and I think it takes brains to disappear. And something had gone wrong with his life in Miami. Bill Long let that slip out. So I think it's a possibility, and it's as important to find that out as it is find out that he was…he… something else happened."

"You mean he was murdered, Jean," interposed Rusty completing the thought she was unable to. "You've got to face it, Jean."

Jean didn't answer, so Rusty asked Jean to tell him what Bill Long had told her about the disabled lady Max had been seeing. Rusty good naturedly remonstrated her for not telling her this before, and she apologized for it. "There's nothing in Beggs' notes about this, so apparently Long and Sanderson, who

122

must have known about it, withheld it from him. We'll try to find the lady."

That caused Jean to squirm. She managed to say, "I guess, if you must."

"Yes, we must, Jean, but we won't implicate you. I'm sworn to protect you, not involve you." Then he changed the subject again. "So far we've talked about stuff that's <u>not</u> in the file. What about what's in it?" Rusty asked.

"Well, again, a lot of what I'm thinking about is between the lines, so to speak. For instance, there's no record that Beggs followed up on the crumpled phone number in Max's car. From the area code and the next three numbers, it was to a phone down in the Keys somewhere. I asked myself why Beggs failed to pursue that. Probably because he felt that it wouldn't connect to Bobo."

"Good point. What do you think about Bobo as a suspect?"

"Frankly," said Jean, "After reading the files, I'm 98% convinced he had nothing to do with it."

"That's a pretty bold statement," Rusty said as he leaned farther across the pull-out work drawer that separated them. "You've told me most, if not all, of the breakfast people think the boy killed Max for the money. Why don't you?" Rusty was intense.

But Jean was matter-of-fact in her reply. "Lots of reasons. One, the coincidence of a Seminole boy finding a man early one Sunday morning on a remote hammock who happened to have $4,500 cash in a money belt stretches credibility pretty far. At least it stretches mine. Second, as I understand it, none of the $100 bills ever showed up—although Don Purvis had some silly explanation for that. Am I right about the bills?" she interrupted herself.

"You are, so far as I know. Go ahead."

"Well, if he was a car thief, as Beggs indicated, why didn't he take the car? It was a nice one, a popular Taurus that wouldn't cause attention. Probably easily fenced. I'm not even sure he was a car thief although the files want us to think so."

"I checked on that. He took some joy rides, usually with someone else driving, but never tried to dismantle a car or fence one," Rusty said. "But to play devil's advocate a moment, the handicap controls might cause suspicion if an able-bodied young guy tried to sell the Taurus."

"Hadn't thought of that," admitted Jean, her ego a little jolted.

That didn't diminish Rusty's growing respect for her. "I don't think it matters much," he said, "But here's something that might. We've found out that he has a car now that might have cost him around four grand."

"If the birders knew that, it would clinch the case against Bobo in their minds," Jean declared. But she was undeterred. "Everyone's except mine. Is it likely that a poor kid would sit on that much money for two years before spending it?"

"I can't rule it out, Jean." But the fair-minded young man added, "He might have a job and bought it from his earnings. We'll check out how he paid for the car. And you should know that since Beggs left, Bobo has been in zero trouble with this office. Zero. Nearly two years clean."

"And aren't his people well respected?"

"Absolutely. Some of them still follow the old beliefs of the Seminoles. My reading of Bobo is that he might be having trouble reconciling his family's traditional beliefs with the world around him. But there I go with Psych 101 again."

"Well, it makes sense to me," Jean agreed. "Anyway, from what I hear, his family doesn't seem the kind that would cover for him with a fake alibi."

"You're probably right, but don't get too sentimental about it. Families do strange things to protect loved ones." Rusty was all lawman now. "I've got to keep him on my suspect list."

"OK. But I have to speak frankly, Rusty." Jean paused, eyebrows raised. Rusty gave a little nod, a go ahead signal.

"It's just that Ed Beggs was so obviously prejudiced against Native Americans, Bobo in particular, and Hispanics that I think he found Bobo a convenient fall guy. He didn't follow up on anything that didn't involve Bobo, like the phone number in the keys. Or at least didn't put it in the record." Jean scooted forward in her chair and was almost elbow-to-elbow on the work surface with the chief deputy.

"And so you're saying that when Ed made Bobo the fall guy, the real guilty party, if I may use that phrase, automatically had a fall guy without having to take the risk of framing someone. How convenient! Isn't it what they call serendipity?"

He was running with the idea.

Jean tamed him somewhat. "Well, at least it's a theory."

"What else have you got?" Rusty asked, trying to recover the momentum.

125

Jean paused a moment, then answered his question with one of her own. "Don't you think it odd that there were practically no fingerprints inside the car? None on the steering wheel or the inside door handles."

"What are you suggesting?"

"Not exactly suggesting. But I doubt if Max Wein wore gloves that hot morning two years ago. He wasn't wearing them in the picture of him the morning he disappeared, which I saw. And I can't think of any reason why he'd wipe the wheel clean."

Rusty simply uttered the word, "So..." and let it drag out so that Jean would continue.

"Well," she picked up, "It's possible that someone else drove the car to the hammock."

"And that Wein's body was disposed of somewhere else," Rusty concluded. He emphasized his excitement with a gentle tap on his desk with a closed fist. Then his face clouded, and he looked right at Jean. "But that could bring Bobo back into the picture. He could have disposed of Wein then driven the car to the hammock as a diversion." A frown creased Jean's face. "Ah, but how would he know this was a popular spot for the birders? And don't I remember that one of the group made it easy to find the car by saying he had planned to meet Wein at the hammock?"

Jean's voice became even softer than usual. "Yes, Bill Long did. I don't think he said they'd planned to meet there, but he'd referred the hammock to Max as a place he thought he'd seen a rare warbler and wanted Max to confirm it," Jean said.

"So Long could have set up the diversion. Got rid of Wein somewhere else and driven the car to the hammock. Right?" Rusty was no longer sensitive to

Jean's feelings for her friends. "No, wrong!" Jean almost shouted. "Bill Long is a thoughtful 71-year-old multimillionaire. It can't be like that."

Jean got up from her chair and walked about as she said that. She was bearing conflicts that she found it hard to master: her high sense of loyalty to her friends against her innate old-fashioned morality that demanded justice; her desire to turn away from something that could become ugly against her need to help straighten out something that may be terribly crooked.

Rusty, the young psychologist, gave her a minute or two to settle down. He looked at her earnestly as she eased back into her chair and in a soothing tone said, "Look, Jean, do you think I like it that a lovely, quiet friend of my wife's, Consuela, is a suspect here? Of course not. I hate it. You have five friends involved—five reasons to dislike these questions and some of the answers that are beginning to suggest themselves. I understand that. But think a moment of why you are here today. You are here because you heard about a prominent man disappearing, and when you asked normal questions of the five people who had breakfast with him just an hour or two before, some of their answers were unsatisfactory."

"I wish I'd minded my own business."

"I'm glad you didn't. Besides, a disappearance, maybe a murder, is everybody's business. And don't forget that by throwing a lot of cold water on the case against Bobo, you shift some attention to the birdwatchers. We're a lot farther along than we were an hour ago, thanks to you."

He looked at her intently. He enjoyed looking at her. Like Arnold Benson and many other people in her life, he had passed from the stage of regarding her a mousy little woman who had an untamed head of hair and wore unfashionable clothes. By now her personality, her mind, her decency, her dedication all but blotted out his awareness of the mere physical presence. Amusement had yielded to admiration. He thought he saw moisture forming in her eyes, but she didn't get out a handkerchief.

He continued softly. "Now then, do you know of any possible motive other than the Don-Doris thing and Sanderson's kinship with Wein?"

"None other than robbery." He obviously wanted to talk more about her friends, and she didn't. Denial was still ruling her judgment. She just sat there a full minute. Suddenly, her voice regained its calm and she asked unexpectedly, "Do you have a detailed map of the area around Big Cypress Cafe?"

"Sure." He went to the wall and pulled down a huge roll-up map. He indicated where the cafe was. Jean pulled out a piece of note paper and started to sketch out a facsimile of part of the map. Before Rusty could ask her what she was up to, Paula stuck her head in and summoned him for a few minutes. That was a nice break for Jean; it gave her time to add more detail. She erased some of the sketch a couple of times to make sure she had it right. Apparently she wanted her sketch to reflect accurately what she was looking at on the map.

By the time Rusty returned, Jean was finished and had put the sketch in her huge handbag. Rusty accepted that the little woman had her own methods of going at things and didn't say anything other than "Can I help with whatever it was you were doing?" He was smiling.

"Not yet," Jean returned his smile.

"You know the rules about withholding evidence," said Rusty now only half joking.

"Sure."

"Somebody may have killed Max Wein two years ago, and if that's the case, that somebody may have his eye on you."

"Not likely," said Jean. "But what I'm going to do with my little map sketch isn't the least bit dangerous. I just want to check out an idea. It won't cost your department a cent. Bye Rusty, and thanks for the use of the map."

"Bye Jean. I'm dead serious when I say be careful. I repeat: We're here to protect you. It could be tragic if you don't let us."

"Don't worry. Everybody was palsy-walsy with me Sunday. They either don't know or don't care that we've met. Guess I've been a little paranoid, but I'll be in touch…and careful."

Jean left, but not without swinging by Paula's cubicle for a warm hello. That gesture was part friendly, part political. She wanted to ensure she'd have rapid access to Chief Deputy Torrance if she'd need it.

~~ 13 ~~

The teacher had not forgotten why she was in Florida. She was mindful that her library research and her visits with Rusty had eaten into the time she was obligated to spend on her project.

She set aside the next few days to catch up and to write a report she owed the Pearson Trust. Her carefully sketched map lay unstudied in a desk drawer.

One day Orville Wilson delivered the word that Doris Groot had phoned and would appreciate a call. By now Jean's deep disappointment in Doris had given way to pity. She called promptly, and Doris told her that a partner in the law firm had given her a couple of tickets to an Andre Watts concert and she asked Jean to go with her. It was to take place Friday evening in the Barbara B. Mann Hall in Fort Myers. Jean accepted readily, and the two women arranged to meet at a moderately priced family restaurant before the concert.

Jean enjoyed herself very much. She hadn't had many meals with other people in Florida and had been to only a couple of other concerts, both times alone. But in spite of the pleasant evening, she couldn't help analyzing almost everything Doris said for clues to whether Con had informed her about the meetings with Rusty. The only indication she could detect was that twice Doris asked rather searchingly about Jean's recent activities "outside of birding and your project." The two questions were separated by a couple of hours—once at dinner and once at the Watts intermission. Both times Jean was noncommittal.

As Jean thought about it afterwards, she took Doris's questions at face value: She just wanted to know what Jean was doing.

Perhaps she was aware that Jean had withdrawn from her in the past few weeks and wished to catch up. At any rate, Jean didn't think Doris a good enough actor to conceal an ulterior motive, i.e., to probe into what Jean was up to with respect to the Max Wein business. And she doubted that the others would choose Doris as an emissary to try to learn more about Jean's activities.

The pleasant evening reinforced the relief Jean experienced on the preceding Sunday. Apparently, Con Smith hadn't connected Jean with Rusty or had chosen not to pursue it.

* * *

On the morning that Jean's report was ready to mail, she took her map out of the drawer and studied it carefully. She placed it on the seat beside her as she started out for the post office. After mailing the report, she headed to Route 29 and proceeded on the familiar route toward the cafe. But she didn't make the second turnoff that leads to the restaurant; instead she checked her odometer and stayed on the paved road. This was fairly familiar ground; she'd hiked up this way on a couple of Sunday mornings, exploring the sloughs and crude paths. She continued another mile or so. Now the road no longer was familiar.

Finally, she stopped opposite an opening in the slash pines and palmettos that had lined the roadside. She got out. The gap revealed twin ruts that indicated that it once had been a passable road. Now branches and fronds littered it, but the ground was firm and dry. She guessed that no one had used the road since Hurricane Andrew had rearranged the landscape the preceding August. Apparently the clean-up crews had overlooked it.

That didn't deter Jean. She had confidence in her big heavy Bonneville, turned it off the pavement, and pointed its chromium nose into the opening. She edged ahead at less than 10 miles per hour. In traveling no more than a mile she had to stop three times to remove large obstructing branches. Once it took all the leverage her little body could summon to swivel a large slash pine branch over to the side to allow the car to get through.

Then, after going maybe a mile and a half, a fallen pine completely blocked the road. Jean cursed her impetuosity in pushing down the road once she realized that it had never been cleaned up after the hurricane. It was impossible to turn around.

She would have to back the one and a half miles, not an easy task on such a narrow road with so many palmettos and slash pines edging it and even encroaching on the road space. She had no choice but to leave the car where it was and to proceed on foot. She climbed over the obstructing pine, snagging her old blouse on a branch as she did so and tearing it as she dropped to the ground.

In the next couple of miles on foot, she encountered more barriers created by trees felled by Andrew. She managed to squeeze her little body under one, snagging her blouse again on a limb, ripping it further and scratching the skin on her back. She tried to skirt around the stump of the next fallen tree, but that put her on deceivingly soggy ground and she sank ankle-deep into swamp muck.

Roadside water also was a problem with the next barrier tree. But by holding on to a sturdy branch above her, she was able to keep her feet at the edge of the dry road while using her body as a cantilever over the muck, much like the crew does while projecting over the water in a sailing race. She was congratulating herself on accomplishing that slick maneuver without further snagging her clothes, adding to her scratches, or getting any wetter, when she saw she was being examined by something long and dark in the ditch at her side, not more than a couple of feet away. Its contrasting white mouth opened hideously. Was it merely yawning or was it preparing to sink its menacing fangs into her?

Jean had never seen a cottonmouth in the wild, but the pits behind the nostrils and spade-shaped triangular head told her what it was. She had a bizarre first thought. She remembered how every year she taught her biology students, "Don't worry about the cottonmouth. One never has been positively identified north of the Ohio River." A lot of good that knowledge did her in South Florida! She elected to wait it out. That's what the reptile was doing; she'd play his game. She knew that to make a threatening move might incite the snake. Now it was only staring.

So she waited. And waited. Jean had no idea how long she held a statue-like pose. Maybe it was two minutes, maybe three but it seemed longer. Finally, the moccasin moved its head to one side and the other. Its tongue darted in and out. It swung its neck around so that its head faced away from Jean, and its six-foot body followed in a graceful arc. It swam away down the slough in ess-like swirls.

Before the incident with the cottonmouth, she had noticed the vegetation to her left had become less dense, and she could see a saw grass marsh beyond it. As she resumed her walk down the road, there was less debris to hinder her; the small vegetation had given way to ancient bald cypresses that were better anchored against the hurricane's forces. She observed two large hammocks shooting up from the saw grass, one off to her left and the other a few hundred yards farther along.

She sloshed along. As she neared the second hammock, she looked up to see an adult bald eagle gliding in to a nest. Her sight angle was different, but she was sure it was the same nest she had visited a few weeks before; now she was on the other side of it. She tramped farther. Soon the road, now much better defined, widened briefly, then split. One branch veered off to the right, away from the black marshy pond and saw grass and on to the pond that was no doubt the fishing grounds for the eagles. She followed the left spur, which continued a few yards around the marsh's edge, then became no more than a path. She looked up at the nest. Now it was nearly at the same perspective she'd seen it when she approached it via West Road #2 while shielding her presence from Doris and Don. She was at the crest of the wishbone formed by the two crude paths on each side of the marsh.

She had proved to herself that Don was wrong (or deliberately lying); a person with Max's handicaps <u>could</u> have made it to this choice spot to view the eagles. Before the hurricane had all but blown the road out of existence, he could have driven to where it split, walked the few level, dry yards down the spur and the path beyond, and had glorious viewing. At the wide spot where the road split he could easily have turned his Taurus around and driven out. But he could not have managed the much longer walk if he'd gone up West Road #2, the route that she and Doris and Don used a few weeks ago.

On the walk back to her car, Jean was prepared for the barriers and had an easier time of it. She started her car and began the laborious trip in reverse out to the paved road. As good a driver as she was, she couldn't avoid the palmetto fronds, saw grass spikes, and fallen branches that littered the road and scratched the sides of her car. She would face a painting bill, but she was satisfied that she'd accomplished something for her effort. Now the little piece of the yarmulke, if that's what it was, she found back there could be explained.

Jean had wanted to tell Rusty about finding the alternative way to the eagle's nest and to hint at the significance she attached to it, but he was away on sheriff business. The adventure advanced her theory that whatever happened to Max Wein didn't necessarily happen at Panther Hammock where his car was found. It could have been in the area of the eagle's nest or somewhere else in the vicinity. She was mindful that she'd taken off on this investigation without informing Rusty and hoped her brash act wouldn't put a crimp in their smooth relationship.

But Rusty's reaction could wait. Meanwhile she would go to breakfast with the others in two days. She would be easy doing so; none of them could know where she'd been on Friday or why she went there. The last breakfast had been one of the best, affirming her good standing in the group. Con Smith's apparent silence about Jean's meeting with Rusty had been a great relief, and the innocence of Doris when they went to the concert was reassuring.

She was so comfortable that she hadn't even noticed that all five cars of the other birders were already on the parking lot when she drove up. Then she walked into the gloomy, dank room. In an instant, she realized her comfort was misplaced. There was the "tribunal" she had dreaded facing two weeks before. All were seated and served, looking uncharacteristically solemn.

The confrontation she had dreaded merely had been postponed.

As she approached the group her mind frantically tried to reconstruct the preparation she had made two weeks ago. The answers weren't coming back. When she got to the table, she was in for a second surprise: Sandy Sanderson and Don Purvis had exchanged their usual places. That put Sandy in the center of the threesome along the wall facing Jean, symbolically in the position of chief high priest in this little Sanhedrin.

Jean spoke first, meekly, "Hello, everybody. I guess my watch is slow. I seem to be a little late."

Mumbled Hello's and How-are-you's from around the table. Sure enough Sandy was the chosen speaker. "No, you're on time. We all just happened to get here a bit early. Sit down, Jean."

"'Just happened to,' phooey," Jean said to herself wondering if the imagined sarcasm showed on her face. But all she said aloud was, "Thanks" and she acknowledged Con, who was pouring her a cup of coffee. The atmosphere around the table was as cold as an Oak City winter although the restaurant itself was oppressive.

Sanderson cleared his throat and said "As a matter of fact, we were just talking about you, Jean."

"Nothing good, I trust." She was gamely trying to impose a light-hearted tone on the interview, still trying to adjust to accepting that her most congenial friend, Sandy, was the inquisitor. She anticipated that it would have been either Don, who had organized the group, or Bill its unanointed leader and who usually was the dominant personality.

"Well, maybe it isn't so good at that," Sandy responded.

"But it's something I know we can work out. You see, Jean, we know you have been talking with the chief deputy sheriff, I think his name is Torrance, about our dear friend, Max, my cousin Max, and we just wish you would stop."

Jean shot right back at him, ignoring the rest of them who, she was aware, seemed to be nodding affirmatively more or less in unison. "But don't you want to know what happened to your cousin? Not that I know anything about it," she added quickly.

"I <u>do</u> know what happened to him," Sandy countered. "He was robbed of $4,500 cash he had on his person. After two years, I can finally say it another way: He was <u>killed</u> for the money."

Jean noted that this statement didn't exactly square with earlier conversations with Sandy.

"You see, that's news to me," Jean said trying to sound surprised and innocent. "I didn't know he was killed."

"Oh, come on, Jean," Don butted in. "You and I talked about Bobo Jumper, who everybody knows is the prime suspect. Don't say you didn't. That's what the others told you, too, when you quizzed them."

Jean wanted to come back with, "How do you know what conversations I've had with the 'others'?" But instead she decided to ignore the last of Don's remarks, at least for the moment. She was casting about for sympathy from at least one of them and knew she wouldn't get it if she answered in kind. So she replied, turning from Don to Sandy, "Prime suspect in a burglary, yes. But I didn't know you thought he killed your cousin. If he did, don't you want justice done?"

"Of course. And it will be done. The old sheriff couldn't make anything stick; your pal may be able to." The emphasis on "pal" was freighted with sarcasm. "But we don't want to go through another trial-by-media," he continued, "where there were veiled and not-so-veiled suggestions that someone from the breakfast group might be involved. Beggs, with all his faults, knew better than that. It was a hellish time, Jean, and we're finally satisfied now. Let things that don't concern you alone."

Jean thought that the trial-by-media charge was a cop-out. The papers she scanned were more than generous to the group. She let it pass, however. She didn't want them to learn she'd read the 1991 newspapers and open herself to another assault.

Instead, she answered simply, "I'm glad you have found your answer. Believe me, Sandy, I am. You are acting as if I'm on some sort of a crusade here to save a young Native American I've never seen. That's not true. But I'll admit I was interested to find out what happened to a respected birder who sat at this very table and tramped the very paths I've been exploring with you people. Don't you think my interest is, or was, natural?"

Then she added, speaking to the group as a whole, "You act as if I was some interloper from the north who was sent down here to solve some dark mystery. Not so. Not so."

The discussion to this point was accompanied by the usual quiet noises of breakfast: coffee cups against saucers, knives against plates, hot coffee sloshed onto cold coffee, waitress scurrying about removing cutlery and crockery. But after Jean's last statement, even those noises ceased. People stopped eating.

The silence was broken by a surprising source, Doris, and in a surprising way. "'Not so' you say, Jean. But isn't that really what you are doing? You see, we know who you are. We know about the kidnapping of the little girl and the murder of her uncle and how you worked that out when you came on the scene years later.

"Same thing here. Something odd happened in the past—perhaps a crime, although I'm not sure of that, and it involves ornithology. I don't know who sent you to look into this, but the parallels are just too obvious. I'm sorry, Jean. You are a terrific birder, but we aren't fooled about why you are here."

Jean was down in the mouth. Her skin took on a gray pallor, intensified by the combination of the unshaded light bulbs and the heavy early morning sky outside the dirty window. But she'd give it a try before she would bow out.

"Doris, don't you remember when you first told me about Max Wein? It was when you came to the trailer to explain about the dinner. I don't think you could say I prompted you. You may recall I had only the vaguest recollection of his name and that something had happened to him. That's all I knew at that point. If it was a crime for me to ask you a few questions about such a curious story, then I plead guilty."

"Yes, Doris told us how the subject came up," Don put in. "But we agreed you could have been acting, faking it, to get information for the people who sent you."

The doughty little teacher was angry. She hadn't much practice in handling anger in a life where most people respected her, but considering her inexperience, she handled it rather well.

"I'm sorry, Don, but that's just plain ridiculous and frankly an insult." An unwanted tremor in her voice gave away her anger. "It also would astonish my high school drama teacher, who found me hopelessly unable to act. Besides, I didn't invite myself into the group. You and Doris did."

Jean then looked right at Doris, pointedly ignoring Don. She continued in a firmer, more controlled voice, "But Doris, if you think I was quote sent unquote by someone to probe about Max Wein's disappearance, you are mistaken. If you want to know who actually did send me and why, OK, I'll tell you. It was the Pearson Trust of Oak City, and yes that's the family of Georgina Pearson, the girl who was kidnapped. They and the principal at my school thought I should get away for a sabbatical after a difficult period, helping identify the gangsters and then dealing with the trial. I hadn't told you this because, well, why should I? I was being true to the reason they sponsored me, to get away and further my research. Besides, you just don't go up to people and say, 'Hi. I'm Jean McKay. I helped solve the notorious Pearson kidnaping and murder.'"

Sanderson wanted to regain his role as spokesman. "So, you see, Jean," he put in, "You can understand how we feel. You wanted to forget about what you call a 'difficult period' and that's just what we want to do."

Jean saw herself approaching her Rubicon, so she decided to plunge in. "Except that there's a fundamental difference."

"What's that?" Doris asked. Her color was now a bright pink even in the dim lighting. Challenging Jean had embarrassed her, yet she kept the conversation going.

"It's that the Pearson case is closed. The crimes are solved, the guilty people were tried, and they are in prison. The Max Wein case is hanging. That's a big difference, and frankly I still don't see what's wrong with a few innocent questions to try to find out what happened."

Don was almost belligerent. "Come off it, Jean. Making dates with the chief deputy to talk about the case hardly constitutes 'innocent questions.' You act as if we don't want to find out what happened. We do, but what we don't need is somebody coming down from up north to tell us how to do it. It may surprise you that we are fairly bright people down here and have been capable of digging into what happened to our friend ourselves. You didn't even know him."

Bill Long spoke for the first time, looking at Don. "Take it easy, Don. Jean's our friend, or at least she's mine. I think she understands how we feel now. Let's hit the trails."

Was this someone on her side at last? She couldn't see Bill very well, but she gave him a pleasant smile anyway. "Well, I've been doing so much talking and got a later start than the rest of you, so I still have some eating to do." She paused, wondering if they'd gotten the mild sarcasm in the crack about the later start. Then she said, "But before you go out, let me say that I've decided that this will be my last breakfast with you."

Both the women muttered protests, but Jean went on. "I feel very flattered that you invited me to join you, and I think you are a terrific group of birders. More than that, I've learned a lot from you and enjoyed your company very much. Each one of you." And there she got up her courage to look at Don. "But I seem to have a meddlesome personality, and you don't want me meddling—understandably, I guess."

"Don't say that, Jean. You've been a special part of the group," Con finally said something.

"Thanks, Con. But groups don't function well when there are factions, and this group has two factions—you five and me.

Sandy responded. "I think you are overreacting. We weren't two factions two weeks ago, and we aren't now. I'll admit we talked about asking you to forget about pursuing what happened to Max, and we still feel that way. Or at least I do. But that doesn't mean you aren't a respected member of our gang, and more than that, you're my friend."

"Well, maybe," is all that Jean said. She still had a half-eaten waffle and some luscious strawberries, but the others began to leave. Each said something to her.

Doris was first, still bright pink and near tears. "See you back here at 8:30, dear. I hope you will have reconsidered by then. But whatever you decide I'll be in touch."

She was followed by Don who extended his hand and said, "No hard feelings, Jean." "None," she fibbed. She noted that he didn't ask her to reconsider.

143

Sandy Sanderson forced a smile over a pained look. "Want to come out with me and watch me take some pictures? I know where there may be some summer tanagers and the light is getting better."

Jean's warm smile and almost imperceptible head movement told him she declined but appreciated the gesture. He went on. "It'll be a long time before I forget the time we went out together and got the pictures of the marsh wren and the glossy ibis with the snake. I've sold them both, by the way."

"I'm glad, Sandy," she said. She still felt warmly toward him despite their earlier harsh words. She would be devastated if he was somehow involved in his cousin's disappearance—but at least she was finally admitting the possibility. Despite their cordiality, he didn't ask her back either.

Bill Long and Con Smith dallied over their coffees a couple of minutes before Bill got up to leave. He said, "I don't like this at all, Jeanie, but I guess I understand it. Still I really hope I see you two weeks from today sitting in that very seat. You are real asset to our gang. A real asset. And a guy with a background like mine doesn't like to lose an asset."

Jean thanked him, dabbled at her remaining strawberries, then started to leave herself. But Con laid a graceful hand on Jean's arm to detain her. It was clear that she had waited for the others to leave. She turned her lovely face and looked into Jean's small gray eyes with her large black ones. "I guess you think I'm an awful snitch," she said.

Much as she wanted Con not to feel bad, Jean couldn't totally deny it. "I understand, Con."

Con tried to explain. "Once in a while my English gives me a little trouble. The others kept asking me if I knew about anything you were doing. Once I stumbled and hinted at what Rusty had said to me. I guess you know I kept the information to myself for quite awhile. Anyway, the news that you were in touch with Rusty didn't seem to surprise them very much. It was as if they were looking for me to confirm something they already knew. The most important thing is that you come back."

It was spoken tenderly and quietly, but in a way that little speech hurt Jean more than any of the others. It confirmed to Jean that the others did have a network that excluded her. Even Con met with them although according to her story the others were a jump ahead of her. And, Jean hated to think it, she couldn't recall a time when Con's English wasn't textbook.

That lady, usually so reserved, seemed to want to continue to talk. She said, almost irrelevantly, "By the way, I think Rusty and Dawn are a wonderful couple."

"I don't know her, but I do admire him. Yes, I've been to his office, but I hope you and the others remember that he wasn't here when Mr. Wein vanished. How would he have any first hand knowledge of the case?" She wished she'd had the full group asssmbled for that one.

Con didn't even try to reply, so Jean smiled warmly and said, "Well, good-bye, and I do hope we see each other some more. I mean it."

Con still wasn't ready to say good-bye. She bit her lip and fumbled with her napkin and then blurted out, "Do you think one of us did it?"

"Did what, Con?"

145

"You know. Had something to do with Max's disappearance?"

"Ed Beggs didn't think so. Rusty Torrance doesn't know anything other than what is in Beggs' files. Who am I to dispute the record of law enforcement people?" It was a nifty evasion, but not really convincing.

This time they really did say good-bye. Jean started the drive home, relieved that she'd acted to sever herself from the group. She wished she could have been a fly on the wall when they decided to face her. Who lead the discussion? How did it come about that Sandy Sanderson did the dirty work? Was Con there?

Her initial relief gave way to uncertainty. She said she wasn't coming back, and if she could leave it at that, that would end it. Three of them specifically asked her to reconsider. But on what terms? Were they saying, "Come back, Jean, but with the stipulation that you drop it. No more talking with Rusty Torrance"? If that was the tacit understanding, she had gone too far to accept the terms.

She needed an advocate among them—or at least a listening ear—but dared not to approach any one of them to play the role.

The person approached could be exactly the wrong one.

146

～ 15 ～

A couple of nights later Jean was working late. She hated air-conditioning, and by now the sounds of the night filtering through the trailer's small opened windows were as familiar as the daytime "what-cheer" of the cardinal: the prattle of cicadas, the croaking of frogs seeking to impress potential mates, a late-singing mockingbird, the rhythmic hoots of a great horned owl, the distant bellow of an alligator, maybe the rustle of an opossum or raccoon slinking along.

Tonight, though, she sensed an unfamiliar faint shuffling amidst the chorus of familiar night sounds. A bobcat stalking a victim? Doubtful. A human being? Unlikely. Who else would it be other than Orville Wilson, and he produced a distinctive strong footfall rather than a near continuous rustle. Besides he nearly always was whistling a tune that approximated "Low and Lonely."

Now the sound was closer. Then it stopped and was supplanted by three firm knocks on her door. It was a human, and now that her troubled relationship with the other birders was in the open, Jean was frankly wary. Before she responded she flipped on the powerful spot she had installed over the little stoop at the trailer's entrance. The whirr of wings of two or three nocturnal birds that reacted to the bright light pierced the other night noises.

Apprehensively, she peaked through the door window and beheld two men, strangers, whose features and dress suggested they were Indians. Both wore bright satin shirts with dark Western-style hats low on

147

their foreheads. One might have been 65 or older, the other not much more than 20. The younger man wore jeans, the older buckskin trousers. Both sported elaborate silver belt buckles.

Jean hadn't known any Native Americans other than the waitress, Marie, but she detested the bromide that "they all look alike." Nevertheless, these two did look alike, and it wasn't just their high cheekbones, copper skin color, and other classic Indian features. It was the positioning of the eyes wide on the face, the prominent ear lobes, and the similarity of their stern miens. They not only looked alike as Indians, but as a father and son or grandfather and grandson might.

The elder of the two men spoke in a rich, sonorous voice through the still unopened door. "Jean McKay?" Although she was at least concerned if not quite frightened, the manner in which he said the two words did not seem menacing to her. "Yes," she replied, half a statement and half a question. As she did so, she opened the door part way.

"Please come with us," the older man said.

There was absolutely no reason why she should venture outside her trailer with two strangers at 8:30 on a dimly moonlit night. Yet there was something about the quiet, firm manner of the invitation that weighed against outright rejection. She decided to seek more information. She stated her case:

"I can't go out in the night with two persons I've never seen before. Who are you?"

Unbidden, they moved inside. The older man said, "I cannot tell you who we are or where we are going. I can tell you we will have you back safely, if you don't resist us, before midnight tonight. In about three hours. Please come with us now, Jean McKay."

She noted that he had a slight accent, saying "tree" for "three" for instance. She concluded that he may have spoken an Indian tongue before he spoke English.

"How do I know you will have me back here safely in three hours?"

"You have my word." For him, that was all the answer that was needed. For her, it was no answer at all.

There was a long pause. The two men had moved to either side of her, and each laid a hand gently on the elbow closest to him and applied slight pressure to move her out the door. The harmony between their movements was remarkable.

Jean could feel her heart beginning to pound. Until they touched her, she had been intrigued albeit concerned by the adventure; now she was scared. Suddenly she stepped backward so that the men no longer touched her.

"Please do not resist us. It won't do you any good. Please come with us," the older man repeated, unwavering in his purpose.

"I can't. I won't." Jean was close to screaming. The young man, who had not said a word, looked around outside as if to ascertain whether she'd alarmed any one or any thing. He looked at the older man and made a barely perceptible nod, indicating, Jean thought, that there was no discernible reaction to her little outburst.

The old man was silent for a minute or so, then said, "You may call deputy Torrance and tell him that if you are not back by midnight, he should investigate. Do it now. We are losing time."

His offer reassured her a bit, but she suspected that he knew that she didn't have a phone and therefore it was a bluff. She decided to call it. "I'll do that and come with you if you tell me your names and where we are going. Otherwise I won't come."

"I won't tell you our names or where we are going, but you are coming anyway." Again they took her elbows, this time more firmly, and propelled her gently out the door, turning out the spotlight as they did. The old man was correct in saying she would come with them. He had won the upper hand and knew it.

Jean soon understood why she hadn't heard distinct footsteps when the pair approached the trailer. The older man scooted his his feet forward like a cross country skier. Jean wondered if he had an affliction such as Parkinson's disease or whether he had affected the walking style to muffle his approach. The silent younger partner was extremely light on his feet and moved noiselessly.

As they approached the Wilson's trailer, Jean hoped to make the deal she couldn't make in her own trailer. "May I tell the man in this trailer to call the sheriff if I'm not back by 11:30?"

"Wilson is at his lodge meeting. It's his wife's bowling night." Jean wondered if a faint smile might have crossed his face as the older man said this. He'd done his homework. She knew enough about the Wilsons to know that this was their Tuesday night routine. "May I leave a note?" she asked.

"Do you have a pencil and paper?"

"No."

150

"Neither do we."

"I do back at my trailer."

"Too late," said the older man. That was final.

Now she saw the dim outline of an old beat-up pick-up truck 20 or 25 feet away. The night was too dark and the truck too weather-worn even to tell its color, but the Wilson's outside flood light reflected off the chrome letters "TSUN" on the side of the hood. She reasoned that they were what remained of the chrome nameplate "DATSUN," and she was familiar enough with cars to know that Nissan had stopped calling its cars Datsuns some years ago. She was being taken off in an old Datsun truck. It wasn't much of a clue, but she was pleased that her mind was alert enough to pick it up.

The men stopped, and the old one spoke. "I'm sorry, Jean McKay, but we can't let you know where we go from here. So we are going to blindfold you for a little while."

Jean wrenched and squirmed. It was a way of letting them know that she didn't like what they were doing; it was not a realistic effort to get away. She knew she couldn't outrun the younger man. They reacted to her physical protest by holding her a little tighter, but not enough to hurt her. The old man placed what apparently was a bandana over her eyes and tied it snugly in the back. "Is that too tight?" he asked. "Yes," she snarled. So he loosened it. She wasn't sure whether or not she was being kidnapped, but if she was, her abductors certainly were considerate.

They gently helped her into the truck. The young man slid behind the wheel, Jean was in the middle, and the old man was on the outside. Other than the latter's odd walking style, Jean was able to note very little identifiable about the two men from the moment they appeared. She felt she might be able to recognize the older man later by the deep quality of his voice and his interesting accent. So far she had picked up nothing notable about the young man. He hadn't spoken a word, and he was dressed like a lot of young men she'd seen.

He started the engine and with three or four short back-and-forths, turned the truck around and groped along the crude road with lights off. He finally turned on the lights after they'd passed under the Wilson's funny entrance sign and turned onto the county road.

Jean noted that they turned right when they left the campground. She conceived a plan of memorizing the sequence of left and right turns and starting the chronometer on her Timex after each turn. Later she would convert times to approximate distances between turns, thus allowing her to reconstruct loosely the route to wherever she was going.

But the young driver thwarted her plan, perhaps by design, by changing speeds, thus messing up her time estimates. Then he seemed to backtrack and use devious routes. At one point, the older man initiated the only words exchanged by the two men, "This stretch is often patrolled. Be careful and don't hurry." The young man said, "Right," the first word Jean had heard him say. His voice was high and the word was swallowed. It would not be an easy voice to identify. Twice the older man, who never called the young one by name, asked Jean if she were comfortable. The second time she snarled a strong, "No!" even though she was. He let it go, but she could feel his body next to hers jiggling as he suppressed a chuckle.

Finally, when she estimated they'd been out about an hour, reckoning from the 9:00 o'clock ding on her Timex, they slowed considerably. The road jostled them about a good bit, and she could hear the rustle and scratching of branches against the truck's cab.

After only a couple of minutes of this rough stretch, they stopped. The old man said, "We get out here. Soon we will remove your blindfold." Jean raised her right hand toward her forehead, and he took it and lowered it again, saying, "But not yet."

They walked her forward about 50 paces and helped her up three steps. Then she felt she was on a firm floor. They removed the blindfold, and after her eyes had a few moments to adjust, she gradually began to take in objects in the subdued light. She saw she was in a long room with what appeared to be a thatched roof supported by wooden poles. The sides were open to the night. The room was electrified; she made out a television set and a few dim electric lights suspended on the support poles. Her eyes were drawn to the far end, perhaps 30 feet away, where she counted four human figures.

It dawned on her that she was in a chickee, one of the open-sided dwellings of the historic Seminoles. Its cypress stilts boosted it above the rise and fall of the changing wetland floor and its roof was thatched with palmetto fronds. This was a real chickee, not one of the quaint facsimiles that she'd seen used as pool houses at condominium complexes on her beach walks. Its length surprised her. As her two escorts led her toward the little cluster of people, she saw that a small woman was seated in front. Tiny as she was, she was the focal point; it was she that they were approaching and that the others were attending.

They stopped, and Jean's older captor greeted the woman in another language, presumably Seminole or Miccosukee. She replied in a squeaky, broken voice, apparently bidding them to come closer. When they did, Jean beheld perhaps the oldest woman she'd ever seen. Her body was shriveled, and her wrinkled, sunken face reminded Jean of the pictures of the deeply creased landscape of some distant planet or moon under a space vehicle's telescope. She was the only female in the group. Her skirt, which was spread about her as she sat, was brilliant even in the dim light. It featured horizontal stripes of patchwork, mostly oranges and bright purples. She was smoking a little pipe.

She said something, and Jean thought she detected the words "Jean McKay" in the otherwise squeaky garble. "She'd like you to come a little closer so she can see you better. Granny doesn't see very well," interpreted the older of her escorts. She obliged, but edged forward only a few feet.

Granny said something else, which she climaxed with a weird cackling laugh. With that the men all laughed heartily and genuinely; even the silent young driver of the Datsun permitted himself a chuckle. "She said that she sees that you are as tiny as she is. She wonders if you are as smart as she is," explained the older man. He laughed some more. So did the others.

Then the ancient woman's mood changed, as did that of her small entourage. Jean listened intently to what she said next, hoping to pick up some kind of clue. She did; she was sure she heard the phrase "Max Wein." The interpreter explained: "Granny says she has asked that you come here because she wants you to promise to keep on trying to find out what happened to the bird man called Max Wein."

Jean was astonished and blurted out "Why?" Her interpreter started to respond, but Granny raised her skinny left arm and he stopped. She apparently understood Jean's bafflement and wanted to answer her herself. When she was through, the old man, whose name Jean still didn't know, explained. "Granny says because people say her great grandson did it but he didn't. She thinks you can prove that he didn't. She thinks you are very smart."

Jean instinctively turned slightly toward the younger of her two abductors, who was at her left. He remained impassive, but the older man gave a slight nod. Now she knew that the younger man who had driven her here was Bobo Jumper. She assumed the older man was probably his grandfather, Granny's son.

"But he hasn't been arrested, and whatever happened occurred two years ago. Why is she so concerned?" Again, the grandfather started to respond in English, but Granny raised her hand. She wanted to know what Jean had said. Her son told her, and she replied at some length, at one point waving her arm around over her head as if to indicate the chickee itself.

"Granny says she knows that some of your friends still think Robert did it and talk about it," her son interpreted. Jean noted that it was "Robert" not "Bobo." His grandfather went on. "She knows that these people want you to stop asking questions about the little bird man. As long as people think Robert has something to do with what happened, our family is disgraced. She is angry that the sheriff didn't believe us when we told him that Robert was with us that night, right here in this chickee, after one o'clock. That is an insult to the word of our family. She says she is 96 years old and will die soon. Before that happens she wants proof that Robert had nothing to do with the little bird man's disappearance and that we told the truth. She believes you are the only one who can prove that before she leaves the earth. Please don't give up, she asks."

Jean felt a crushing pressure to make a promise to the ancient woman on the spot. But if she did, she would have to risk digging farther into a situation that she'd been warned to stay out of. She stalled and decided to try to take the offensive. "Ask her if she knows what really happened," she directed the grandfather. He complied. Granny's brief response ended with a smile. "Granny says she don't know. That's for you to find out."

That ended the interview. Granny extended her bony hand and smiled a toothless smile. She said, "Thank you for coming," in clear but heavily accented English. The three men who comprised her entourage were introduced as uncles and shook hands with Jean. All wore traditional dress; two of them sported the feathered turbans that Seminole men sometimes make. All thanked her for coming ("as if I had a choice," thought Jean). It occurred to her that she had learned everyone's name at the interview but that of her chief escort and interpreter. She was feeling more warmly toward him than she did in the doorway of her trailer, an event that seemed ages ago but had actually occurred only about an hour and a half earlier. So she asked him point blank what to call him. His rather surprising reply was "Harding." Perhaps he was born during Harding's presidency.

Then Bobo and Harding turned and escorted her out of the chickee. Before they left the platform to step down to the earth outside, Harding took out the bandana and re-blindfolded Jean, saying under his breath, "I must be sure that Granny sees me do this." When they were outside heading for the pick-up, Jean again started to raise her hand to release the blindfold. Again, Harding restrained her. "No, not yet Jean McKay. But it won't be so long this time. I'll untie it when we are along the way on a main road."

"But why, Harding? Now that I know who you are it would be easy for me to find out where your mother's chickee is. It would be in the county records."

"Maybe," he replied. "Except I'll bet you don't even know what county we was in. Anyways, in our family and our culture we respect the wishes of a 96-year-old granny. She don't want her culture invaded by white people. She thinks this way protects our way of life—her way of life. You were a very privileged white person to go there at all."

Jean was fascinated by Granny, and on the way back she and Harding talked easily about her life. She had grown up living a nomadic life in the Everglades and Big Cypress, the heritage of a generation or two before hers when the Seminoles were opposing the efforts of the white Government to round them up and repatriate them in Oklahoma. When the Tamiami Trail was slashed through the area she was already a grandmother in her forties, and she resisted the lure of becoming an airboat concessionaire or curio shop proprietor. She felt that was selling out to the white invaders of her beloved dark swamp and mysterious glades. She was a leader in maintaining their native language, customs, and culture. She taught her ancient ways to her own large family, not always with success but with a passion that always brought respect. In this brief interview, Jean, too, was engulfed with respect for the tenacious old lady.

Bobo was still silent on the return trip. True to his word, Harding released the blindfold when they were well along on a smooth road. None too skillfully, he tried to wheedle out of her what she thought happened to Max Wein and what she was going to do. She couldn't respond directly because she herself didn't know what she was going to do. Instead, she tried to turn the tables on them. "Well," she asked, turning toward Harding, "What do you think happened?"

"One of them bird people killed him. But I don't know why or what they did with the body," Harding replied.

That was no help. She turned her head toward Bobo. "How about you, Bobo. What can you tell me that would help clear your name for Granny."

Bobo started to say something, "I…" then was silent for several seconds and started over. "I…" After a couple more seconds, Jean prompted him, "You what, Bobo?" This time there was no hesitation. "I don't know nothin' about it except that I didn't do anything to that man." Jean was disappointed in what he said and the bitterness with which he said it. But she wouldn't forget the false starts before he spoke. She felt he knew something and it was significant. She didn't know how she'd get back to Bobo, but she'd try—if she decided to pursue her quest further.

Then she asked about the thing that puzzled her most. How did Granny know about her and her interest in the Max Wein disappearance? More than that, how could the ancient woman possibly know that Jean was being dissuaded from pursuing the case?

"Old grannies have secrets," is all that Harding would say.

Eventually they turned into the campground. They drove all the way to her trailer with lights on, no pretense of stealth. "It's 10:50. Back an hour before I'd promised," Harding said cheerfully, almost as if it had been a routine evening. "Please clear Bobo so Granny can die happy. And please don't try to find where we've been."

Jean made no reply, but on the way back she had activated the plan she had conceived going out for retracing the route. As they left the chickee, she began to memorize the sequence of left and right turns. She had turned off the alarm bell on the Timex and started the chronometer, punching in laps whenever they made a turn. She was pretty sure the two Indians hadn't noticed what she was doing. This time Bobo's driving was steady and seemingly without deviations. Now, all she had to do was play out the times between turns, convert times to distances, reverse their order and the turn directions, and she could make a pretty good guess at where she'd been.

But she wouldn't try. When she got inside the trailer, she deliberately erased her chronometer. The interview with Granny had produced so much respect for her—respect that only increased as Harding talked

159

about her—that it became unthinkable to play some sort of secret game to track her down.

She climbed into her narrow bunk pondering a tired cliche: She found herself between a rock and a hard place. Honor Granny's request and investigate at her peril; play it safe and let Granny (and Bobo and herself) down.

~~ 16 ~~

The interview with Granny had been a powerful emotional experience. It became almost an imperative to clear Bobo's name before Granny died.

Almost, but not quite. She had half-promised the bird watchers that she would cease her probe into Max Wein's disappearance, and she had voluntarily left the group. Most of them would probably welcome her back (with conditions)—at least they said they would—and Doris Groot had already called her at Wilson's, somewhat emotionally beseeching her return. Certainly, it would be easier to dig out more information inside the group. Within or without, however, she'd have to face potential danger if she furthered her investigation.

Denial at last was behind her. She no longer was shutting out words like "potential danger" as she weighed her dilemma. The danger was real. If one of the birders was guilty of some dreadful crime, she would place herself at terrible risk if that person invited her to go for a tramp back into the swamp. How could she excuse herself without giving herself away? How could she protect herself if she accepted?

But what other avenue of investigation was left? She was convinced that Bobo wasn't directly involved although he may have known something relevant. No trace of Max had been found to support a conclusion that his disappearance was voluntary.

Still, maybe there was another possibility, and it began to haunt her. Ed Beggs himself. He had left the area in a hurry, and he had bent the standards of fairness to try to implicate Bobo. The idea of his involvement nagged her.

It was time to get back to Rusty. Initially she had held off because she thought it would be awkward to sound him out about the possible involvement of a fellow officer. But when Rusty left a message with the Wilsons that he'd welcome a call "just to catch up," she made an appointment to see him the next day and resolved to pose some questions about Beggs.

Rusty was fascinated by her encounter with Granny and readily perceived the difficult spot the old woman's request put her in. He grasped the potential danger any time she was alone with any one of the five—and the huge task of finding the truth without reconnecting with them. He strongly advised that she forget Granny's request. He peppered her with questions, the most unanswerable of which was, "How on earth did the old Granny know about you and your interest in Max Wein?"

Jean just sat there a moment, throwing out her hands, palms up, in a helpless gesture. Then she said, half jokingly, "Maybe what Harding said is true: 'Old grannies have secrets.'" She thought of Indian women she had met, then the answer came out loud. "Marie…"

"Marie?" he asked. "Who's Marie?"

The revelation was still sinking in. "Marie. Of course."

"Marie Of Course? What the heck are you talking about?"

"I'm sorry, Rusty. The little mystery has been solved. Marie Billie is a waitress at the cafe," she explained. "She's an Indian. She's really chummy with us and was no doubt serving us when they were lowering the boom on me and I told them I'd withdraw. I remember now, although their voices were lowered, Don kept shushing us and nodding his head in her direction."

"So you think she picked up what was being said and passed the word on to Bobo's family."

"That has to be it," Jean said with assurance. "She goes back several years with the group. She knew Max Wein and liked him. I remember now she once told me, 'I sure wish they'd find out what happened to that nice little man.' In retrospect, I think she was telling me that she didn't think Bobo was involved."

"Well, at least it's helpful to have an explanation of Granny's special powers." Rusty chuckled, "So the Seminoles had a mole in your cafe."

The concept intrigued Jean.

The upshot of their meeting was that Rusty advised Jean to lie low for a week or so and expend her energies on her work for the trust. "The best way to let the group know that you aren't probing is to do simply that—not probe. For a while.

"Meanwhile I can do two or three things. I can find out about Max's friend, the disabled lady in Miami. Who knows? Maybe she's heard from him. And I can have an FBI check made on the birders.

"One's already been made on Bobo, of course. And we can look into the phone number down in the keys. Was the name Owens?"

Jean nodded, then hesitated. She drew in more breath than usual. "Maybe you can do one, or maybe two, more things."

Rusty eyed her curiously, knowing she was having trouble asking and wondering why. "Shoot," he encouraged her.

"Well, I wonder if you could find where Ed Beggs is and whether he's been around here."

"I guess I could try. Why do you want to know?"

Rather hesitantly at first, but gaining confidence in the absence of a challenge from Rusty, she reminded him of the chief deputy's quick exit to parts unknown and how the files revealed that he went to some effort to point the finger of suspicion at Bobo. She concluded with an apologetic, "Of course, I realize he's a fellow officer."

"<u>Was</u> a fellow officer, Jean. You're not the only person who has had these thoughts. I've had 'em too. I can talk to a sharp old-timer in the office named Joe Bob Carey and a couple of the others about Beggs if you think it's important. I think I can pull it off without giving away why you're interested if that's what you want. He sounded accommodating but didn't convince Jean that this was something he wanted to do. She noticed he said "you're interested" instead of "we're interested."

"What is the other favor?"

"Could I see some of the items that were in Max's car?"

"I guess it's possible, but if you are going to lie low I don't think you should keep coming here. Let me give you a copy of the inventory list before you leave and then you can tell me what items you wish to see. If we have 'em, we'll send them to you."

"If you have them?" Jean asked, surprised.

"Well, I've found that things like this tend to disappear or get misplaced over time, and it's been more than two years."

The interview was comforting, but it didn't end the questions that were bedeviling her. "How can I let Granny down?" "Can I allow the disappearance of Max Wein just continue to sit there?" "Should I show up next Sunday morning?" "Would my life be in danger if I did?"

Her concerns were not in the least assuaged by a call from Paula a few days later. She had located all the items Jean had requested except one. Jean had wanted to see the small notebook with bird notes, the copy of the <u>Journal of Ornithology</u>, the camera, the "Owens" scrap of paper with the phone number. Paula was sending everything except the journal, which she said she couldn't find. That struck Jean as strange, and she asked Paula to recheck. True to her obliging nature, the secretary cheerfully said she would.

When she got the camera, Jean looked to see if it had film; it did, and it was advanced to picture 11. She wanted to remove the film and have it developed, but first called Rusty to find out if that would be tampering with evidence. He thought it was a good idea and hoped that the film would still be good after a couple of years. Jean thought it was odd that Beggs hadn't had the film processed. Then her cynicism about him took over: Of course, the film would not likely have anything that implicated Bobo. She immediately took it to a one-hour developing place.

While she was waiting, she opened Max's notebook, an act that gave her the guilties, and began to read it. It contained little more than the routine notations that any birder might record. Nothing rare or unusual. The book was new when it had been found, with notes on only three pages. The last one was dated the day before he vanished. On it was scrawled "Rm 132 H.I." She assumed it would match up with the Holiday Inn receipt found in his car—if it were still available.

Only eight of the 10 pictures came out. Early in the roll were three pictures taken by flash in a high-style living room. The subjects were a pretty little woman in a wheel chair, a handsome middle-aged woman expensively dressed, and Sandy Sanderson. Jean concluded the woman in the wheel chair was Max's friend whom Bill had told her about (and Sanderson hadn't). The next four shots were typical south Florida scenes, presumably in an estuarine inlet. The tangled roots of red mangroves were reaching out to open water in two of the pictures and another was a beach shot. Jean made out the silver tip of an aluminum canoe at the bottom of one of the prints, suggesting Max was taking pictures from the bow. In another a robust-looking fellow in a ranger uniform, about 50, was waving.

The final of the eight pictures was the most interesting to Jean. It was a candid portrait of Con Smith's beautifully shaped head in profile, half in shade, half in sun. The part in the sun caught her handsome mouth, slightly smiling, in the act of speaking. Her white, even teeth complemented the white streak in her hair and both contrasted strikingly with the shadow across her smooth dark cheek and raven hair. The other pictures betrayed the cheap camera, but not this one. Jean wondered where it was taken and when. Perhaps at the cafe although the background was too diffuse to tell because of the close focus on the woman. It struck Jean that it might be a worshipful picture of an unattainable quest. She was beginning to acknowledge something similar in her own life the past few days. The picture saddened her.

But it didn't trouble her the way the missing copy of the <u>Journal of Ornithology</u> did. When Paula's continuing efforts were unavailing, Jean made inquiries to several academic libraries in Florida, but could find no copies. She finally called the publisher and asked if she could buy past issues of the bimonthly. She specified the first three issues of the year in which Max had disappeared and, thinking about the mistake in recording the date, all six issues of the preceding year. The issues were in stock and would be sent as soon as Jean's check was received.

She admitted to herself that ordering the May/June issue of the year in which he disappeared in March was probably wasteful, but sometimes copies are mailed out far in advance of the listed date. She was particularly eager to see the July/August 1990 issue. She guessed that it might have been the issue Max had with him; the sloppy clerk at the sheriff's office might have mistakenly entered the current year date instead of the preceding one.

Whatever issue it was, why would Max have placed it in a locked compartment for valuables and concealed the compartment itself under a beach towel? And why couldn't Paula find it with the rest of the inventory items? Those questions joined the many others that kept recurring.

167

* * *

Two mornings later all of Jean McKay's questions were rendered moot: That was when she found the wires from her external receiver deliberately cut. She knew that someone was out to get her.

Part Two

Discovery

~~ **17** ~~

After pawing half-heartedly for "clues" out at the dish on that sultry morning, Jean returned to the trailer and played the tape from the start to the point at which it cut off. The predawn noises were normal. She identified nothing suspicious until the owl screamed its alarm call a few seconds before the tape stopped.

She rewound the tape and replayed it slowly, a few revolutions at a time, listening intently. She *might* be hearing an automobile driven at very slow speed, seemingly close by. She listened again; still nothing conclusive. She listened for footfalls prior to the alarm cry. She couldn't really distinguish them amidst the noises of the awakening day.

In the final few seconds of the tape, the microphone picked up the ghastly call (even more ghastly because of its proximity to the mike), then an unmistakable whoosh of clothing against the foliage, a second rustling of clothing, followed by an expiration of air, a human grunting sound, then silence. No doubt, the trespasser had planned to cut the wire anyway and was about to do so when the cry sounded. Whoever it was, was cool, aware of being recorded, and would not give in to any kind exclamation that the tape would pick up.

The sounds on the tape painted a picture for Jean: A person was startled by the alarm cry, turned around, and probably turned around again when the light came on. The person found the wire, then emitted a release of voice and air as the wire was cut.

171

Yes, she could picture exactly the way it might have happened. But the person in the picture is shapeless, featureless, voiceless, genderless. She replayed the tape several times trying to determine if the small sound immediately prior to cutting the wire was made by a male or a female. She can't make the call.

Jean needed Rusty. She has his home phone number and pondered what phone to use. The Wilsons and Annie Crews probably were up, but calls from their phones might alarm them if they should overhear her end of the call. So she jumped into her car and hurried to the nearest phone booth. She called the number even though it was barely 7:00. She identified herself to Dawn Torrance, and the name registered. Rusty was on the phone right away.

"Hi, Jean. What's up?"

"Something that frightens me. Someone deliberately cut the wires that go from my receiver to my tape recorder this morning..."

Rusty interrupted, "Receiver? Tape recorder? What are you talking about, Jean?"

She had forgotten that he knew very little about her project. Jean explained quickly but in a way that impressed on him why she considered it an ominous, deliberate act. "So you see," she summarized, "Someone didn't want his movements recorded on tape."

"His?" asked Rusty.

"Or hers," admitted Jean.

"Be over as soon as I grab a bite." Jean gave him directions and suggested that they meet at Wilson's office. Rusty asked for 40 minutes, but as he hung up

172

he thought, "This is a call for help from Jean McKay, and she'd be last person to do that unless she meant it." He bolted a piece of toast on the run and used the privilege of the squad car to obliterate speed limits to get to the trailer office in 30 minutes instead of the promised 40.

Jean was already standing outside the Wilsons' trailer to greet him. She had talked to Orville Wilson. Without telling why she was asking, she fished for information from him. "I thought I heard a car back this way earlier this morning. Did you or Dot hear anything?"

"Not a thing," Wilson had replied. "Why? Is something missing or something?"

"Oh, no," Jean had said calmly. "Just a woman's curiosity."

Rusty came very close to hugging her fragile little body when he got out of the squad car. Jean sensed that impending gesture and picked up the concerned look on his face as he asked if she was all right. She wanted to establish a rational rather than an emotional footing, so she averted the hug and said in a perfectly natural voice, but quiet enough to make sure Orville didn't overhear her, "I'm fine now. I shouldn't have called you at home, but I thought if there are any clues to this funny business lying around, the sooner you could take a look, the better chance you'd have of finding something. I hope you didn't think me a panicky little old lady."

"Jean, Jean," he comforted her. "You are about the least panicky person I've ever known. You did exactly right to call as soon as you did. Where do we go from here?"

Jean showed him the road to her trailer. They examined it as they walked. Rusty doubted that any car had been along it that morning.

"But someone could leave a car out by the gate and walk. It isn't very far," Jean suggested.

"If they know the way. Not much moon last night," said Rusty. Several times he squatted down to examine the road closely. "Can't make out any recent footprints except very light indentations that are probably yours coming from the trailer.

"Any other way to get back here?" he asked.

"He—or she—could have used an abandoned road to go around on the other side of the swampy area. It doesn't go by Wilsons' office trailer. It connects with this road just before it reaches my trailer. Actually, my dish is a little more accessible from the abandoned road than from this one."

"Who knows about the other road?" Rusty asked.

Jean remembered her barbecue and how Con's son Peter accidentally took the abandoned road. "Well, all the birders who came to my barbecue. That's everybody except Doris. She's been here, but I don't remember if we talked about the abandoned road or not. Probably not, but of course any of the others might have talked to her about it."

"Everyone in your Sunday group, then," said Rusty. He removed a notebook from his shirt pocket and listed the birders who certainly knew about the road. "And Bobo and his grandfather were back here, weren't they?"

"Yes, but I don't think they knew about the abandoned road." Nevertheless, Rusty made another note.

174

"But as you say," he persisted, "they could have left the car outside the gate. They know how to walk quietly. We can't dismiss Bobo despite Granny's plea. Anybody else?"

"No one," Jean assured him.

Rusty put his hand to his chin, withdrawing it only to wave away a mosquito. Then he changed the subject. "I want to see that abandoned road and the parking area out at the main road, but first show me where the wire was cut."

It was easy for them to discern where someone had pushed through the lush vegetation and across the fern matting in the direction of the receiver. Yet no definitive footprints could be found. Noting the person's direct path to the receiver, Rusty observed that "the person either knew exactly where that receiver is or has the nerve to beam a flashlight around. But it looks to me as if he—or she—knows your set-up exactly." Both of them were being a little silly in their efforts not to use prejudicial pronouns. Rusty did remark, however, that what was left of the swathe the person made suggested "a person of considerable size."

They came to the dish and then to the place where the wire was cleanly snipped. Rusty examined it carefully. "You're right, Jean," he concluded. "Snip. Snip. Clean and deliberate." He identified a footprint of Jean's made when she was out there an hour or so earlier. They didn't find any others, nor a piece of thread or a button or any other object that often is so conveniently left behind by miscreants in crime fiction.

Rusty paused to think. Motioning with his head toward the dish, he asked, "That thing got a switch on it?"

"Yes it does, and you are probably wondering why the person didn't use it. He, or she, may not have known about it, and also it's kind of tough to snap open the cover that protects it."

"Just the same, we'll dust for prints on the cover. At least it's a possibility."

"I'm afraid you'll find mine," Jean sighed. "I snapped the cover open to see if the switch was on."

"And it was, I suppose." Jean nodded. "We'll still try," Rusty continued, sounding a bit discouraged. "Maybe the wire cutters were back-up if he couldn't manage the switch although frankly I doubt it."

The sun now was fully up, and they were getting hot and frustrated. Jean suggested that Rusty come inside, have some iced tea, and listen to the tape. He accepted readily. She didn't play the whole tape, but did go back far enough so his ears could acclimate to its sounds. "There," she said suddenly. "Sound like a car back there?" They replayed it several times, and Rusty concluded it was a car but he admitted he didn't know what it signified as a clue.

They figured it was about 4:45 when the car approached. When they played and replayed the three or four minutes before the tape cut off, Rusty listened intently. "I can't prove it, but I think that's a male. The rustle through the grasses sounds fast and heavy. Same way when the person whirled around when the owl shrieked. Boy, that's some kind of shriek!" He smiled at Jean, then continued. "That grunt, or whatever you want to call the noise just before he snipped the wire sounds more male than female. But as I say, I can't prove it." Jean didn't want to add that both Doris and Con are tall women, fast walkers, and have rather low-pitched voices.

"We'll want to get this to an acoustical engineer who's worked with the department before," Rusty said. "We'll make a perfect copy of it first for you to study."

He had been deadly serious the entire time. He was even more so as he leaned his big frame forward in the small chair. "Now then, Jean, who has been to the dish out there?"

She tried to envision the parade she and Con's son Pete led to the dish at the barbecue. She had been so absorbed in explaining the set-up to Pete and one of the Purvis boys that now she wasn't fully sure of who else was there.

"Well," she began hesitantly. "I think that Sandy, Don, and Con inspected my set-up at my barbecue. But I can't be sure about Bill Long. He may or may not have stayed behind with his wife. Somebody did, I'm sure."

"And Doris Groot?"

"She wasn't there, but I showed her the dish and recording stuff at another time." She seemed unhappy to admit it.

Rusty wanted to get this just right. He took more notes, then asked, "What about others at your party? Con's son, for example."

"The son, Pete, was there for sure. Maybe Susan Purvis. Isn't this getting a little remote?"

"Not when somebody is trying to harm you. How about the Wilsons? Ever show it to them?"

"Oh, please, Rusty. I suppose so."

He ignored the tinge of exasperation in her voice. "And I'll bet it would be an ego trip for Wilson to show your set-up to his friends."

"If you say so, but that's absolutely it." Jean, showing the strain of the morning, was getting a little testy.

"Well, again don't forget that everybody's prime suspect, Bobo, has been to your trailer."

Jean answered so fast that he barely got the word "trailer" out. "But not to the dish." Then she paused. "Besides, he ain't <u>my</u> prime suspect." The little grammarian's deliberate fluff broke the tension. Rusty permitted himself a smile, then after several seconds asked, "Who <u>is</u> your prime suspect?"

"I guess I should be honest and admit that Don Purvis is a little ahead of the others, but that's probably because I'm so disappointed in him. The theory that Max might have threatened to expose Doris and him is so weak as to be virtually nonexistent, but even if it were strong, I can't think that I'd tipped him or Doris off that I know about them."

Rusty was interested. Inspecting the tall ice tea glass, he said, "OK, so Don would top your list. Can you rank-order the others?"

"No, Rusty, I absolutely cannot. It's a four-way tie for 'totally-out-of-the-question.' And that's really the case with Don, too." Jean was fudging a little with that reply, but she felt it was far too early to air a couple of dim theories she was beginning to develop.

"Let me try another tack," Rusty suggested. "Aren't you forgetting another possibility?" Jean looked at him curiously and slowly shook her head.

"How about the reason you are down here in the first place? The kidnappers."

"No, not a chance," Jean said quickly. "They're in prison. I never even think about them."

"Well, maybe we should. They have a motive, revenge. And they have more than nodding acquaintances with killing. And somebody is threatening you. Wouldn't a convicted kidnapper with a revenge motive be a more likely suspect than, say, a junior high science teacher without a clear motive? Or a millionaire retired lawyer? Or any of the other birders? I'm going to check with your friend Francis Sheehan to see if he knows what they're up to."

"Oh, I don't want you to do that, Rusty. It would needlessly worry Francis over nothing," Jean pleaded.

"Trust me. I'll think of a way to talk to Francis so he won't worry about you…any more than he probably already is."

Rusty gulped down the rest of his tea and said he'd like to search some more for outside clues. They went out and started to tramp the abandoned road. He was methodical in his inspection. He never gave the impression of hurrying or mentioned that he had a full agenda of meetings and a report deadline awaiting him at his office.

Even the ruts of the abandoned road were overgrown with matted vegetation near Jean's trailer. Yet Rusty pointed out how the vegetation had been beaten down. He speculated that the visitor had used that route on foot rather than the normal road, where he'd found no signs of recent movement other than Jean's. At one point he got down on his haunches and took a metal collapsible tape measure from his pocket and measured the distance between very slight indentations in the matting.

"If these indentations were caused by a person's foot," he explained to Jean, "and I can't be certain that they are, that person has a long stride."

Jean was fascinated watching Rusty do the part of detective work that she knew nothing about. She thought that this is practical stuff, unlike his grilling her about remote possibilities.

After a while he lost the indentations then picked them up again, a little more clearly demarked. He showed them to Jean, but in answer to her questions, said, "I can't be sure even that they are footprints or were made this morning. But they are recent enough that I would bet that your visitor came or went this way."

Now they were at the point where the two roads join and footprints and tire tracks were all over. Rusty pointed out his own car's tracks with a smile.

They proceeded to the gate, and Rusty was able to make out where a car had turned around on the berm. He picked up part of a candy wrapper and a cigarette butt, both clean and recently discarded. "Any of them smoke?" he asked. Jean said that Don Purvis does rarely. She thought about her changed feelings for Don. At first she thought of the handsome ranger as "very much the Eagle Scout." Now he's an adulterer with a surly personality and a smoker.

"Know his brand?" asked Rusty. Jean didn't but added that she'd find out. "How are you going to manage that?" Rusty asked. She'd forgotten for the moment that she'd bowed out of the group. They shared a rueful laugh when she realized that. His broad freckled face and timely smiles have reassured her time after time during the brief time she has known him.

"Any of the birders a candy nut? It would take a nut to be nibbling a Snickers at 4:30 in the morning while trying to be invisible and planning to harm somebody." Jean thought to herself that both Doris and Sandy like to gobble M&Ms any time of day.

Rusty was just as meticulous in inspecting the abandoned road on their return. "Who lives in that trailer?" he asked, pointing to the only one visible from the old road.

"Annie Crews," Jean replied. "A retired schoolteacher in her seventies. She's not well but is as sharp as she can be mentally."

"Does she use the abandoned road?"

"I think she does sometimes." Jean gestured toward the trailer and a car parked in front of its carport. "See, she's got that nice old Plymouth. She gets out in it once in a while."

"So the 'abandoned road' isn't really abandoned," concluded Rusty. He added that he saw suggestions of tire tracks on the abandoned road nearer to where it veers off from the regular road, but thought they were made before this morning. "Must have been made by her car," he observed. "Does she know about your dish?"

"Rusty, she's a great grandmother with arthritis."

"It's happened before," he said quietly.

They looked again through the growth of live oaks, weighted by Spanish moss, toward Mrs. Crews' trailer. The robin's egg blue Plymouth, dating back to the fins era of auto design, was at the end of a sparsely graveled drive. Rusty asked, "How's your relationship with her?" Jean assured him it is fine. "I'd like to talk with her, but I've got to get on to other things first."

He backtracked to examine a couple of places where the undergrowth appeared matted down, then returned to Annie's driveway. He stared at the ground some more but offered no further comment.

They returned to Jean's trailer. While she was pouring some more iced tea, he asked, "Do you know what bothers me most about this thing?" She didn't. "Why would he (and I'm just saying 'he' because it's easier) why would he take the chance of showing his hand this morning? The answer: Because he thinks you are getting close. Tell me the truth now, Jean. Have you learned something that flushed whoever it is out this morning?"

"Believe me," she said, "I've been wracking my feeble brain about that, and I can't come up with a thing."

"Motive, motive, motive," Rusty crescendoed. "That's what we must find out!" He sat a moment, allowing his little soliloquy to sink in. "You know, maybe I'm wrong when I say our friend thinks you have latched on to something. Maybe he just wants to scare you off before you do. He has a lot of respect for your cleverness. He thinks that if you work at it you will find something incriminating. Either way, he's told us that there's something out there that will tie him to the disappearance. You've either found it already, or he's afraid that you will. That tells us something, anyway."

Jean was doubtful, and Rusty changed topics. "How much do you trust Orville and Dot Wilson?"

"With my life. Why?"

"Maybe that's what you're going to have to do. I think we're going to have to clue them in. Oh, not all the way. But beginning right now I'm going to set up a 24-hour patrol of this place in unmarked cars, and I expect we ought to tell the Wilsons. I'm going to want from him a description of the cars of all the campground residents as well as cars that regularly come and go here—relatives or lovers of occupants, tradesmen, and so forth. Maybe we'll tell Orville that twice you have suspected someone has followed you back here, and we want to put a stop to it. Sound plausible?"

"I guess so if you really think it necessary." Then she couldn't resist a sarcastic jab. "But aren't you forgetting—shudder, shudder—that the Wilsons may know about my dish?"

He ignored the sarcasm. "It is necessary, and I'm also going to insist you get a phone. Look, little lady, whoever cut those wires this morning didn't do it as a random act of vandalism. He knew exactly what he was doing and why. I don't know what the plan was exactly, but I thought I smelled gasoline back there. I suspect the idea was to douse your trailer with gasoline and set it on fire. If it didn't kill you, it would scare you enough to lay off. You can be eternally grateful to that hooty owl for scaring him off."

"I am," Jean sighed. "But I'm not laying off."

~~ 18 ~~

Rusty had to get back to headquarters. Before he left, however, he went over with care his plans for Jean's protection while shopping and carrying on her day-to-day living. He asked her not to venture outside the camp for the rest of the day because it would take some time to set up the patrols.

Naturally, Jean was apprehensive about the need for protection. Rusty tried to reassure her. "You know, Jean," he said, "in a way what happened this morning has made me less anxious. Our friend has to assume that he put you on guard. He may decide that it's safer to lie low than to try again. Of course, we can't be sure of that; it's just one hypothesis. We have to prepare for the worst, and that's what we'll do."

It was a nice try, and Jean was grateful but unconvinced. Rusty said good-bye and swung by Wilson's trailer to get the information he needed from them and to apprise them of why he wanted it.

Left alone, Jean was restless, full of nervous energy. She tried to work on her project, but her mind wandered. She wanted to investigate…what? Something. Anything. Once more, she probed around where the wires were cut looking for clues. Nothing. Next she examined the faint imprints on the abandoned road, which Rusty thought the intruder used on foot. That would point to someone who knew about the road. Annie Crews arises very early. Could she have seen or heard something? She'd call on Annie.

She had been to Annie's trailer three or four times to drink iced tea or Coca-Cola with her. And Annie was at her barbecue. Jean was very fond of the handsome, 75-year-old teacher, retired from a mostly black Virginia school. Annie had told her of some of her trials as she helped take her school from all black to "theoretically integrated." She would smile serenely as she recalled events with pointed irony.

Annie had been a widow for 35 years and had also outlived her only son. She had lived alone most of three and a half decades, and so far as Jean can tell, had done so happily. Jean knew that she had friends from her church and other activities, but because the trailer camp was so remote, their calls were not frequent. Apparently she wanted it that way. Jean understood that her resources were not large, but she seemed to be a prudent manager who could change her lifestyle if she wished.

Jean pictured her as she walked up the lane toward her trailer. She was tall, five feet eight or so, and erect, without a hint of a dowager's hump. Her iron-gray hair was parted in the middle and pulled back in a bun. Her glasses were shell on the top half, metal on the bottom. Her skin was light enough that you could discern a few freckles. Her features were still handsome; Jean wondered why she had never remarried. About her only physical concessions to age were swollen ankles and fingers gnarled by arthritis. Despite the latter, she was skilled in various needle arts, and Orville Wilson once told Jean that Annie's creations had won ribbons in several local fairs. Jean remembered that the trailer had been immaculate each time she'd been there, and so had been the little plot of land that surrounded it. The elderly but well kept Plymouth had been parked just as it was this morning. "Good," said Jean to herself, "She's home."

She knocked several times, giving Annie time to arise from an early afternoon nap. She called her name, circling the trailer. She wondered if Annie was hard of hearing; she didn't recall seeing a hearing aid. Finally, she peeked in the only window she could reach. Everything appeared to be in apple-pie order, but there was no sign of Annie.

Jean thought her friend's absence without her car was a little surprising. She supposed that she had gone out with friends in their car. Impressed by Rusty's techniques earlier that day, she puzzled over tire tracks but couldn't decide whether another car had been there or not. She felt a little foolish.

Although not alarmed, Jean was concerned enough to swing by the office to ask the Wilsons if they'd seen Annie leave or if she had left a message. She found Dot, who said, "Are you all right, dearie? We know. We know. The sheriff told us. You can count on Orville and me." Jean thanked her for her concern and assured her that everything was OK, but wondered if it was OK with Annie Crews.

"S'far as I know it is, but I haven't seen her for a day or two."

"Do people ever come by and take her out in their cars?"

"Yes, I think so. She has friends, and I think they come by from time to time." Jean wished Dot had been more convincing.

One more question occurred to Jean. "Does she usually let you know when she is leaving the camp?"

"Yes, for vacations and trips and things like that. We hold her mail. But other times I just don't know what her policy is. You know, I think she takes the abandoned road some times, and that wouldn't bring her by here. If she's just going out shopping she lets us know if she happens to catch our eye. But if she goes out and doesn't let us know, we don't know whether she's gone out or not, do we?"

Jean wished Dot hadn't been so exasperatingly logical. She walked back toward her trailer, trying to get interested in a little blue heron that was busying itself at the swamp's edge. She recalled the "little blue" was sometimes an alarm caller, playing the blue jay's role for swamp and shore life. Of course, with the thought of the heron's alarmist nature, her preoccupation with what had happened to her that morning returned, accompanied increasingly by her concern for Annie Crews. She concluded that she probably would not have given Annie's absence another thought if she weren't so keyed up by her own predicament. Still she resolved to try to see Annie again tomorrow.

~~ **19** ~~

That night Jean gave thanks for the presence of Rusty Torrance in her life. She slept surprisingly well for someone who presumably was the object of a murder attempt that same morning. She dreamed realistically of her adolescence. Her name was up for membership in a club of six other girls. She wanted very much to be asked. Two of the girls were Con and Doris, two were actual friends from her school days, one was a snooty cousin, and one was nobody in particular. They told her that she had received one black ball, and they promised to tell her who it was. But the dream ended before she found out.

When she awakened it took her several seconds to realize where she was, so vivid was the dream and so true was it to her own young womanhood. In grammar school, she was well liked by the other girls, who admired her grades. She was especially popular with the Girl Scouts, where she was a leader. But when they moved on to junior high school, the girls whose beauty blossomed and whose figures developed attractively left Jean behind as they courted new friendships with the popular girls who came from the other elementary schools. That's when Jean found other interests, mainly in nature study, to substitute for the social life she was denied.

Orville brought down her mail in the late morning. He looked around suspiciously as if to make sure he wasn't being followed, then gave her a couple of letters. "Heard anything?" he asked, barely above a whisper. At first Jean didn't comprehend the reason for

188

the air of mystery. "What do you mean, Orville?"
"You know," he said giving his head a little jerk back
toward the road. He lowered his voice even further.
"Seen anything?" Jean finally recalled that, in order to
get information he needed from Wilson, Rusty had
cooked up the little fiction about someone following
her. Orville was letting her know that he'd been let in
on a very important secret.

"Haven't seen a thing." She smiled at him. "By the
way, have <u>you</u> seen Annie Crews today?"

"Nope," he said indifferently. Then he came closer
to her and said earnestly, ignoring thoughts of Annie.
"Don't worry, ma'am. Me and Dot have our antennas
up, and we have the deputy's private number." He
relished being an insider.

Although at first Jean had a little trouble latching
on to Orville's pose, she had no trouble at all working
up interest in one of the pieces of mail he brought. It
was a #10 envelope of expensive cream-colored stock.
Her name was lettered in a fine old-fashioned hand,
and the embossed return address was "GWL, Jr.," with
a Naples Port Royal street number. Bill Long had
written her.

It was an invitation for her to rejoin the group. It
praised her skills as a birder and complimented her on
"a winning personality that all of us took to right
away." But the letter was more interesting to her
because in it Bill attempted an explanation of sorts as
to why they weren't "friendly to an investigation of
dear Max's disappearance after all this time." He
wrote:

        ... I guess if I could speak
    for the group as a whole I

189

would say that we have an
underlying feeling that you
seem to suspect us, or at least
some one of us. We feel that
Bobo is involved, and we've had
two years to think about a
solution; yet you seem
determined to show that he
isn't. Whom does that leave?
Surely you can't think, Jean,
that a flibbertigibbet of a
secretary, or a quiet
schoolteacher, or a nature
photographer, or a park ranger,
or a has-been retired lawyer—
none with a discernible motive—
could have a hand in some sort
of nefarious scheme. Yet we
sense that's where you've been
heading.

Believe me, dear Jean, we'd
love for you to investigate
with all the zeal you can
muster if you were going after
Bobo, or his carousing friends,
or Ed Beggs, or someone else
none of us knows about. We'd be
happiest of all if you could
determine the disappearance was
voluntary (which I personally
think is still a real
possibility).

But to subtly probe about in a way that makes us think you suspect that someone in our group is involved, and to meet with chief deputy Torrance, just doesn't sit well with the people who extended to you the hand of warmest friendship—a hand that we have withheld from others who have hinted, more than hinted, that they would love to join our group.

Frankly, Jean, I'm less concerned about these things than some of the others are. Therefore, I appointed myself a reasonably impartial committee of one to advise you. I expect it comes as no surprise to you that we have talked about these things in your absence, and I believe I have fairly represented our views, both individually and as a group—including the view that we'd like to have Jean McKay back with us next Sunday!

Despite the letter's inherent plausibility, it didn't sit well. Beneath the courtly tone, there was a second message that seemed to Jean to say, "We know exactly what you are doing." And Jean wondered if all the information had come from Con.

191

She wanted to discuss it with Rusty and planned to leave the camp to make a call to him. Yesterday she had reluctantly agreed to Rusty's request, almost a demand, to have a phone installed in the trailer, but it would be several days before the hook-up could be made. Meanwhile they'd agreed that she would make her calls from three different booths in an established sequence. Although they trusted the Wilsons, they decided it would be better not to use their phone.

After she drove out of the camp, she tried to determine which car on the county road, if any, might be that of the deputies assigned to protect her. She couldn't identify a likely candidate immediately and wondered if the system was working. Then she realized that a nondescript dark blue Ford Crown Victoria sedan had spirited itself behind her and had been there for maybe a quarter of a mile. It had two male occupants. She was relieved.

She was doubly relieved when she turned to head to phone booth #1 and the Crown Victoria made the same turn. When she got out to make her call, she didn't see the car, but now she knew it was around somewhere close.

Paula put Jean's call right through to Rusty in a way that suggested she had standing orders to do so. Jean mentioned the letter as her reason for calling. Rusty said he'd wanted to see her too, but didn't want her to risk showing her hand by coming to the office. He suggested meeting for early supper at a cafe called Bodine's Koffee Klatch and gave her directions. He added with a chuckle, "Look carefully for a big red-headed guy in a sport shirt and shorts. That'll be me.

Joe Bob Carey will be with me, and he'll be out of uniform too."

Jean didn't exactly know how to feel about bringing in Carey, but Rusty was reassuring. "It's full speed ahead on this thing, Jean, since yesterday morning. I'm bringing in Joe Bob because he was on duty the morning the disappearance was reported. We've got some police-work chores to get to pronto, and he's good at them. And he tells me he's never liked the idea of this unfinished business hangin' around. He'll be fine."

She had no trouble finding the cafe and quickly spotted the two men in a maroon leatherette booth near the rear of the narrow eating area. It was uninvitingly dark back there, which was no doubt why Rusty chose that booth. The table, which jutted out from the beige wall, was topped by a marbleized vinyl pattern rimmed with chrome. Jean noted to her satisfaction that it had been wiped clean recently.

Rusty, with Carey following his example, made as much of a rising gesture as the booth would permit as Jean walked up. Both greeted her warmly; she'd met Carey previously at the station.

The men were seated opposite each other, and she chose to sit beside Rusty and opposite Joe Bob. There she could examine a large friendly, weathered face, with round brown eyes and a wide nose. His hair was parted extremely low on the right side, and long dark strands were trained across the top in a not-too-successful attempt to cover his scalp. His sideburns were trimmed at the bottom of his ear lobes, but the effect wasn't very attractive because his facial hair was much sandier and coarser than his scalp hair. His

193

cotton sport shirt featured a pastel plaid pattern and was neat and clean. Rusty looked quite handsome in a tan short-sleeved sport shirt with a button-down collar.

He got right down to business. "Jean, before we talk about Long's letter," he said quickly while making sure the adjoining booths were unoccupied, "let me say that this thing is our number one priority, and I've brought Joe Bob in on it pretty much full time from now on. He's up to speed about recent developments. Anything you want to say at this point, J.B?"

"Well, I reviewed the file this morning," he drawled in a true deep South accent, "and it's pretty much the way I remembered it. Factually, anyway. `Course I didn't go along with the way Ed seemed to want to nail the Indian boy right off, but that was Beggsy. It wasn't the first time I seen him try to convict an Indian or Hispanic kid without much evidence. I also found my own personal log for those days, and it squares up with the record."

Carey's confident manner reassured Jean despite his grammar.

"I understand you were on duty that morning," she ventured. "Were you at the hammock where the car was found?"

"Yes, ma'am I was there before Beggsy was. He was playing golf, as he let everybody know. I dusted for prints, but with almost no success. Fred Billie was our best tracking guy, and I worked with him as we hunted for clues. But the bird guys who were there before us had trampled things up so much that we got nothing from that. Billie's no longer with us, but I called him this morning and he remembered well that

we could get no tracks other than the two men's—
Sanderson and Long."

"So that means if Sandy or Bill had, for whatever
reason, been there earlier that morning," Jean said
thoughtfully, "you couldn't have distinguished those
earlier tracks from the ones they made when they were
looking for Mr. Wein."

Rusty jumped in. This was the farthest Jean had
gone to try to link specific individuals to the
disappearance. "I like you're thinking, Jean," he said.
"Maybe one of them deliberately went there to mix
fresh prints with earlier ones he might have left. It fits
with your theory that someone else drove Wein's car to
the hammock. And Long was the guy who directed
people there."

She barely heard him. She was preoccupied by
thoughts of Sandy not Bill, thoughts she didn't like
about her favorite member (with Con) of the group.
She again worried, seriously this time, that what he
said about his "poverty" didn't square with what she
could see of his lifestyle. Scratching out a living by
selling bird photos for $35 to $75 each didn't explain
the $1,000 or more in new photographic equipment
he'd laid in since she'd known him or his new
Mustang convertible—all the while paying alimony.
She had no idea where he lived; he'd never said. But
she concluded that he must either sell a tremendous
number of photos or is able to push his credit to wild
extremes. Or he had another source of income he
hadn't told her about.

Jean couldn't hide her distress as she thought about
Sandy, but Rusty beside her didn't notice. "What do

you think, J.B.? Could one of them deliberately cover up earlier prints?"

"Sure, it's a possibility. A strong one. Those two guys walked all over the place. But it don't rule out the other bird folks or Bobo or Bobo's friends."

"OK," conceded Rusty. "But this is a good start. Now we want to run down other leads, like Wein's lady friend in Miami, the one that someone said had caused him some distress." He turned to Jean at his right. "I've asked Joe Bob to find her, beginning tomorrow. Can you give us any information about her?"

"Only that she was somehow disabled and was a member of Max Wein's temple."

"No name?"

"No name. I wasn't in a position to ask it when Bill Long reluctantly told me about her. And of course we can't ask him now. I have a picture of the lady I presume was she. In a wheel chair. Sandy Sanderson is in it too. It was on an undeveloped roll of film that was in Max's camera. Just a snapshot. Want me to get it to you?"

Joe Bob looked at Rusty for an answer. "Thanks, Jean, but I want Joe Bob to get going."

"Any ideas," Joe Bob inquired, "on how I go about finding the church or whatever it's called?"

Jean suggested going to the Yellow Pages and matching addresses of synagogues against a grid of streets in the section of Miami where she understood that Max lived. She explained that the synagogues might be distinguished as Reform, Conservative, and Orthodox, and proposed starting with Orthodox, remembering that Max wore a yarmulke in the picture

196

of the group she had seen for a couple of seconds. She thought fleetingly about the little piece of cloth she found near the eagles' nest but didn't voice that thought.

They agreed on a straightforward strategy whereby Carey would pick a likely temple, identify himself, say he's investigating the disappearance of Max Wein a couple of years ago, and ask if he was a member of that congregation. When he made a connection, he would lead the conversation to a disabled woman Wein had been seeing, and that in turn should lead him to the woman. At least that's how it would work in theory. Joe Bob reviewed the strategy with some mock conversations. This was right down his alley; he had something of a reputation as an actor in local theatricals.

"I'll start for Miami right now," said Carey, sliding across the seat to leave and reaching for his wallet. "I think this'll cover my meal." He extracted a few dollars.

"Keep it," said Rusty. "Department expense. Good luck."

"Excuse me," said Jean hesitantly but looking at Carey, "But could I ask just one question before you leave?" Both men nod.

"Are you in touch with Edward Beggs?"

"I sure as hell, er sure as heck, am not, ma'am." (Jean has that kind of effect on people, especially those who are or think they are Southern gentlemen. Sometimes she wishes men would talk like men in front of her.) "He resigned a couple of years ago. Sold his house and took off with his girl friend. Barely said good-bye. I got a Christmas card from an island called

197

Anguilla the first year but it didn't have a return address. Around the office we used to talk about him and wonder what he was up to. But now we're used to having him gone. I don't think anyone else there is in touch with him, but I'll ask around. Anything else?"

"Can you estimate how soon he resigned after Max Wein's disappearance?"

Joe Bob, who was caught by Jean's questions in an awkward half-turned position leaving the booth, sat back down and said, "It'd be easy to look up. We know that Ed was in charge of the investigation, which was in March. But I think he packed off pretty soon after the investigation simmered down without results. Probably in April or May. We had a farewell thing for him—didn't have time for anything elaborate—and I seem to remember it was in Easter week. But I'll look it up."

"No need," said Jean. "You've been helpful. Bye bye."

"And again, good luck in your search," repeated Rusty, then added, "and, Joe Bob, let's not ask around if anyone knows where Beggs is. If you want to ask someone casually about Beggs, clear the person through me before you ask. We want to keep this investigation to ourselves for the safety of this lady here."

After Joe Bob left, Rusty smiled at Jean. "I'm glad he asks his rather naive questions rather than try to wing it. He'll do OK. Bet we hear from him tomorrow or the next day."

Then they talked about Bill's letter, and Rusty said he will not stand in the way if she decides to accept the invitation.

"We'll be nearby," he assured her. "Just don't go alone out in the field with one of the other birders. I don't care if it's Consuela or Groot or any of them. If one of them suggests going out with you by yourselves, we have a live suspect!"

They talked through two iced tea refills about precautions, protection, and people, including Jean's newfound concerns about Sandy Sanderson. When she drove home, her escort appeared and followed her to the trailer. Before she retired, she took a short stroll in the direction of Annie's trailer. She could see its outline, but there were no lights on. Jean reasoned it was fairly late and Annie retires early. Still she would have welcomed seeing a light.

20

The next afternoon an excited Orville Wilson delivered a request by Rusty for another supper meeting at Bodine's. The message cited a specific time, "as near to 5:15 as you can make it." Jean got ready and, ignoring the advice to use pay phones, stopped by the trailer office to use the phone there. She left a message with Paula that she'd be there at the time suggested. Paula apologized for Rusty for the short notice. Rusty broke in from another call to explain that Joe Bob was on his way back and that he would like her to be there to hear what he had to say. Orville didn't try to pretend he wasn't listening.

The rainy season was closing in, and this was a sodden, hot, gloomy day. It seemed oppressively so when Jean saw no sign of Annie Crews at her trailer. Because of the threatening weather, she allowed some extra time to reach the restaurant. Sure enough, the ominous sky opened up as she left the camp. The rain impeded visibility, but as if anticipating this, a nondescript car with two male occupants began to follow her more closely than usual so she could see they were there. Evidence that she continued to be well protected was comforting.

Rusty had timed the meeting so that he and Jean would have a few minutes together before Joe Bob arrived. He based the timing on an estimate of how long it would take Joe Bob to drive from Miami in the rain. As Rusty had instructed him, he had called as he was checking out of the Ramada Inn where he'd stayed and had kept in touch by cell phone.

Jean and Rusty arrived within a minute or two of each other during a respite in the rain. He was wearing a bright yellow tee shirt, but still had on his uniform trousers. Again Rusty selected a booth near the rear, just one booth in front of the one they'd occupied yesterday. He looked around and saw that the only other diners were three older couples taking advantage of special early bird fares. Now he noticed two young men who came in and occupied a booth near the door. He gave them a barely perceptible nod that was reciprocated in the same way. Jean didn't notice her protectors.

With so few competitive noises, Rusty lowered his voice to barely above a whisper as he apologized for asking for the meeting on such short notice. He then filled Jean in on what he knew about Joe Bob's mission to that moment. Carey had called that morning to say he had "struck pay dirt." With a sardonic smile Rusty explained that all Joe Bob had meant was that he had located Wein's temple. The woman who answered the phone had known Max Wein and suggested that the rabbi would be interested in seeing Carey. She offered him an appointment at 11.

"That sounds promising," said Jean.

"Yes, but he called when he checked out of the Ramada, and I have my doubts whether the trip produced anything on target. Joe Bob said his day was 'ver-r-r-ry interesting' but not in the way we had expected. He sounded a little mysterious—the man isn't without a sense of drama—and that's why I wanted you here to hear his story. I didn't want it filtered through me. Oh, there's J. B. now."

By this time it was raining hard again. Joe Bob had maneuvered his big cruiser into a spot across the street. By the time he entered the restaurant he was sopping, and the combination of very high humidity and 92 degree temperature was more than Bodine's air-conditioning system could handle effectively. Carey's aviator glasses fogged up. His chief went to the front of the restaurant to meet him and escort him back to their booth.

After Rusty slid into the booth, Carey flopped down beside him and opposite Jean. He was winded from his dash across the street and occupied himself by drying himself off and defogging his glasses, but he managed a polite hello to Jean and Rusty.

"Whew!" he gasped. "Well, good to see you both." And he began to talk about the weather and a couple of storms he'd driven through on Alligator Alley. That of course wasn't what Rusty wanted to hear, so he finally gave him a nudge.

"C'mon, J.B., you said what you learned today was 'interesting but not what we expected.' Get to it, fella."

"Well, where to begin?" He now had caught his breath and was beginning to string the account out a little. Rusty waved off the waitress who solicited their order. A forefinger to his lip was a signal to Joe Bob to keep his voice down.

"Well, begin somewhere," coaxed Rusty, a little annoyed but quietly so. "How was the rabbi? Did he know Max Wein? Did you meet the woman?"

"OK, I'll start when I met the rabbi this morning. Golly, was it just this morning? So much has happened. Anyway, I didn't have to wait at all, and he seemed anxious to tell me anything I wanted to know.

He spoke highly of Max Wein and hoped that our investigation solves the mystery of his disappearance."

Then Joe Bob told how he segued to the subject of the lady. He quoted himself as saying, "We understand that he was suffering some despair over a relationship with a lady he knew in your congregation who was disabled." (He chuckled a moment as he told how he actually used the word "parish" instead of congregation, but his listeners weren't all that appreciative.)

Joe Bob continued. "So I asked him 'Do you know who that lady would be?'" Here he again interrupted his account to say, "I'd never talked with a rabbi before, but he's just a nice, regular guy. He's real interested in the Dolphins and the Marlins teams. Doesn't like pro basketball much."

"How and why did you get on sports?" Rusty asked impatiently.

"Well, the lady, her name was Eleanor Gluck, was one of the few females who get Lou Gehrig disease, and that led to baseball."

"Did you see her?" Rusty asked anxiously.

"No, she died a year ago." A cloud came over Rusty's usually pleasant face. Sitting beside him, Joe Bob didn't notice and went on. "The rabbi explained their problem like this. They were two people who were attracted to each other because, among other reasons, both had suffered a tough physical break. But Max's came in childhood, and he had always lived with it. The rabbi thinks that Max couldn't quite empathize (Is that the word?) with someone whose disability came on in later life and didn't understand why Eleanor didn't try harder to keep her book store going. It had been quite successful. From her side, she thought that he didn't understand a disease that continually ate away at her ability to function. I guess she had it a long time before it was diagnosed as ALS, as the rabbi calls it. Anyway she called it off with Max, didn't want to see him again. The rabbi thought this was awful because essentially they were so good for each other. But he believes she just couldn't stand to have Max see her die, especially since he kept pushing her to do more. Apparently he felt seriously guilty when he finally realized how bad off she was."

"Serious enough that he might have gotten so depressed that he might have killed himself or walked away from that part of his life?" Rusty asked.

For the first time, Joe Bob seemed a little off guard. He squirmed and said, "Well, I didn't exactly ask it like that. But he did say that he doubted if there was a connection between their problems and his disappearance."

"Well thanks, J. B.," Rusty sighed, playing with his fork. "Good work, but we might as well face it that we didn't learn much."

"No, now wait a minute, chief," the other man said with his voice rising. Rusty shushed him. "I'm not quite finished," Joe Bob resumed quietly. "The rabbi asked if I would like to talk to Eleanor's sister, Mrs. Stein, who he said was close to both of them. I said 'sure' and he called her up. In another hour I'm having coffee with this good-looking lady in her fancy apartment on the 26th floor of some ritzy condo overlooking the ocean." (Jean's mind turned to the pictures on Wein's little camera showing Sanderson with two women, no doubt the sisters.)

Joe Bob continued, "I can't get over how nice these folks were to me."

His naivete irritated Rusty and was embarrassing to Jean.

"OK, J.B., we don't need a sociology lesson right now," said Rusty. "What, if anything, did she have to say that has to do with why the department sent you over there?"

J. B's forehead scrunched up in wrinkles that produced a hurt look. He decided that he'd toyed with his boss long enough.

"Well, here's what's interesting. She told me that maybe two, three months after Max disappeared Eleanor got a post card from him!

"From California."

21

"What?" nearly screamed Rusty, then realizing he was the one making the noise now, he repeated "What?" just above a whisper, as if correcting himself. He looked around the restaurant to see if he had attracted the attention of the other diners. Jean didn't say anything but looked as startled as Rusty. Both were clearly caught by surprise.

"Wait a minute. Don't get too excited," cautioned Joe Bob with exaggerated quiet. "The post card could be spurious." He seemed proud to use that adjective but had a little trouble with the pronunciation. This produced a faint smile on both Jean's and Rusty's faces. But the two, usually so harmonious in their thinking, had opposite reactions. Jean, hopeful that the card was genuine, blurted out, "But could it also have been real?" Rusty seemed to want to buy the idea that it could spurious and asked almost at the same moment, "A fake, eh. Who'd do that?"

Carey raised his large left hand, palm out, and said gently, "One at a time." Turning to Jean and smiling, he said, "Maybe it's real, but it seems that Eleanor was suspicious of it. It wasn't a crank letter—it was very sweet and nice—but she just didn't think it sounded like Max—the wording, that is. Also, it was typed, and she hadn't known Max to type stuff before. The signature resembled Max's, but she was suspicious of it, too. So she took it to a handwriting guy, and he said he couldn't swear that it was Max's signature or a forgery for that matter. No help from that so-called expert."

"Where's the post card now?"

"Mrs. Stein doesn't know. She saw it once; Eleanor showed it to her. But it wasn't in her personal effects when they cleaned out her apartment after she died."

"Oh boy," said Rusty. "If it was a fake—and I bet it was—it means that whoever sent that is our person. Probably sent it hoping it would get back to Beggs if he was still there, or at any rate the sheriff's office, so that the case wouldn't be reopened. But apparently Eleanor never sent it over. If we could just find that post card, we could compare signatures and typewriter impressions."

"Also we could find out who took a trip to California that spring," added Jean. Although she hoped the card indicated that Max was alive somewhere, she accepted that it was probably a vain hope.

"Right! We'll get right on that, Jean." Rusty acted almost as if he reported to Jean.

Carey also was impressed and said so, then added, "But there's one more thing. Maybe very important." Joe Bob the actor again was stringing out what he was saying trying to add suspense.

Jean and Rusty let him play his little game without interrupting him this time, so Carey has no choice but to go ahead. "Mrs. Stein asked about Mr. Sanderson."

"How did it come up? What exactly did she say?"

"She asked if we'd talked to Sandy Sanderson 'that nice cousin of Max's on the Gulf Coast.' Direct quote. I didn't know how far to go so I stalled by saying that I wasn't familiar with all the pieces of the investigation and knocked the ball back in her court by asking

207

whether she thinks we should talk to him. She said she had no special reason to think so."

He went on to report that he asked Mrs. Stein how she knew Sanderson, and she replied that he was over several times both before and after the disappearance and was a real comfort to Eleanor. You see, although Eleanor had engineered the bust-up, she was pretty unglued by the disappearance. Mrs. Stein met Sanderson on some of these visits."

"The pictures on Max's camera verify that," Jean murmured.

She was preoccupied by another question, one that she didn't like asking.

"Did you ask her if she thought Sandy knew about the post card?"

"I sure did, ma'am, but her answer wasn't of very much help. She said she didn't know, but he could have. She was pretty sure he'd been over after Eleanor got the post card but before Eleanor died."

"Wouldn't it have been logical for her to tell Max's cousin about the message?" Jean asked no one in particular. "And wouldn't he have been the logical courier if she planned to send the post card over here?" The men nodded and Rusty said deliberately, "Of course, we don't know that she didn't give it to him. I'm afraid, Jean, your friend Sandy moves higher on the suspect list."

Jean didn't deny it, but added a qualifier, "<u>If</u> he knew about the card. By the way, what was the substance of the message?"

"Mrs. Stein didn't remember any specific details. Basically, 'I'm well, don't try to find me, I understand things better now,' that sort of general stuff."

They were ready to order. While waiting for the food, they discussed strategies for combing airline manifests and travel agency records for names of passengers who had booked space to California two years earlier.

"Also Amtrak," suggested Jean. She added that Doris Groot had once confessed to a serious fear of flying and that she took a convoluted train-bus route to see her parents in Sun City, Arizona, once or twice a year. While she was out there she also sometimes visited a sister in California.

"Oh boy," said Rusty, more in confusion than excitement. "That puts her up there with Sandy."

"I suppose so," Jean conceded without enthusiasm. Her mind went back to a conversation she and Rusty had about the possibility that Doris might be trying to protect her sweetheart.

The fake post card, if that was what it was, could have been an amateurish attempt to do that. Jean didn't want the lawmen to close in on Sandy and Doris as their prime suspects yet, deflecting attention from the others. She was still quite willing to accept any scrap of information about any of her five companions and put it into her mental file.

They left with Rusty's usual admonition to Jean to be careful. Pretty soon a Crown Victoria appeared from somewhere and trailed her back to the trailer camp, through Wilson's funny gate, and to her trailer. The men got out of the car and silently saw her up the little path.

Rusty came by for a follow-up session the next morning, looking none too cheerful. It was depressingly humid, but not raining. He told Jean that they'd already started the pick-and-shovel activity of running down airlines for trips taken by "the five" during the period when they estimated "Max's" post card might have been sent. But he acknowledged that the sender "probably used an assumed name for the California trip, so I'm not optimistic. I'm not optimistic about something else, too," he added.

"What's that, Rusty?"

"That telephone number on the scrap of paper among Max's things. It's the number of a nature preserve down on White Heron Key. Certainly, there's nothing out of the ordinary about Max making plans to go down there."

"Did you talk to 'Owens,' the name on the scrap of paper?"

"No, I wouldn't have the foggiest idea what to say to the guy. I did talk to my counterpart down there. He said the preserve is a quiet, peaceful place and described Owens as the ranger there and a 'good guy.' But really I think we have higher priorities than talking to a ranger down in the keys. Am I wrong?"

"Well, no. But since Max was a specialist on sightings of rare birds and those that may have been blown or wandered away from their usual habitat, it might be interesting to find out if they were seeing anything special down there."

Rusty rarely disagreed with Jean, but now he did. "Interesting to you perhaps, but frankly, Jean, even if they sighted a dozen dodo birds, I don't see how it could tie to Max's disappearance. How could it, pray tell?"

"It can't," she admitted. "Still…"

"OK, OK," he capitulated. "Do whatever it is you are thinking about down there and then explain it to me."

"It's a deal." She smiled.

One of the reasons Rusty had come by the trailer that morning was to see if there had been any progress in getting a phone in the trailer, and while he was there the installers came. That pleased him more than it did Jean. He really didn't want to continue the charade with the Wilsons in order to reach Jean.

After Rusty left, the phone people finished their work. Later that day Jean got her first call. The loudness of the bell penetrating her quiet environment jarred her. So did the message.

It was Rusty. His voice sounded lower in his throat than usual, making Jean wonder if her new phone's connections were faulty. But it proved to be emotion. He said, "Jean, the FBI has gotten back to me. They had something on two of the birders, but one we can easily dismiss. Bill Long. He's in their files because of a part he played as an expert witness in the prosecution of some big-time Wall Street swindlers. He was on the right side. No problem there."

Rusty paused. Jean filled the gap. "And the other one?"

The deputy had a hard time getting started. "This is tough, Jean. It's Consuela. Consuela Martinez-Tomaso-Smith, as she is known to the FBI. Many arrests. Mostly disturbing the peace but also destruction of property, resisting arrest, carrying unregistered firearms. The FBI also said she was an Olympic-class pistol shot, by the way. She was an important figure with groups in Miami that were pledged to restore Batista to power. By force. Finally she was kicked out of a teaching position in the schools over there."

Jean interrupted. "I can't believe it. Was this at all recently?"

"No, that's the good news," Rusty assured her. "Last arrest was nearly six years ago. But she was in enough big trouble that the FBI still keeps tabs on her regularly. The agent was intensely interested in why I was checking on her and the others. If he could find a way, I think he would have entered the case then and there and focused his sights on Con."

Jean recalled that when she examined the microfilm of the Miami <u>Herald</u> at the time of the disappearance, Con was identified as a former Miamian, the daughter of a right-wing Cuban physician named Martinez. She reminded Rusty of that, adding, "But she's so devoted to teaching and helping immigrant children," as if illogically expecting Rusty to be able to do something about the situation.

"So she is, but that's of little interest to the FBI. The Bureau is more interested in the fact she faked credentials to get the teaching job over here. She could never teach again over in Miami or thereabouts. Maybe over here they needed teachers in these migrant communities so bad that they overlooked her past. More likely they just didn't know about it. When she came over here she assumed the name 'Smith.' Not very imaginative. According to the Bureau, she was never married to anyone named Smith, by the way."

"Are you sure this is correct? Same woman? Our Con?"

"Positive, Jean. The FBI agent felt it was important enough to call me. A written report is coming by Fed Ex tomorrow."

Jean grasped at straws. "I seem to recall that her father is dead. Maybe when he died, she got out from under his political thumb and resolved on a totally new direction for her life."

"I hope so, Jean. You know that Dawn and I think highly of her. So does her pastor, Fr. Bernard." Rusty was revealing that Consuela was the one birder in whom he had an emotional investment. Still he was a good law officer. He said, "But no matter how highly we think of her now, we can't just forget that she's been in serious trouble in the past. And she was there that morning when Wein disappeared. And she's tough."

"People change," said Jean.

They were so upset that their good-byes weren't very warm.

Left alone and feeling lonely, as she rarely did, Jean found it nearly impossible to believe Con had ever been involved in violent crime—irrespective of Max's disappearance. But she also realized that Max Wein could have easily known about Con's former life and had been in a position to blow her new life apart. Then she remembered his adoring picture of her. It wasn't possible.

22

Flaming orange streaks intermingled with steel-blue reached upward in the southeastern sky as Jean followed the oblique course of the Tamiami Trail toward Miami. It was an hour after dawn, still cool, and her convertible top was down as she pierced first through Big Cypress Preserve, then edged along Everglades National Park. The birds appeared as black silhouettes with the sun in front of her, but she had no trouble identifying the many great blue and little blue herons, the ibises, the egrets, and the scruffy kingfishers sitting on the telephone wires. A myriad of sparkles glinted off the meandering watercourses and roadside sloughs.

Some distance back she had sped by a sign that warned "Limited services for the next 60 miles." She berated herself severely for not stopping there as she watched the fuel gauge needle dive relentlessly toward the E.

Still her concern didn't thwart her from pulling off the road at a place Bill Long once had told her she might add the endangered snail kite to her life list. Of course, she hadn't told Bill or anyone else of her trip to the Keys, but she had taken a note when he had described a location just off the trail in a section called "40-mile bend" where the rarities were nesting and were "easy" to see. She had learned to discount some of Bill's claims, but she gave herself half an hour to look for the kites. The habitat was a mosaic of open water and emergent saw grass and cattails where the birds could spot their exclusive diet, the apple snail, as it climbed up on the vegetation to breathe or feed.

Even if none of the endangered birds appeared, seeking them provided a diversion from thinking about the troublesome news about her friend Con. Then, at about the 28th minute of the allotted 30, a slate grey male swooped low over the water, made a splash, and apparently found its little meal. Jean marveled at how this species was so perfectly adapted to eat this one specimen among nature's millions. It shuns practically everything else and faces possible extinction as a consequence. Is stubbornness a character flaw of some birds as well as many humans?

Watching the snail kite was a thrill and she vowed to come back to record the female's cackling, which entices the males to bring her the precious snails. But that didn't put gas in the tank, so she nudged the big Bonneville gently forward.

Since coming to South Florida, she had come to love the barren glades, but now she would like to see one intrusive gasoline station. Now and then an official road sign proclaimed an Indian Village. At roadside, the "village" was usually just a single building housing a curio shop or the launching point for an air-boat ride. But finally there was a somewhat larger building that sported a cafe. Jean stopped and asked where she could buy a couple of gallons of gas, enough to get her to Route 1 where she would find complete services. She was in luck. The proprietor told her she could get gas just half a mile down the road.

She pulled away and to her relief soon spotted a sign, "Gas"—no brand name in evidence. A broad-faced young Miccosukee with only half his complement of teeth pumped in the nameless fuel. He explained that the government had closed the other gas stations in the parklands, but since he was an Indian, he could stay open. As she watched the gas needle creep up, she was grateful for his exemption.

She and the young Indian talked about family names; he stated that Miccosukees tend to "take white names," but Seminoles have names like Cypress, Osceola, Jumper, and Tigertail.

The name "Jumper" brought a picture of Bobo Jumper's rather surly face to mind. She had resolved to track him down and talk to him about why he hesitated when she asked him what he thought had happened to Max Wein. The chat with the young gas attendant also brought back in vivid detail her conversation with Granny in the remote chickee.

At the time, she treated the ancient woman's plea as a strong request, but one that she did not fully commit to fulfilling. At least that's how she rationalized things then. Subsequent events, however, had made Granny's plea an imperative. As a step in carrying out that imperative and at the same time furthering the investigation, today she was seeking out "Owens" at White Heron Key. Why did Max have his telephone number on a scrap of paper locked up in his glove compartment?

Rusty didn't want any part of the trip to White Heron Key. Nevertheless, he arranged for her protective escort to be standing by at her early departure. An unmarked patrol car followed her for the first 20 miles or so of the trip.

When she had called down to White Heron Key yesterday to confirm her visit, she wasn't prepared to explain her purpose on the phone and luckily didn't have to. Jean took a shot and asked for Mr. Owens. The woman who answered said he was not available that day; he would be in tomorrow. She had planned to work out her tactical approach on the way down, but had been too interested in the glades environment to consider how she would try to guide the conversation with Owens or even how she would introduce herself.

She turned off of the Tamiami Trail and pointed straight South through the devastated city of Homestead. The post-Andrew clean-up and rebuilding had been heroic, yet the remaining visible scars ate at Jean's heart. She hurried on, edging along Everglades National Park briefly.

Her thoughts turned to one of her heroes, Marjorie Stoneman Douglas, whose books and articles had done so much to energize forces to save the "river of grass," the Everglades. Jean was grateful to Mrs. Douglas and others whose foresight had resulted in the preservation of 1.5 million acres of these beautiful wetlands in the National Park. She was sickened when she considered that four times that amount had been lost to development, greed, and poor planning. She could hardly deal with the fact that scarcely 5% of the South Florida wading bird population of the early 20th century remained today. Were there that many plumes on ladies' hats? That put her in mind of another hero, Helen Hemenway, that Boston blueblood pal of Cabots and Lowells, who led the charge against using bird plumes as a badge of fashion among ladies in her own social class. Hemenway and Douglas both lived more than 100 years, Jean mused, a long time to do their good works.

She resolved to become more active in the preservation of dwindling wetlands and wild country around Oak City, where so little of the original wetlands were left. She had read somewhere that three quarters of the leadership in environmental causes had come from dedicated birders. She recalled that each of her five birding companions had talked of commitments to environmental causes. It was cathartic for her to think constructively about these people for a change. She found it incomprehensible that among them could be a...killer.

After she crossed the uppermost neck of Florida Bay she reached Key Largo and mounted the Overseas Highway, the strand that binds the necklace of keys for 180 miles southwestward.

Now she was angling back westerly, recrossing the longitudinal markers that she had crossed just an hour or two earlier 50 or so miles to the north. She wished she would have the opportunity to record the croaks of the great white herons whose world wide habitat is confined chiefly to a few keys. Why, she wondered, had the largest of all herons chosen to nest in such a restricted area when its powerful wings could take it almost anywhere. Maybe, unlike the rest of us, the huge wader has found its paradise.

A little redstart flashed vivid orange and black and white markings as it flit across the highway in front of her car.

She marveled that this tiny warbler, scarcely five inches from bill tip to tail tip, might fly over hundreds of miles of open waters and land masses, from the Caribbean and South America to as far north as Labrador, while the great white heron, with its wingspread of six to seven feet, was for the most part a year round homebody confining its life chiefly to a few square miles in the dense mangrove estuaries.

The highway took her on to Great White Heron key and directly to the entrance to the ranger station. The temperature had been climbing a degree or two every quarter hour, and it was blazing hot under a full sun as she stopped before the small, square, white-painted cement block building. She still wasn't quite sure how she would connect herself to Max Wein without seeming an insufferable busybody. The only strategy she could come up with was to volunteer as little as possible about herself.

She entered a stark white lobby that was sparsely furnished with a couple of old upholstered chairs and several card-table chairs, all unoccupied. A detailed mariner's map and a framed photo of President Clinton adorned the bright walls. A counter about two-thirds of the way back divided the room. The air-conditioner was noisy but effective. The contrast between the cold inside and the hot wind she'd felt in her open car caused her nose to stuff up.

Behind the counter a woman of about 45 and a man in a ranger uniform were giving directions to an older couple poring over a map. She assumed the ranger was Owens. Jean was thankful that no one else was waiting. She hoped that she could have the ranger to herself when the couple departed. She wished now that she'd made an appointment.

The ranger and the lady wished the older couple luck, and the man looked at Jean and said, "Ma'am, can we help you?" Jean thanked him and approached the counter. She spotted "Owens" on the badge on his shirt; her guess was correct. He was older than most rangers she'd met, perhaps 55. His gray-brown hair was in a crew cut. His wide face was heavily creased by years of working outdoors in a blistering climate. Apparently the veteran, working in a comparatively isolated post, no longer felt it necessary to be as fastidious about his uniform as someone like Don Purvis was.

The top two buttons of his tieless shirt were unbuttoned, and it could have used a pressing. He sported the requisite aviator glasses of his trade. His large gnarled fingers were hairy, and the top of the fourth finger on his left hand was missing. He had the mark of a rugged outdoor guy of long standing. A warm smile of greeting revealed a gap between his upper front teeth.

In response to his offer of assistance, Jean decided on a direct approach. "I'm Jean McKay, Mr. Owens, and I want to ask you something. Do you remember an ornithologist named Max Wein who might have come here a couple of years ago?" Jean was prepared to describe Max although she disliked using a person's handicaps to characterize him.

Owens didn't hesitate. "Sure I remember him. I knew him. Little crippled fellow. Very smart. He was here several times over the years to identify Caribbean birds that accidentally found themselves up here. Very respected in that field."

The ranger paused, looking thoughtful. "You ask about a visit couple of years ago? I'd say that was about the last time, but I can probably check that. Say...(he dragged out the word as the focus of his thoughts changed) have they found anything more about what happened to him? I was sick when I heard that he'd…disappeared was it? Or was he killed?"

"That's what I've come to talk to you about."

"Is that so? Well, come on back to my office here. First, meet the Missus. Millie this lady…"

"Jean McKay"

"Sorry I missed it the first time, Jean. I'm Clyde Owens."

Then, turning back to his wife, he added, "Jean knows our little crippled friend. You remember, Max Wein, who used to come here every year or two."

Jean and Millie reciprocated "Glad to meet you's," and Millie added, "I admired Mr. Wein a lot." Clyde told her he'd like to visit with Jean about Wein and asked Millie to mind the counter.

He lifted a hinged section of the counter and ushered her through an unpainted door behind it and into an eight-by-ten foot cubicle with a steel desk and file cabinet, two side chairs, and a somewhat incongruously handsome print of the great white heron on the wall. He motioned Jean to a chair.

Jean opened the conversation by correcting Clyde. "Actually I didn't know Mr. Wein, and I didn't mean to leave that impression. But I'm associated with some people who knew him well."

"Bet I know who some of them are," said Owens. "Don Purvis? Bill Long? A Dorothy or Doris something? Large gal." Jean nodded at the mention of each name and commented, "You're right. The woman is Doris Groot. We're all good friends, and they were close to and fond of Max Wein."

She looked at him with keen interest, hoping that he would continue. But Clyde missed the cue and, instead, waited for Jean to tell her story. She offered almost no background at all, and even bypassed describing how she became acquainted with Max's friends. She waded right in. For all Clyde knew, she could be working for the law. Or was just a Nosy Nelly.

"As you may know," Jean began, "Mr. Wein's car was found the morning he disappeared more than two years ago. The chief deputy sheriff in charge at the time had some ideas about the disappearance, but he resigned before he had any success in making anything stick. Now, the new chief deputy sheriff for the area is reviving the case. Reviewing the evidence, he noticed that a crumpled note with your number on it had been found in the car and apparently hadn't been followed up."

"Excuse me, Jean. That would be William Torrance, I guess. Our local deputy called me to say he might be coming by."

"Yes it is," agreed Jean hurrying on so she wouldn't have to explain why she was there instead of Torrance. "So that's why I'm here: To find out whether Mr. Wein came here two years ago, in early March, and why."

"My log may or may not help us. I'll check in a minute." He put his huge hand over his mouth and parts of both cheeks as he thought back. Suddenly he snapped his finger. "Wait a sec. I do remember the last time he came. There'd been a storm. There were reports that it had blown some Caribbean birds up here, little bananaquits and grassquits, things like that, and Max came down to try to identify and count them. As I recall he was quite successful. He took careful notes and asked me to help with the counts. He even asked me to sign on that his counts, identifications, and other research were accurate. I think I have a copy of it somewheres."

"Can you relate the timing of that visit to when you heard about the disappearance?" Jean asked.

"Not really," Owens replied. "Somehow I missed the story of his disappearance in our papers down here. I didn't know about it until Bill Long came by and told me. He's another good guy and very sharp about birds. He came here several times with Max, and I think he might have been along that last time. Anyway, Millie and I were pretty broken up about it when Bill told us."

The ranger paused to rummage around in the middle drawer and located a log book. He licked his large finger and deftly turned the seldom-used pages. "March. Ah, here it is. Wein underlined telephoned on March 9 wanting to come down in a couple of days. But there's no indication he ever came." He fanned backwards through a few more pages. "The old memory seems to be playing tricks on me. Apparently the last time he actually was here was August of the year before. I remember now. It was a summer storm that blew the bananaquits and other strangers up this way. Doesn't say whether or not Bill Long was with him although I see that Long was here again a few days later."

Owens noodled around among his entries. "Long was here March 16, too, and see, here's a note that says, 'Told us bad news about Max Wein.' Here's something else. I met Don Purvis at a meeting a couple of days later, and he introduced me to Doris. My log says they were upset that Max was missing too. Noted right here. Apparently, the last time I saw Max Wein was the August before. I'll go over my log again if you'd like."

Jean thanked him warmly and assured him it wasn't necessary. She did give him her new phone number "just in case anything else comes to mind."

Owens offered to show Jean around the preserve. They spent a pleasant hour in the keys environment, on the beach and in the red mangrove swamps. The highpoint was a quiet canoe glide among the gnarled exposed roots of the mangroves, playing hide and seek with some moorhens and a small alligator. It was so still; the dominant man-made sound was the lovely slap of their paddles on the clear water. If one strained one could hear the highway noises not very far away. But who wanted to strain?

The ranger invited her to continue their little trip, but Jean thought she'd better be leaving. They pulled the canoe ashore and walked to the parking area. As she got into the open car, he leaned over the driver-side door and said, a little uncomfortably, "By the way, I guess I should have asked you for some sort of credentials before I opened up the log book for you."

"Unfortunately, I haven't any to offer you," Jean admitted. "I suggest you call Rusty Torrance, that is William Torrance, to verify that I'm legitimate." She wrote the number on a piece of scrap paper, adding, "Although I'm not a professional, I helped a little on another criminal case—not that this is necessarily a criminal investigation. All we really know is that someone disappeared. Anyway, Rusty found my experience helpful for doing some informal gofer tasks. This way he wouldn't lose the services of a deputy for a full day to come down here, for instance, since I wanted to come to see the Keys anyway."

She hesitated before going on. "I guess what I'm doing is a bit confidential. For now it would be best not to mention this visit to Bill Long or Don Purvis or Doris Groot if they should happen by. I'll let you know when this changes. By the way do you know a Bob or Sandy Sanderson or a Consuela Martinez or Con Smith?"

"The names ring a vague bell, but I don't think I know them. Should I?"

"No, just wondered. They were other friends of Max Wein who are interested in ending the mystery. It's probably just as well that they don't know I've been here either." Even on such short acquaintance, Jean felt she could trust him. Perhaps that's what a canoe trip in the mangroves will do to build a quick friendship.

He agreed to keep their visit confidential and reached across the door to shake hands, saying, "Well, I'm glad Torrance sent you, Jean. I've really enjoyed it and hope I've been a little help, although I don't see how."

"You have been, Clyde. Thanks for showing me your set up here, and tell Millie I enjoyed meeting her too. I'll be in touch if we make progress."

Jean had wanted to swing down to Pine Key to see if she could observe some of the 300 or so little Key deer that remain on the planet. But she was worried about Annie and wanted to digest what, if anything, she'd learned at White Heron Key on her return trip. So she began to head back homeward on Route 1.

As she pushed forward onto mainland Florida, large raindrops began to pelt her windshield. It wasn't much of a rainstorm, but the lightning flashes in the northern sky before her were dazzling. They branched erratically in crazy paths and bright bursts. Then they repeated in more wild and brilliant patterns.

The accompanying rolls of thunder seemed foreboding. The electrical storms of her Midwest summers seemed tame by contrast.

Her escort picked her up again a good 20 miles from Wilson's camp. The car followed her through the gate all the way to her trailer. As she stepped inside, her phone was ringing. It was Orville, who would have seen her car pass the trailer-office. He was unusually terse and serious. "Sheriff Torrance wants you to call immediately. Got his home number?"

Jean did, and Rusty answered her call. Voice was solemn. In his job, he frequently was the conveyor of bad news. He had developed the technique of coming directly to the point. "Jean, Annie Crews' body was found today in a canal." He heard Jean gasp and waited a moment for her to regain her composure. "She was bludgeoned. From the state of her body, the coroner said it probably happened four or five days ago. That would jibe with the day you found the wires were cut. Poor Annie probably saw something."

Then Rusty's tone changed. "God damned reports! God damned meetings!" he snarled.

Jean had never known this side of Rusty and was taken aback by his outburst and let him seethe. Finally he explained himself.

"I'm sorry Jean. It's just that if it hadn't been for all the paperwork this job requires, and the meetings, I wouldn't have had to leave so soon that morning at your trailer. I <u>knew</u> those were traces of footprints on the old abandoned road. And then they disappeared for a little distance. That would have been when whoever it was went up to Annie's trailer and came back a little farther down the road. I <u>knew</u> that when they resumed again, they were a little stronger. The extra weight of Annie's body would have accounted for that. But no, I didn't stay to pursue it. I had my meetings and my reports to make. God!"

"But, Rusty, she was dead," said Jean summoning her most comforting voice.

"I know. But the trail would have been just three or four hours old instead of several days. That makes a huge difference."

After answering a couple more questions by Jean, the suddenly calm Rusty said, "I've posted an all-night guard there, and I'll be by at 8:00 tomorrow morning. Be careful, Jean, promise me you'll be careful."

Jean promised.

23

Rusty didn't come by the trailer at 8:00 the next morning; in his anxiety, it was more like 7:15. Jean was fully dressed in suntan pants and a brown short-sleeved blouse when she answered the door. They said nothing; she just trained her gray eyes into his, shook her head very slightly and slowly, and shamelessly lifted a handkerchief to watering eyes.

He finally spoke: "Rotten business." He put his arms around her. She responded.

"Awful. Wonderful lady. Does her family know?"

"That's all being taken care of by professionals, Jean."

"Good. Any clues?"

"I'm afraid not." He was going to try to spare her the graphic details of Annie's death.

Rusty accepted her offer of a seat in the small living room area and was embarrassed when she remained standing, gazing out the window in the direction of Annie's trailer. She openly sobbed. "I feel so responsible," she managed to say. "If I had just minded my own business, that dear old lady would be alive."

To Rusty, it was so unlike the doughty little woman to be crying that he was moved to get up out of his chair and stand beside her. He placed his hand on her shoulder. Again she responded. "<u>You</u> feel responsible," he said, "Think how I feel, supposedly a professional, leaving the scene the other morning to go to a damn meeting. No, don't blame yourself, Jean. If you hadn't gotten interested in the case, a murderer probably would go to his grave with the secret."

"He still might. We're not getting anywhere." Jean was still disconsolate.

Rusty waited a moment. Jean was gaining control. "Are you frightened, Jean?" he asked.

"No, not frightened. Mad. I just want to get on with it. I don't want to work on my project for the Pearson Trust. I don't want to go out in the field. I just want to help figure this awful business out." She wiped away one last tear rolling down her cheek and offered Rusty some coffee and a toasted English, which he accepted.

Jean was now composed. Rusty felt comfortable about going ahead. "What can you tell me about your friend Annie that might be helpful?"

She had been thinking about that herself, so she was ready with an answer. "Well, for one thing, she sometimes arises...arose...very early in the morning. She could have been up or awakened when the alarm cry and my light scared whoever it was out there. You seem pretty convinced that he used the abandoned road by her trailer, aren't you?" Rusty nodded, and Jean continued. "If she saw him, she probably could have identified him."

"Why's that?" Rusty was skeptical. "Do you really think she could have gotten that good a description of a stranger hurrying along on a dark morning before the sun is up?"

"Not of a stranger, no. But the person probably wasn't a stranger. Which brings me to another point I've thought about. This terrible event could help eliminate Doris as a suspect."

Rusty looked up suddenly, surprised, and asked why.

"Because Annie had met all the others at the little barbecue I had here. Doris didn't come. So if Annie saw someone hurrying down that abandoned road at 5:00 in the morning and perhaps turned on a spotlight, she might have known who he or she was by name."

"Interesting!" exclaimed Rusty, then added thoughtfully, "But not Doris." After dwelling on that briefly, he changed the subject.

"A couple of people are going over her grounds carefully for clues right now—we can't hide that. But we don't need to let on that we've tied Annie's death to an attempt on your life or to Wein's disappearance. The only one of our suspects who knows about your early morning visitor is the person himself, or herself. The bastard doesn't know that _we_ know he was there and that he probably killed Annie. I'd like to keep it that way for now. I don't even want to ask the birders for alibis for that morning. We can't show the killer our hand."

They walked outside on an already steamy morning. The oaks and cypresses seemed to be drooping under the weight of the Spanish moss. Waving some bothersome gnats away, Rusty asked Jean about her day yesterday, and she recounted what she'd learned from Owens. He was interested in the discovery that Long, Purvis, and Doris Groot all were in touch with Owens shortly after Max disappeared, but then commented, "Frankly, Jean, I still can't see what Wein's proposed trip to Great White Heron Key has to do with the price of eggs. But if there is a

connection—and this is your department, not mine—
we can't entirely eliminate Doris as a suspect."

"I suppose not," Jean agreed but looked sour.

As they went back into the trailer to escape the
mosquitoes, she shifted to the second item on her
mental agenda—a talk with Bobo. She reminded Rusty
that she thought Bobo might know more than he let on
that night she was with him. She suggested that a one-
on-one talk with the young man might be productive.

Rusty was skeptical. "You know he's still a
suspect, Jean," he reminded her.

"Officially, yes. But not with me, he isn't." This
was said with a smile, the first she'd permitted herself
since she'd heard about Annie. "However, I get your
point."

"How do you think you are you going to find
him?"

She told Rusty her plan for doing this, which she
put into action over his mild objection immediately
after he left.

She went to the library and perused phone books
for several nearby areas looking for the name and
number of Bobo's grandfather, Harding. On the third
try she found it. She returned home, rang the number,
and Harding answered. His voice brightened when she
identified herself. He asked what he could do for her.

"Harding, I've thought a lot about Granny's
request that I help clear Bobo's name. It would help if
I could talk with him. Can you tell me how to reach
him?"

Harding was eager to oblige. "He don't have a
phone. He's living with a girl named Carol, Carol
Musgrave." Jean's steel-trap mind recalled that was the

name of one of the girls Bobo was with the night before Max disappeared. "The family don't approve of the arrangement—Carol is white." Harding went on, "And I don't think you'd have any luck if you show up where they're living. Best bet, I think, would be to catch him at work as he leaves the bakery."

"The bakery?" asked Jean.

"Yes, he's been driving a bakery truck for about a year. Doing real well. Gotten a better route. Of course, he blew most of what he's made on an old Camaro, but really he's settled down—more to white man's ways than ours, I'm afraid."

Jean liked hearing about the car. It would help convince Rusty that he hadn't taken Max's money to buy it. Harding then told her where the bakery was and that Bobo got off work at 5:30 unless his route delayed him. He wasn't very hopeful that he'd open up for Jean, nor was she. But both felt it was important to try.

That afternoon she found the bakery and at 5:15 parked across the street where she could see the rear of the garage. A route truck drove into the garage. She didn't think the driver was Bobo. After a few minutes, a man she presumed was the driver emerged from a small door alongside the wide garage door and headed for an adjacent parking lot. Jean speculated that he had probably changed out of his uniform and signed out, perhaps a fifteen-minute task. She was right; it wasn't Bobo, but it suggested to Jean a pattern for his probable behavior when he got back. She plotted how she could intercept him.

She glimpsed the driver of the next returning truck and thought he could be Bobo. She drove onto the parking lot and parked near an older Camaro convertible, probably Bobo's. Sure enough, in several minutes a skinny young man in a cowboy hat emerged from the door next to the garage door and headed to the lot. She got out of her car, and as he neared her, she saw that he had changed into jeans and a Grateful Dead tee shirt. His black hair was long but halfway presentable. Maybe Carol was having an influence on him, Jean thought. As he came closer, she observed a silver cross bobbing on a necklace and a single earring, which she recalled from their previous meeting. He would come right by her if she guessed right about his car.

He did. When he got within 10 feet, she said, "Hello Bobo." He looked up to see a small female in dark clothes. He didn't answer. He looked puzzled, but didn't slow his pace.

Jean was not daunted. "You remember me, Bobo. Jean McKay. You and your grandfather kidnapped me and took me to Granny's chickee the other night."

She chose the word kidnapped for its shock effect. It worked; he scowled and stopped. "Hey, we didn't kidnap you. We don't do that stuff." He wasn't a particularly prepossessing young fellow, but Jean realized that maybe he'd be more attractive if he were not scowling at her.

"Of course, you don't kidnap people." Jean's wide mouth widened further, flashing her most winning smile. "I just said that to be sure you'd remember me. I have something very important to talk to you about, Bobo. About clearing your name."

"I told you I had nothing to do with that other thing. I'm late. I gotta go." But his instincts kept him from leaving Jean abruptly.

Jean sensed that he might be curious and willing to talk a little despite his objections. "Bobo, when we were in Harding's truck the other night, I asked you who you thought was responsible for the bird watcher's disappearance. I sensed that you started to say something, but then you apparently had second thoughts and said you didn't know anything other than that you didn't do it.

"What was it you started to say?"

"Nothin' Well, it was something but it didn't mean anything, and I didn't want to talk about it in front of grandfather. Maybe we could talk about it after Granny dies. That'll be in a few days."

"Oh, I'm sorry to hear that," Jean said genuinely. "But that's the point. Let her die with your name cleared. I know you didn't do anything, but I need to convince others. We may be getting close to the truth, and your cooperation would help a great deal."

Jean paused to let that sink in. Keen observer that she was, she saw that the surly young man was on the verge of relenting.

"What was it that you started to say?" she repeated.

Still no response. The young man was looking at the pavement, at his feet perhaps. Jean went on, playing her trump card as she had rehearsed the scene to herself. "No, you and your grandfather didn't kidnap me, but you <u>did</u> blindfold me and take me on a rough ride on a dark night without telling me where you were going. I put up with all that. It seems to me you owe me something in return."

"It's...it's that it's hard to talk about."

"Can I buy you a cup of coffee...or a beer?" Jean suggested. Bobo looked at her doubtfully as if wondering if she'd know very much about how to go about buying a young man a beer.

But he'd become quite civil and simply said, "No thank you, Ma'am." It was the first time she'd seen him that way. "I really do have to get home. But maybe we could sit in my car for a little while." He motioned toward his convertible and even held the door open for her and then went around to the other side and slid under the wheel. Bobo kept his top up because of the threat of afternoon rain. That afforded them considerable privacy, which the young man seemed to be seeking.

From her students, she knew what cars mean to young men, and she complimented him on the Camaro.

After thanking her and making a technical comment about its engine, he turned his dark head directly toward her. "Are you Indian?" he asked.

Jean's impulse was to laugh, but she was able to control it and only looked at him and smiled. "No, Bobo."

"Not even a grandfather or great grandfather?" he persisted, unaware that he was amusing and intriguing Jean. "Or great uncle?"

"I'm afraid not. Why do you ask?"

"Well, because if you was Indian I know I could trust you to take an oath and keep what I tell you secret."

Jean thought that Harding would be pleased to know Bobo hadn't entirely forsaken Indian ways. She was no longer smiling when she said, "You can trust me, Bobo." She looked at his black eyes to emphasize her sincerity.

"Well, it's important to me because I've changed. I've grown up. I never was as bad as that jerk Beggs said I was, but I did get into a little trouble sometimes. Now I've held a good job a year. I have a perfect safety record on my route, and I've got me a fine woman. I don't want to lose them things."

"You won't on my account, Bobo."

Bobo paused several seconds. "OK, I want to get rid of this. I guess I trust you. So this is for Granny. I haven't told what I'm about to say to my mom, my grandfather, to Granny, or to my girl." He paused as if to stop. Jean nodded to him to continue, and he did.

"What happened is that when Beggs was trying to pin the thing on me I got a package with $5,000 in it." Jean sucked in her breath and expelled a low whistle. Bobo continued. "Yeah, five thousand bucks. It was in two bunches, one for $500 and the rest in the other. All in hundred dollar bills. But that ain't all. There was a letter that said that there would be $15,000 more for me if I'd admit that I found the bigger pack, the $4,500, and turn it in. I didn't have to admit to anything about the man's disappearance, just that I found the money."

Jean was eager. "Do you still have the letter?"

"No, I got rid of it. Right away."

"Oh, Bobo," Jean agonized in disappointment. "Why?"

"Well, I was scared. The guy who wrote the letter said to destroy it and made some sort of dumb threat if I didn't. So I did. I knew Beggs hated me and I was afraid it might look even worse for me if I had the letter. He'd say I faked it. I think it was on plain paper, typewritten. Nobody signed it."

"Could you tell where it was mailed from?"

"No. I remember that I tried to read that on the envelope, but couldn't."

"What about the money?"

"That's why this is a secret. I kept it."

"Spent it?"

"Only the $500. I hid the $4,500. The papers said the bird guy had that much on him, so I figured Beggs was trying to frame me. It was probably marked or they knew the serial numbers. No way was I going to spend them bills no matter how tempting it was."

"So you think..." Jean hesitated hoping Bobo would fill the gap.

He did. "...that Beggs sent the money. I don't think it, I know it."

"How?"

"Because I know Beggs."

"But would he have $20,000 cash lying around to spare?"

"Well, he only gave me $5,000, and he'd probably crap out on the rest if I'd cooperated. But even if he did come through, $20,000 wouldn't be anything to him. He had all kinds of dough. Dope money."

"Dope money?"

"Yeah, the narcotics dealers—coke, heroin, crack, all of the stuff—paid him off. I can't prove it, but it was common knowledge. I took a little coke in them days, and the guy I got mine from told me." He paused and looked at Jean's innocent, troubled face. "Don't forget your oath, Ma'am. I'm clean now and I plan to be the rest of my life."

Jean assured him his secrets are safe.

237

Bobo's vitriol toward his tormentor was running over. "Besides look where he's been the last couple of years. Living like a millionaire on a boat with that damn old girl friend down in the Islands. That takes dough. That LaWanda don't come cheap."

"LaWanda?"

"LaWanda was his honey. She was a waitress at one of the places where we was the night before the little man disappeared, and she just plain lied about how much we had to drink. You know, the old guff about Indians and firewater. She was in on the thing." Jean remembered that the files had identified the night waitress at the Big Cypress Cafe as LaWanda Carter. When she was questioned, she had stated that Bobo and his friends were drinking heavily.

Jean was fascinated by the young man's story. Once he had decided to release his secret, it had all gushed out. Yet she felt obligated to try to sort cold facts from the boy's animus. So she went on, "But I understood he sold his house. Couldn't that have financed his life in the Caribbean for a couple of years?"

"Well, yes," Bobo admitted, "for a few years maybe. But he'd better have enough to stay down there the rest of his life. If he comes back here, if Torrance has any guts he'd arrest him as soon as he sets foot in Florida. But we won't see Beggs again. He's a rich man without selling that house. Remember he offered me the twenty grand before he sold his house."

Bobo settled back a little. "Ma'am, I really do have to go."

"Sure, Bobo," Jean was sympathetic, but of course privately didn't share his leap to the conclusion that

Beggs had sent him the money. She hadn't interrupted him, however, because she was learning a lot about Beggs and she was sure the unbottling of his secret was helpful to the young man. She did beg to ask "one more question" and without waiting for Bobo's assent, wondered, "With Beggs out of the picture all this time, why haven't you come forth with the money before this?"

"Because Beggs wasn't the only one who said it was me. All them people who had breakfast with the little bird guy that last morning also thought so. And that includes that ranger, Purvis."

"Aha, 'Marie the Mole' at work again," thought Jean, then aloud:

"I really appreciate all this, Bobo. But please do me one more favor." Bobo didn't say he would, but merely looked doubtful. Jean went on. "Could you get me the serial numbers of those bills? There's a record of the ones that were stolen. If they match, it would help clinch the fact that whoever sent you the money was trying to frame you."

"If I have it, they'll think I swiped it."

"I don't think so, Bobo, not after two years and not after you voluntarily surrender the bills. I can assure you Sheriff Torrance is a very fair man. It is clear that you were being framed."

"It was Beggs. My girl Carol goes to class tonight. I'll go to where the dough is hidden and jot down the numbers. Want to meet here tomorrow?"

Jean could have kissed him. But more than ever she would like to know more about Beggs' last days in office. She'd move that item up to the top of her priority list. She'd begin to look into it quietly, beginning in the morning.

~~ 24 ~~

Much as Jean admired Rusty as a competent and compassionate law enforcement officer, she wished he were a little more zealous about including Ed Beggs in their inquiry. Long before she heard Bobo's unsubstantiated accusation that the sheriff was in the business of taking payoffs from drug dealers and had tried to frame him, Jean was convinced that Beggs was a bad man. She saw him as a self-promotional and unscrupulous mini-potentate who wouldn't give a Hispanic or Native American a fair shake. And now she was nearly convinced he knew something about Max Wein's disappearance. He even could have killed him for reasons that she hadn't figured out yet. When he had realized he couldn't pin anything on Bobo Jumper, he cleared out fast.

Rusty had said without enthusiasm that he was interested to find out where Beggs was now, but never proactively sought to connect him with the events of the disappearance. Jean thought she understood the psychology of Rusty's reluctance: He was unduly conscious of being Beggs' successor, and he didn't want to convey the image of someone who comes in and stabs his predecessor in the back. "Rusty is wrong about that," Jean thought. "But if he won't try to find out more about the circumstances of Beggs' departure, then I will."

She resolved to do just that immediately after she and Bobo had their talk. However, the next morning, before she had a chance to initiate the steps she had in mind, she received two phone calls. The first was from

Rusty, suggesting that they meet for coffee in an hour to catch up. She wished to meet also, but would have preferred to do so after she had the serial numbers of the bills Bobo had sequestered. Still, she couldn't put off Rusty.

Then, just as she was leaving the trailer, the phone rang again. Both the caller and the content of the call were surprises.

The caller was Don Purvis. His tone was the friendliest it had been since he first introduced her to the Sunday morning group.

"I've been thinking a lot about our last breakfast, Jean," Don began, "And I'm a little embarrassed about how we ganged up on you. I overheard a couple of the others say they hoped you'd reconsider, and now that I've thought things through I really do hope you come back next Sunday."

Jean, caught off guard, stumbled a bit in her reply. "Well, that's nice of you, Don, and there's no reason to apologize, but, well, I don't know…"

"I mean it, Jean. I have woken up to the fact that you're right; we should get behind any effort by anyone to find out what happened to Max. Then I read in the paper this morning about your neighbor, the lady we met at your picnic. I don't imagine there's any connection, but what are we trying to shield?

"Anyway, whether or not you choose to pursue whatever it is you are doing about Max, you are welcome back with us. We've learned a lot from you, and I for one want to see more of you before you go back up to Oak City. When will that be, by the way?"

Jean told him of her plan to go in two or three weeks and thanked him again. She said she will "seriously consider" coming Sunday (this was Friday) and would call Doris or him if she decided to be there.

"Well, we all want you," Don said.

"All of you?"

Don was perceptive. "Well, we haven't gotten together and taken a vote," he said good naturedly, "but I expect you're worried about Sandy since he was the MC, so to speak. It happens that he's the one person in the group that I have not seen or talked to since then, but I'm sure he wants you to return, as I'll bet he has told you."

Jean thought, "You'd lose your bet," as Don continued. "It's probably no surprise to you that we did get together before the last breakfast, and frankly Bill, Doris, and I asked Sandy to lay out the case because we thought that you had a lot of respect for him and that he'd do it fairly."

They rang off. On one level Jean was pleased at Don's gesture of rapprochement. But on another level she was troubled as she drove to meet Rusty. Three questions nagged her. Did Don want her there so he could keep an eye on her…or worse? Second: Was this just a device to find out how much longer they were— he was—going to have to put up with her presence? If he knew that, he, or someone else, could plan a strategy that would keep her at bay for the short remaining time.

Most nagging of all: How did Don know her phone number? She wracked her brain, but she was sure she hadn't given the number to anyone other than the Wilsons and Rusty's office, nor had she told any of the Sunday morning group that she was getting a phone. She'd called none of the birders. They all knew she didn't have a phone when she had her barbecue. Again: How did Don know her number?

She tried a couple of answers on herself. Maybe he forgot she didn't have a phone and called Information. Or perhaps he called Wilson's office with the idea of leaving a message, and Orville told him her number. She decided the latter explanation was plausible, and yet... She would ask Orville if he'd gotten a call for her from Don Purvis.

Rusty had designated a different meeting place, an undistinguished breakfast-lunch cafe snuggled amidst various look-alike store fronts in a small strip mall. As she drove onto the parking lot, she spotted Rusty and Joe Bob waiting for her in an unmarked car. They intercepted her and the three entered the drab little cafe. It was the kind of place where the patrons, mostly local tradesmen and delivery people, all knew each other and the employees. They were engrossed in their own banter. Rusty steered the others to the rear of the establishment, three tables away from anyone else.

He wanted to bring Jean up to date on a couple of things. The acoustical engineer had finished his work, but the result was inconclusive. "I can't pick up anything that's helpful," he said.

"I've brought a copy of the enhanced tape along with your original. Play the new tape in the quiet of your trailer, Jean, and let me know if you can pick up even the slightest hint of something you hadn't heard before. Fingers crossed on this, because it can be a piece of evidence that we'd have a chance of making stick."

Rusty added that examination of the Snickers wrapper and Carlton butt had yielded nothing, and that

Francis Sheehan had called back to say that the likelihood that the little girl's kidnappers were after Jean was virtually nil. "I guess that'll have to be good enough for me," he added, unconvinced.

The chief deputy also had to concede that afternoon rains during the five days between Annie's murder and the discovery of the crime had wiped out exterior clues. A deputy did find a smudge of blood of her type on her front stoop, so the working hypothesis was that she was killed there, put into a car, and dumped in a canal some 13 miles away. That fit with Rusty's and Jean's belief that Annie might have identified her killer as he or she scurried away, frightened by the owl's alarm call and the light Jean turned on.

Jean had a couple of questions for them. The first concerned the post card sent from the West by "Max Wein." Rusty seemed glad to have something else to talk about. He spoke about their technique for running down the trips of the suspects. "You were right about Doris, Jean," he said admiringly. "She went to see her folks in Sun City and was out there at the time the card was sent, but of course Arizona isn't California."

"Close to it," said Jean. "But don't get me wrong. I'm not implying anything."

"Maybe you should. I think it's the best answer we have so far to that bizarre turn of events, but I haven't a clue what it would mean."

Jean reminded Rusty that Don had been called in for brief questioning a few weeks after the initial flurry of interest had died down. "Perhaps," Jean posited, "Doris sent the card to divert attention from Don. And she does know how to type, and Wein didn't use a typewriter. But this is sheer speculation."

"Well, it's another reason we should keep her on the list, but we still have a lot of work to do on that one. What was your other question?"

"Anything on where Beggs is?" she asked a little hesitantly, and not looking right at Rusty.

"Not yet," he answered curtly. J. B. shook his head.

The chief deputy had barely smiled when he greeted Jean on the parking lot and had been talking through clenched teeth ever since. "He's not like himself," Jean thought, "Something worse is coming." She was right. As he reached into his brief case and pulled out a sheaf of papers, he was even more grim. He looked around and lowered his voice. "Here's the stuff from the F.B.I., and it's not a nice picture. Consuela was involved with some pretty radical people in Miami. A real activist, hate-Castro group. Would stop at nothing. I don't like saying it, but there's violence in our friend's background."

Rusty cut off talk altogether when the waitress brought donuts and coffee. The men helped themselves as Jean scanned the FBI summary and shuffled through the attached documents. "I don't see anything yet that says Con actually used a gun or committed any direct violence," Jean said hopefully. "Nor do I," Rusty agreed. "But she sure as hell was there when guns were fired and people were beaten up. She knows what the inside of a jail looks like, and with justification, I'd say."

"But look at the end of the report." Jean read slowly, a word at a time. "'Subject has not engaged in suspicious behavior in the last six years and appears to be living a useful life as a teacher although unlicensed. During this period, however, she has lived with two different men, neither her married spouse.'"

"Oh, for goodness sake, that last is irrelevant," Jean snarled. "Shades of J. Edgar Hoover!"

That uncharacteristic outburst at last brought a smile to Rusty, and Joe Bob laughed outright. "Atta girl, Jeanie," he said.

Jean was quickly back to business. She asked, "Have you read the whole file?" Rusty nodded. "Do the names of Max Wein or Robert Sanderson appear in it anywhere?"

"No," and again he smiled and changed the subject. "You got anything for us?"

Jean said that she had tracked down Bobo and that he's doing well in his job and presumably bought his car with his earnings.

She explained that Bobo thinks Ed Beggs was connected to the disappearance and added that she will see him again this afternoon. She said nothing about the money; she wanted to wait until she had the serial numbers in hand. Rusty was skeptical about going any farther with Bobo. Joe Bob was more direct. "You wouldn't expect Bobo to do anything other than try to implicate Beggsy. It's human nature. I don't blame him, I guess, but I don't think it'll get us anywhere." Jean kept quiet but thought she knew better and hoped to be able to prove it in a few hours.

Rusty asked if there were anything else, and she reported Don's surprising phone call beseeching her return. "That's an interesting twist, coming from him," Rusty commented, "and it could be dangerous."

"Yes," admitted Jean. "and there's something else a little funny: I don't know how he knew my number." She explained that as far as Don and the others knew she didn't have a phone, and she hadn't told any of them that she was getting one. She admitted that a lucky stab at Information or a call to Wilson's could have produced the number.

Joe Bob looked as if his mind were a thousand miles away. Suddenly, he returned to earth. "I can guess how he might have gotten your number. I haven't mentioned this before, but I know Don Purvis, and…"

"You know him?" interrupted the surprised Rusty. "I think you should have told me."

"You're right, chief. Well, I don't exactly know him, but I knew who he was. So did the rest of the old-timers at the post."

"What are you getting at?"

"I thought you knew that he used to hang around there a lot. Here it is, Rusty, straight: He was sweet on Paula and often picked her up after work."

Jean and Rusty looked at each other with expressions of disbelief.

Rusty, clearly perturbed, said, "Go on."

"Well, it just now came to me that if the affair is still on—and I don't know that it is—she could be feeding Don everything that's going on in the office, such as Jean's new phone number."

Rusty was even more stunned than Jean. She at least had had the experience of stumbling on Don and Doris and had pegged him as an unfaithful husband. Nor had she made any kinds of moral judgments about Paula the way Rusty probably had.

So it was Rusty who broke the silence. "Are you sure, J.B?" The question was painful, almost like the fabled youngster's "Say it ain't so, Joe" when he heard his idol Shoeless Joe Jackson had taken bribes to throw the World Series.

"Am I sure? Well, I'm not at all sure that Paula's been feeding Don information about the investigation if that's what you mean. That's just guesswork on my part about how he got Jean's phone number. But I am absolutely sure that they were sweet on each other once."

Joe Bob pondered a moment, then drawled, "Wait a sec. Now I realize why you didn't know about them. Don stopped comin' around at about the time you came aboard. The office scuttlebutt was that Paula and Don thought it best to cool it with a new boss around. They knew you were a married man, went to church, and probably it would be better for Paula not to start out flaunting the fact that she had a married lover hanging around. That was the speculation, and it made sense."

"That's ironic," Jean observed. "Don also is a family man and goes to church."

"Well," said Rusty, trying to sound resigned. "We're making a lot of fuss about a telephone number. After all, Jean has given a couple of logical ways Don might have gotten it—from Orville Wilson, for instance."

Joe Bob and Jean agreed, but privately Jean attached considerable credence to Joe Bob's theory. She could recall several instances where one or more of the birders had information that surprised her, notably their sudden knowledge of her involvement in solving the Pearson kidnapping case.

Then she remembered Rusty's comment when she figured out that Marie the waitress was advising Bobo's family about the breakfast group's activities. He had said, "So the Indians had a mole."

That had been amusing then. That Max Wein's birding companions had a mole in the sheriff's office wasn't the least bit amusing.

~~ 25 ~~

Joe Bob got up to leave the little cafe, but Jean placed a restraining hand on his arm. "Please, can you stay just a minute or two longer?" Although she was nervous about her crowded agenda for the rest of the day, she wanted to talk about something she thought might be pivotal to solving the mysteries.

Joe Bob sat back down. Jean looked at Rusty and said, "I'm going to respond to Don's invitation to rejoin the group for breakfast Sunday."

"Oh, Jean, I wish you wouldn't," Rusty pleaded.

But she was determined. "We've got a bunch of ideas and some circumstantial evidence. But I can't think of any other way to flush the person out that would <u>prove</u> guilt. So I intend to exercise my freedom of choice and go to a breakfast where I've been invited. That's a given. Now let's talk about how you are going to protect me if I need it."

Rusty shrugged his broad shoulders. Then he mused for a moment on how Jean's attitude had changed since Annie was murdered. Not long ago she had recoiled at the use of the word "murder" in connection with the Max Wein disappearance. Even the admission that there might have been some sort of foul play involving one or more of the five bird-watching friends had been slow in coming. Her interest had seemed more in proving Bobo's innocence than it was in implicating one of the birders. But now she was aggressively taking risks to find Annie's killer. Now she accepted the strong probability that one or more of her friends were involved.

Of course, both Jean and Rusty realized that the person or persons responsible for the disappearance weren't necessarily part of the group, and it was at this point their ideas parted company. Rusty and Joe Bob were reluctant to eliminate Bobo as a suspect; Jean already had. On the other hand, Jean clung to the idea that Ed Beggs could have been involved somehow; the other two, while not rejecting the notion outright, had little enthusiasm for doing the work necessary to find the link, if there was one. So Jean decided to start doing that on her own—today.

Rusty was concerned about privacy in the cafe. At his suggestion they went out to his unmarked patrol car to continue the discussion. There Joe Bob proposed that they hire Fred Billie, the former colleague who was a tracking specialist, as a consultant and deputize him. He knew of no one else who could cover Jean more skillfully while concealing himself from the other hikers. Rusty agreed and asked Joe Bob to handle that. Then the two men planned to have lunch at the Big Cypress Cafe tomorrow, Saturday, so they could acquaint themselves with the lay of the land first hand.

Jean described the hiking route she planned to take. Rusty would bring home detailed maps from his office, and Jean would go to his house to trace on them more specifically her planned route. Finally, they devised some signals to keep in touch Sunday. As they drove off in their separate cars, Jean felt quite secure about Sunday. Rusty didn't.

It was now about 10:15. Jean needed to be precise in her timing to accomplish her plans for the rest of her tightly scheduled day. She would go to Annie's services at 2:00 and meet Bobo at 5:30. Those two destinations would take a lot of driving time. She hadn't had time to do her usual practice-driving the routes to unfamiliar places.

She also had one more "must" for the day: to set in motion an inquiry about Beggs immediately. It too would entail driving unaccustomed routes. Her destination was the courthouse for some research. This Friday morning would be the only opportunity for her to go there before Sunday's breakfast; it would be impossible to work it in that afternoon between Annie's funeral and her meeting with Bobo, and the court house would be closed on Saturday.

On her way, she couldn't get into the rhythm of the stoplights. It took ten minutes longer to reach the courthouse and park her car than she had allotted. Once inside, she asked directions to the recorder's office. There she asked to see the recorded deeds for real estate transactions of the previous two years. Unfortunately, the clerk, a heavy, bored woman of about 60, probably held the job as a political plum and could care less about Jean. She went to the vault painfully slowly, made a couple of mistakes as she spun the combination lock on the vault, and then brought out the wrong book. She received Jean's request for the correct book without apology or smile, but finally fetched it. Jean wondered if the perverse creature had deduced that she was in a hurry and was deliberately taking her own sweet time.

The woman watched over Jean as she flipped through the pages, finally getting to the months she wanted. It took her a while to get the hang of the format of the pages—no help from the clerk—but once she did, she scanned them quickly.

Ah, here it is. Edgar and Valerie Beggs to Daniel and Wilma Blakely. The specific location of the house, selling price, and lot dimensions were listed. She jotted down the information, thanked the unhelpful clerk, and asked for a telephone book. "We don't have one," the crone said although Jean could see one on the desk right behind the woman. "Go to the public booth down the hall on your right."

There actually was a book in fairly good shape hanging on a chain. She had a general idea of the location of Beggs' former house, so she turned to the section of the book that covered that area. No Daniel, Dan, or D Blakely at all. No Wilma. No W. She looked under Beggs, thinking that the book might be outdated. No Beggs. She tried listings for adjoining sections of the county. No Daniel, Dan, D, Wilma, or W Blakely; no Beggs. She called Information. No number.

She was losing time. She could drive to the house and talk directly to the occupants if they were home. She also knew that the sheriff's office had a criss-cross directory from which she could get the occupant by starting with the address. She elected to call Rusty. She got Paula, who greeted her warmly but said Rusty was in court testifying in a case involving a series of burglaries. (Jean was chagrined to be reminded that a busy chief deputy sheriff could not spend all of his time on the case she was interested in.)

"Something I can do for you, Jean?" asked Paula sincerely. "You sound concerned."

It was time to fish or cut bait with Paula, "mole" or not. The time she could save by phoning rather than driving to the house was crucial. Yet she imagined how the wires might sizzle when Paula told Don of her mysterious call from Jean—if she did tell him. And if Don was "the one," what might he do with the information?

"Jean? You still there?" Paula was solicitous.

"I'm sorry, Paula. Yes, I think you can help me." Jean had decided to take the risk and enlist Paula's aid. Without explaining why she wanted the information, she told Paula what she wanted, and Paula obliged.

"According to the directory, the occupant of that house is Terry Davis. I don't know whether that's a guy Terry or a gal Terry."

She was disappointed that the Blakelys no longer lived there, but said, "Thanks a million, Paula." She rather awkwardly started to apologize about being "a little mysterious," but decided it was better to leave well enough alone. "I owe you one. Thanks again."

"Any time," said Paula sounding as though she meant it. If she noticed Jean's clumsy fumble, she didn't let on. Her desire to help seemed genuine. Still there were all those times when Jean wondered where the birders get their information about what she and Rusty were doing. Joe Bob's hypothesis could be correct.

Jean raced through the phone book wishing that Davis wasn't such a common name and hoping they didn't have an unlisted number. She found a T. Davis at the address and noted the number. She called it. No answer. No answering machine. She decided to race back to the trailer to grab a bite to eat and make herself more presentable for the funeral.

She was scarcely inside when she was startled by a knock on her door. She opened it to find a young man at least 6' 3" tall dressed in south Florida garb—a salmon tee shirt and light green shorts.

"Sorry to bother you, Ma'am," he said politely. "I'm Deputy Murphy, and I've been assigned to be your honor guard, so to speak, today. I've got to tell you that you led me at a pretty fast pace from the courthouse. If I hadn't known it was you, I'd have pulled you over for sure. Better cool it a little."

Jean could feel the red reaching the tips of her ears in embarrassment. She thanked him and promised him to watch her speed. "But there's so much I have to do today," she thought.

With the warning about speeding from the deputy, Jean decided that something would have to give if she were to get to Annie's funeral on time. That something would be lunch. She showered quickly and got into her nicest summer dress. She did what she could with her hair, and it came out pretty well. She looked at herself in the mirror, as always disapprovingly. But others who knew her and were fond of her would have approved. Jean could make herself more attractive than she thinks she can—especially to people who admire her. After one more futile attempt to get Terry Davis to answer, she drove off to Annie's church.

The funeral was gut wrenching. She studied the mourners, dressed in their best black suits and dresses. To her they were beautiful; she wished she had the talent of an Edward Steichen to photograph their marvelous, grieving, respectful faces. A half dozen white people stood out in the group of about 30. One was Dot Wilson; Jean determined she would have to avoid the chatty woman afterwards even if meant being rude. She surmised that a couple of the younger white men were from the sheriff's office. The Baptist minister was not brief, but he was compelling. The church choir sang a couple of moving spirituals. Sweat and tears mingled on the cheeks of the mourners in the sweltering early afternoon.

Jean finally got away and, after a brief stop at home and another futile attempt to reach Terry Davis, arrived at Bobo's bakery about 5:20. She waited for him. 5:30. 5:45. 6:00. She remembered that Harding said he was sometimes delayed along the route. But might he sometimes arrive early—before the 5:20 that she got there? A little after 6:00 she decided to make an inquiry. She went to the little door that the drivers used alongside the large garage door. Locked. The office was closed.

Discouraged, she went back to her car just as a truck barreled into the bakery driveway, tires squealing. It was Bobo. He entered the little door with a key, and from the inside opened the truck door and drove in.

Jean moved to the door to meet him when he came out. When he did, he spotted her right away and greeted her. "I'm so damn late that I only have a minute, but come to the car. I didn't forget." He was smiling, no longer the surly young man she had met the night they took her to Granny's chickee. When they reached the car, he unlocked the passenger door. Jean moved to get in, but he said, "No, no time to talk. Hang on a minute. I've got a surprise for you." He unlocked the glove compartment with a separate key and took out a small metal box, which he unlocked with a third key. He was still smiling and with a trace of mischief in his eyes, said, "You can write down the serial numbers yourself. Here's the dough." With that he took out a stack of $100 bills.

Jean was flabbergasted and hesitated to accept them. "Take `em or leave `em, Ma'am. I don't want `em no more. They're all there except for the $500 I spent."

"Oh my goodness, Bobo. This'll help your great grandmother die in peace."

"I hope so," said Bobo. "And I'm trusting you. You could easy say I swiped them off the little man's body. But I didn't; I'll swear to that."

"You won't have to, Bobo," Jean assured him.

When Jean finally got back to her trailer, she was famished. She'd had nothing to eat since her light breakfast more than 12 hours earlier. But she wasn't so starved that she didn't have time first to open a package that had arrived in the mail. It contained the issues of the <u>Journal of Ornithology</u> she'd written for. The publishers had sent all the issues for the year in which Max had disappeared and those for the preceding year.

While she wolfed down some barely warmed leftovers, she scanned pertinent copies of the <u>Journal</u>, especially the January/February and March/April issues of 1991, the year in which Max disappeared, which would have been current at the time, and the July/August 1990 issue, thinking that perhaps the careless person who had typed the inventory had inadvertently put down the wrong year. She found nothing beyond the usual well written, well researched subjects. She couldn't make a connection, a reason why Max would have secreted one of these issues. She looked ahead to the May/June 1991 issue, on the chance that it might already have been mailed when Max vanished. Again, on quick reading, she couldn't see why on earth he would have locked that issue away.

She didn't allow herself to become too absorbed in the journals before she called Rusty to determine when he wanted to see her in the morning. He suggested they meet at his house at 8:30. "I have the area maps," he assured Jean. "So if you brief me in the morning, I can fill Joe Bob in on the scene when we have lunch at the cafe."

"Will Fred Billie be with you too?" Jean asked.

"Not for lunch, but he's on board. Looks forward to it, he says. We didn't want him at the cafe with us because, as you know, his cousin, Marie, is a waitress there. I remember she was the 'mole,' who fed information back to Bobo's family. I didn't want to risk any other kind of leak."

Jean agreed that was sensible and assured him she would be there at 8:30. As she said good-bye she added, "I'll have a surprise for you," using the same words that Bobo had with her. She hadn't told him about the money and enjoyed her little tease.

After her meal, she unsuccessfully tried the elusive Terry Davis again, then eagerly tackled two tasks. First she washed out her ears with alcohol on a Q-tip and listened to the enhanced tape. She listened. And listened again. The sounds were clearer, but no more definitive. Sometimes she thought that the person whose grunt and whoosh of air she heard was probably a man. Another time she could picture Con and hated it, maybe even Doris. Although Jean had all but eliminated Doris as a suspect in Annie Crews' death

259

because she and Annie never met, she remembered that she had shown her friend the recording setup when Doris called. She'd know where to snip.

After 45 minutes with the tape, she gave up and settled down and tackled the second task: a more careful reading of the issues of the <u>Journal</u> that she'd set aside. She raised her index of suspicion about as high as it could go, yet found nothing that remotely suggested why Max Wein might have saved and secured an issue. "I mean," she asked herself, "Why would he squirrel away a scholarly dissertation of the canyon towhee or a study of the feeding habits of avocets?" She turned out her light.

~~ **26** ~~

A solemn Rusty greeted Jean when she knocked on his door the next morning at precisely 8:28. While she was still on the little stoop, he stepped around her and looked up and down the street of neat starter homes. He spied the Crown Victoria he was looking for, smiled, and showed Jean inside. Making a hand gesture toward the street, he said, "Murph out there tells me he had to have a little talk with you about your heavy foot. Who do you think you are, some kind of a NASCAR driver?"

Jean took it good-naturedly, assured him that it wouldn't happen again, and was pleased that Rusty wasn't so grim that he couldn't tease her a little. Dawn, who was in her fifth month and beginning to show, brought them coffee and sticky buns, then vanished.

Rusty blew on his hot coffee. "Well, Jean," he began, "Before you spring whatever your little surprise is, let me tell you that this meeting has one objective as far as I'm concerned. And that is to talk you out of going tomorrow."

"Then I'm afraid your objective will not be met," Jean said earnestly, looking into her friend's broad, handsome face. To thwart his putting any more pressure on her, she told of her disappointment that further listening to the cassette yielded no clues. She added that she received the copies of the Journal of Ornithology but found no logical explanation for why Max locked up an issue in his station wagon's compartment for valuables. She was sorry to be so unhelpful.

Rusty frowned. "And that's your famous surprise?" he asked with unaccustomed sarcasm.

"No, hold on a second." Jean began to fish around in an unusually large cloth handbag, which the observant deputy had already noticed as an unusual addition to her usual ensemble. She took several seconds to get her right hand around the entire bundle of cash in the depths of the bag. Finally she produced the bills with a flourish and scattered them on top of the current <u>Newsweek</u> on the coffee table in front of them. "Voila!" she exclaimed, jiggling her coffee cup so that some sloshed into the saucer as she watched for Rusty's reaction.

She was not disappointed. "What the… What the hell is that?" he stammered.

"It's the money Max had on him. I'd bet my trailer that the serial numbers will match the ones on the bills the jeweler Robinson paid Max with. Same amount: 45 hundred dollar bills." Jean's voice was firm and confident, triumphant.

"Where on earth…" Rusty still was having a hard time grasping what he was seeing.

"From Bobo. Yesterday evening. He's had it hidden all this time."

Rusty looked displeased. He curled his lower lip over his lower teeth, and bit down on it with his bared upper teeth. "So Bobo probably is our man after all. He stole the money." Rusty said it with finality but was none too happy with his conclusion.

"No, Bobo didn't steal it," Jean said a little condescendingly. "I'm more positive than ever he is not the person we want." Then she reminded Rusty of her nagging feeling that Bobo had wanted to tell her something the night he and his grandfather took her to Granny's chickee. She guessed that, whatever it was, he didn't want to say it in front of Harding. She described how she had confronted Bobo Thursday evening at the bakery and, after considerable coaxing, he recounted his story of receiving the money through the mail with a letter promising $15,000 more.

Rusty listened to Jean's story attentively, started to interrupt two or three times but thought better of it. Then when he heard of the accompanying letter, he burst out, "That's great! That letter can tell us a great deal."

Jean smiled wanly. "Sadly, he doesn't have it. Whoever wrote it demanded that he destroy it. He was scared, so he got rid of it."

"Then his story isn't worth diddly-poo. Whether he stole the money or not, there was stolen property in his possession. With his record, it's going to look like he took it," said Rusty realistically.

"Nuts to his record," Jean contended, almost exasperated with the young man she so much admired. "He'll swear in court to the truth of his story. Besides, why wouldn't he spend a wad like that sometime over the two years? He spent the $500 that wasn't part of the loot without a qualm. He's the first to admit he was a troublemaker back then. Why would he risk handing over the $4,500 now when he's got his life nicely under control? Good job, a girl he wants to marry, clean from drugs. Why now?"

"Is a puzzlement," shrugged Rusty, quoting The King and I.

"Is _not_ a puzzlement," Jean insisted. This uncharacteristic back-and-forth sniping was partly a

263

product of their nervousness about the next day. Jean continued, "At least is not a puzzlement to me that someone tried to plant the money on the boy. He was scared, but he wasn't dumb. He thought that Beggs was trying to pin something on him by sending him the money so he could pounce as soon as he spent the first $100."

"Do you agree with Bobo that Beggs sent the money?" asked Rusty somewhat mollified. The war in his mind between the logic of Bobo's stealing the money and the sentiment of hoping Jean was right was tilting toward sentiment.

"Not necessarily. But I do think if Beggs didn't send it, at least he knew about it. Anyway, if the serial numbers on these bills match the record of the money that Max got from the jeweler—and they will—we'll know for sure that someone removed the money belt from Max Wein's body, dead or alive," Jean stated flatly. It's now "Max Wein's body"—no evasion or euphemism.

"And it still could have been Bobo," Rusty insisted.

"But I repeat," Jean answered, "Why would he come forth with the money now? Is he going to risk his happy new life by producing the money if he'd stolen it?"

"Maybe you are right, Jean. I guess I'm a little wary because you've had some sort of emotional investment in the kid's innocence all along. Let's lay that aside. What's in it for Beggs?"

"Perhaps living in the lap of luxury in the Caribbean somewhere. That's the word on him now."

Rusty wasn't convinced. "How would he pull that off?" he asked skeptically.

"Well, for one thing, Bobo says Beggs was being paid off by drug dealers."

"We've heard something about that," Rusty said, "and between you and me, we have plans to look into it. But even if it's true, the payoffs wouldn't continue down in the islands. Would what's left be enough to finance him down there? I doubt it."

Jean studied Rusty a moment, then shifted her position in her chair and leaned forward. Her soft voice was even lower than usual. "Then try this idea. Suppose someone else is helping to underwrite Beggs' fancy life down there wherever he is. All Beggs had to do to get paid a lot of money was to point the evidence toward Bobo and clear out. For his trouble, he lives the life of Riley away from his possible prosecution for his drug connections."

"Wait a minute, Jean." Rusty is excited. "Are you suggesting that someone might have paid off Beggs to diffuse the investigation and keep the focus on Bobo?" She didn't answer; she didn't have to. "Who could do that?" Rusty resumed, thinking out loud. "Are you suggesting Bill Long?"

"I'm not suggesting anyone in particular, just a theory. But Bill could afford to do it."

Rusty was turning crimson. "Motive, Jean. Motive, motive, motive!" His voice was rising and echoing a similar outburst when Jean first showed him the cut wire. He settled down a bit and asked. "Well, what about Bill? We haven't talked about him very much."

265

This launched a clinical review and search for a motive among all five of the birders as they had done a couple of times earlier, one by one.

They started with Bill. It helped Rusty to jot cryptic notes about each.

Long. Impeccable background. No discernible motive. Would be able to pay off Beggs if that's what happened. Suggested (knew?) where Wein's car would be found. Had opportunity to obliterate evidence.

Groot. Might have sent the spurious (?) post card from the West purportedly from Max Wein. Why? No evidence that her affair with Don Purvis was taking place at time of Wein's disappearance, but even if it did? Annie Crews would not have recognized Doris.

Purvis. Romantic involvement with two people linked to the events. Outspoken opponent of Jean's probing. Mood has swung from friendly to Jean, to unfriendly, back to friendly. Probably used Paula to obtain info about what Jean was doing and passed it on to others. Probable ringleader of "network." Blackmail victim?

Sanderson. Motive of money may be a little far-fetched but real. Lives above his earnings from photography. Did not share certain info about Max's personal life. Had opportunity to obliterate evidence. Surface friend of Jean's but never completely forthcoming. Presumably Wein's closest heir.

Smith/Martinez. Mystery woman: not even sure of her name. Has violence in her past. Max may have known her when she was a convicted felon, but no real discernible motive. Her reserved personality contrasts with her history.

Jean thought the discussion of Con ended it, but Rusty added Bobo to the list. Jean did not contribute to his summary notes.

Bobo. Known to department because of trouble-making past. Had the missing $4,500. Accepted at least $500 payoff money, maybe a lot more. Known to have been drinking in the neighborhood the night before the disappearance. Was prime suspect of not only Beggs but also Purvis and Sanderson and probably others.

So Rusty had his say about Bobo, and Jean asserted hers about Beggs.

Beggs. Made fast, unexplained exit. If not directly involved in disappearance may have cooperated with one of the others. Motive: Money or escape from prosecution for accepting payoffs from drug people. Said to be living in luxury somewhere in the Caribbean. Reputation for being rough on Indians, migrant workers, and Hispanics.

It was cleansing for them to review the dramatis personae once more. It diffused their emotions and helped them turn their concerns to the practicalities of the next morning. Rusty got up and opened a closet door in the hall. He brought out a large rolled-up map which he spread on the dining room table, holding down the corners with books. They pored over it, and Jean traced her planned walk for tomorrow. She had chosen the route because Rusty or someone else could watch her from across the saw grass prairie while being concealed in a hammock—a dense cluster of hardwoods.

Moreover, she could satisfy questions about why she would choose that route. Although the time of day would not be the best for recording the deep grunts of king rails, they had been heard along her planned hike. She would also tell her companions that she would be trying to record limpkins, gallinules, and possibly Virginia rails. She assured Rusty that this plan hung together as typical of the projects she pursued on Sunday mornings. In truth, for a moment she forgot her predicament and looked forward to the walk as an opportunity to add to her soon-due research report.

Rusty quickly grasped the layout. Then he paused and asked the question that both of them had been avoiding: "What if one of them asks you to accompany him or her along some other route, perhaps to an isolated area?"

She exhibited her wide-mouth smile and said without hesitation, "Then I'll go along." If that were the case, she conjectured that whoever it was might head to the site of the eagle's nest deep in the bald cypress swamp.

"Why there?"

"Because that's where I think something happened to Max Wein," she responded calmly. She reminded her friend that this was where she found the piece of fancy cloth, which she now was convinced was from the yarmulke she had seen Wein wearing in Sanderson's photo. She then carefully pointed out on the map the two trails to the nest area.

Rusty assured her that he, Joe Bob, Fred Billie, as well as a couple of other deputies he was planning to assign to the team would acquaint themselves with those two paths as well as Jean's primary route.

They talked earnestly about contingencies until it was time for Rusty to leave for his lunch at the Big Cypress Cafe with Joe Bob. As they moved toward the door, he said, "Will you be home this afternoon? I'd like to call you if either of us has any questions about the layout."

Jean nodded that she'd be at home, and Rusty said, "Good. Dawn and I will not be home tonight, but I'll reach you before we leave if I have a question." Then he paused and surrounded her little right hand with his two large ones. "I've got to say once more that I hope you will give this up." She gave him no satisfaction, only another smile.

On the drive back to the trailer, Jean chose a route through a suburban neighborhood. She was aware of a flash of color out of the corner of her eye. Could it be a painted bunting, a little beauty that she didn't see in Oak City? She understood that it was a little late in the season for the bird to be in South Florida, but a few stay year round. This bore investigation. She stopped her car at the curb along a paved street lined with wide lots and well kept homes and yards. She grabbed her field glasses, noiselessly got out, and scanned the trees and shrubs in several yards in the direction she had come from.

A boy about 12 asked her what she is "spying on," and she explained. She asked him if he'd ever seen a painted bunting. He was not sure. So she asked him if he'd ever seen "a little bird with a blue head, a scarlet belly (the lad grinned at the word), and green and purple back. A little bird."

His face lit up. "I have. I have seen that bird. I thought it was a teeny budgie. I have seen it in our yard across the street there," and he pointed with pride to an orderly yard fronting a yellow Spanish-style house with an orange tile roof.

The two new friends scanned various yards for the colorful little fellow, but without success. Jean did spot a pair of cardinals and let him view them through her binoculars. It was the first time he had really observed the handsome female.

Although the quest for the painted bunting was unavailing, Jean was grateful for the interlude. Here she was, on the eve of potentially the most dangerous day of her life, taking time to teach a boy about a bird. For the moment, she got away from the problem that nearly overwhelmed her. For the moment, she felt like what she really was: a gifted teacher and observer. For the first time, she ached to get back to Oak City and the classroom.

When she arrived at the trailer, she tried to reach the occupant of Beggs' former house, Terry Davis, again without success. That disappointment didn't prevent her from enjoying the first hearty, nutritious meal she'd had in 48 hours. Its centerpiece was a vegetarian vegetable soup that she had concocted.

Before turning on the radio to the Saturday afternoon opera, she called Don, as she had promised, to tell him she would join the group in the morning. His quiet little wife, Susan, answered and said with touching pride that he was at one of their son's Little League game where Don was a coach. Jean left her the message, and Susan was almost pathetically glad to help her husband in one of his activities.

But after Jean hung up, she wondered if what she did was very smart. The message would give Don and whomever he wished to share the information with a half day to plan for her arrival. Well, too late now, so she decided to call Doris also about her plans. She seemed ecstatic at the news. "Between you and I," she gushed, "I wondered if we would ever see you again, Jean."

"Good old ungrammatical Doris," Jean thought but said, "Not a chance that I wouldn't say good-bye to you and the others before I head back up to Oak City." Doris acted relieved, then asked if Jean were calling "from your new phone." They talked about that a bit and then rang off, after which Jean thought, "'New phone' indeed! They no longer even try to hide that they share everything they can learn about me and my activities. One of these times I'm going to challenge somebody and say, 'How did you know that?'" But this wasn't the time to rock the boat.

She was glad the opera was a light-hearted one, L'Elisir d'Amore, without a tragic heroine. Under the circumstances, she didn't want to have anything to do with tragic heroines.

The opera and the painted bunting episode were a couple of examples of how Jean managed to keep in touch with her regular life during these difficult days. They helped her keep a firm control of her emotions. But once she briefly gave in. She was at The Nature Center of the Conservancy of Southwest Florida in Naples, where she liked to go to learn more about sea turtles, fish, flora and other natural elements of the region. While there an injured great horned owl was brought to the wildlife rehabilitation facility. "I wonder if it could be 'my' owl," she mused. Then she realized what 'her' owl meant to her—possibly her life. She walked down a nature trail and had a good cry.

At the operas intermission, she tried Terry Davis one more time. Finally there was an answer on the second ring. It was a young-sounding female.

"Valerie?" asked Jean launching one of her little artifices.

"Who?" said the voice.

"I'm sorry," said Jean. "Isn't this the residence of Valerie and Ed Beggs?"

"Oh, my no. They haven't lived here for a couple of years."

"Oh goodness," faked Jean. "Do you know where they went? I went to high school with Val and was down here for a few days and thought I'd look her up."

"Well, they didn't leave together, I know that much," said the helpful voice. "She went to Jacksonville to be with her mother. We forwarded her mail for a week or two until the change of address form caught up, but I've lost the address."

"And Ed?"

"He went the other way. We sent a few pieces of mail to the general post office at Charlotte Amalie on St. Thomas, I think it was, but they soon stopped coming."

"And you say you bought the house from them a couple of years ago."

"No, we didn't buy it. We rent. Our landlords, the Blakelys, bought it. They live out west. We've never even met them."

Jean would have liked to ask her a few more questions, but decided against it. She'd learned a lot. She told the voice she was sorry she had bothered her and hung up. She sat there a couple of minutes, a faint smile on her face, thinking and sorting.

Her reverie was interrupted by a call from Rusty. He reported that he and Joe Bob got a good feel for the areas where she would be walking tomorrow. Later, away from the cafe, they'd gone over the area with Fred Billie, who felt he could cover Jean if she stuck to her route. They also had tramped both ways up to the eagle's nest. "Boy, that's a wild area," Rusty commented. "I don't see how that little disabled fellow could have gotten back there."

"Apparently he was a determined man. Also, remember the second route was much more drivable two years ago, before Andrew," Jean reminded him. "I checked that out with the weather people."

"Is there no end to your ingenuity?" Rusty asked with a chuckle, trying to be lighthearted at a deadly serious time.

Jean smiled and agreed that it was a desolate, nearly impenetrable area for someone who didn't know it, adding to herself, "That's why nobody has ever found Max Wein's body."

After a light supper, she tried to divert her mind by editing some of the material she planned to send to the Pearson Foundation, but her thoughts wandered. So she retired early and for bedtime reading decided to look around in the issues of the <u>Journal of Ornithology</u>. She was nagged by the thought that there must be a reason why Max had sequestered one of the issues and that later someone else stole it from the case file. If only she knew which issue it was. If only that sloppy secretary hadn't mistyped the year.

Or had she? Jean concentrated for a long time. Then she snapped her finger and turned to the July/August, 1991, issue, the date that the clerk had typed. She scanned contents, raced to one of the articles. Bingo! Here was an article that would have interested Max Wein intensely, that he surely would have saved. But it was in a late summer issue, and he had disappeared in the spring!

She threw her legs over the side of her narrow bed and sat there thinking. She looked at her watch. 8:20. She got to her feet, went to her phone, and called Information for a number in a Northern area code.

Jean awoke refreshed just before 4:15, when her alarm was set to ring. She tumbled out of her tiny bed, then took her time getting ready to leave. She dawdled over a cup of coffee and a slice of whole wheat toast while considering what might eventuate in the next hour or two. She checked out both her own tape recorder and a mini-model Rusty had given her. It was fitted with clasps that she attached to her underclothing. As she had the previous evening, she practiced once more how to start and stop it through her clothing without detection. She had inserted fresh 90-minute tapes in both machines, 45 minutes per side.

Even though Rusty had told her he would be away last night, she had tried to call him anyway about her discoveries of yesterday afternoon and evening. There was no answer, so she considered calling him at this early hour, but decided against it out of concern for his wife's condition. Jean is considerate to a fault.

Faint light was beginning to swathe the eastern sky as she stepped outside to get into her car. Stars that were bright when she walked to her car extinguished one by one as she proceeded on the familiar journey. Trees took form first in silhouette then in dimension and detail in the reddening foredawn. She compared the atmosphere of this late spring morning with the shadowy moonlit predawn drives when she first became part of the bird group.

To her the increasing light was a metaphor for the illumination now being cast on the dark puzzle that had absorbed her interest, first reluctantly, now passionately. She was expectant. Will the full light of this morning see the final piece in place?

She smiled as she noted another difference from her earlier Sundays: The nondescript Ford sedan was discreetly following her. "Rusty, ever protective Rusty," she thought with gratification, "always thinking of my safety." Thanks to his concern and thoroughness, she didn't carry the baggage of fear as she progressed toward possible exposure of Annie's killer…and Max's.

Yet if she could have gotten inside of her protector's head at this moment, she would have found that he didn't share her confidence. By the map light in an unmarked car, on a roadside turnoff that none of the birders was likely to drive by, Rusty, Joe Bob, and Fred Billie were once more going over the map of the land around Big Cypress Cafe, working out contingencies and safety nets, which they would pass on to three other deputies who would join them later.

And Jean herself, despite her confidence, couldn't expunge a sense of foreboding, a feeling that this would be her last trip over these familiar and friendly roads. The next hours might bring events that would tear apart the fabric of the breakfast group.

Because of this sense of finality, she drove more slowly than usual so that she could observe and appreciate the familiar landmarks and stirrings of nature as they became more distinct in the brightening morning. Her sense of the beauty of an environment so unlike that of Oak City was heightened: dry and wet prairies, hardwood hammocks, isolated clumps of slash pines dotting the landscape, roadside sloughs now no longer dry, the wakening birds, a bankside alligator.

The road crossed a little bridge that spanned a pretty water trail meandering who knows where, active with moorhens, egrets, and a kingfisher rattling raucously as it tore upstream inches above the water. Jean recognized the bridge and adjacent turnoff as a place she'd stopped once on her way back from breakfast to watch a pair of purple gallinules. That time there was no stream at all, just a damp, gray-brown bed of muck and a succession of little puddles, reminders of its past and future life. Now the late spring rains doused it regularly, enriching it with a healthy life as a bona fide little river searching to join the 60-mile wide "river of grass" that creeps down the imperceptible incline from Lake Okeechobee to Florida Bay. Perhaps, Jean mused, a millenium ago some courageous Calusa Indians might have used the same temporary watercourse to explore inland from their coastal settlements to set up camps in the interior, the relics of which were just now being discovered.

She made the turns that will take her to the cafe. She looked up and wished she hadn't seen three black vultures soaring in lazy, flapless circles as she neared the murky old cafe.

She followed Doris into the rutted parking area. Her friend waited to greet her, bending her large frame down to hug the little teacher wordlessly. Did the awkward woman's emotional display suggest that she too sensed that this could be the last gathering? Or knows it will be?

Anticipation exhilarated Jean. The unusual beauty of her slow-paced drive contributed to her buoyancy, but mostly it was the excitement the hunter feels on the verge of flushing out the prey. Even her walk up the neglected weedy path to the familiar badly patched screen door didn't dispel this feeling. But once inside the large dreary dining room, the heavy air came laden with a sense of gloom and rot that so often engulfed her there.

Jean had no firm views about the actuality of Satan, but if there were an Evil One, she thought surely he was lurking about in the corners of that restaurant on dark and dank early mornings.

Don was already there. His greeting was much more cordial than it had been in recent weeks; she wondered if it were an act.

He said, "Sooze gave me your message. Naturally I was delighted to learn you were coming." Jean noted that he used an affectionate nickname for his wife Susan in front of Doris. She caught a flicker of reaction in Doris—a slight widening of her eyes.

The other three arrived within five minutes. They did not seem surprised to see Jean; the network was still active.

Other than Doris's emotional moment on the parking lot, the social atmosphere was quite like all the other Sunday mornings, on the surface at least. There were no overt references to the outburst of two weeks ago. Maybe there was unusual warmth in Con's face when she said Hello, or maybe Jean just imagined it. Maybe Bill Long was even more courtly than usual, or maybe she just imagined that too. Maybe Sandy Sanderson was trying a little too hard to be funny, or maybe she was being overly analytical.

They slid into the booth in their usual alignment— Doris, Don, and Sandy on the red plastic bench along the wall in front of the unwashed windows with Jean,

Con, and Bill in chairs facing them, left to right. Jean could look into the faces of the threesome opposite, but would be careful to follow her mother's long ago advice not to stare. She didn't want to put anyone on guard. She would have little opportunity to observe Con at her right or Bill at her far right.

They ordered breakfast, and as Marie Billie leaned across Jean to pass plates to the those on the other side of the table, she placed her free hand on Jean's left shoulder and squeezed it.

This act of tenderness was not characteristic of the jolly woman. Jean wondered if it signaled that Marie was aware of what she was trying to do for Bobo and for Granny.

Breakfast chatter was typical. They talked of their projects and unusual recent sightings. Jean wondered if anyone would ask her about her morning plans. Someone did. Surprisingly, it was Con Smith. She <u>sounded</u> innocent when she asked, "And what are your plans today, Jean?" Jean mentioned the king rails and the limpkin.

Talk turned to other subjects, including current political events and warm inquiries about the impending graduation of Con's son, Peter. Bill Long said he was so impressed with Peter at Jean's barbecue, where the young man had made a hit with his ailing wife, Alma.

Then he paused, projected his long neck out over the table, and looked down to Jean. "Oh, Jean, was that nice lady we met there the one we read about so tragically in the paper?" Jean said it was. She sensed they wanted her to expand. She told about the experience of going to the funeral. They were sympathetic.

Doris, the one who hadn't met Annie, surprisingly was the one who asked if "they" were making any progress in finding the killer.

"Not that I know of," said Jean, engulfed in a surreal moment; the killer was probably at that table!

Bill, the unchosen chairman, pushed his chair back and stood. "Well, time I go out and see what I can find." The others rose almost as one and began to mill around taking cameras out of cases, fiddling with their spotting scopes, getting change for Marie's tips, and discussing whether to take along rainproof jackets because of mildly threatening skies.

Amid this disorganized wandering about, one of the birders sidled up to Jean and said quietly and warmly, "I thought we might go out together this morning, Jean." Jean was not surprised by the invitation nor by the person who issued it. The sensible course would have been to decline, then tell Rusty who it was and what she learned yesterday. But she was too much the captive of her quest to do that and thereby forfeit the chance to get the evidence she sought. Her calm reply belied her excitement. "Fine. Want to go with me up the road to listen for the king rails?" But the person was evasive, saying, "Let's go out on the parking lot and talk it over."

Once outside, her companion scanned the surrounding area as the other birders dispersed on foot, then genially made a suggestion: "Why don't we get in my car and drive to where we can hike up to the eagles' nest area? Some wonderful warblers and vireos have been chirping around up there, I understand. You can record some of their spring singing. We can catch the rails on the way back."

Now Jean was sure that this was the anticipated showdown. She proceeded with a plan she and Rusty had worked out. She had deliberately left a microphone in the car. "Sounds interesting," she said to her companion with perfect calm. "Wait a second while I go to the car and get my other mike. Does a much better job picking up songs of little birds than the built-in one does," and before the other person had a chance to dissuade her, she was hurrying to her car. While there, she got the mike, and making sure she wasn't observed, she raised the car's aerial. This was a prearranged signal that she was out alone with another birder and was not going on the marsh path as planned. One of Joe Bob's assignments was to check the car and radio Rusty and Fred if the antenna was up.

Jean returned with the mike. Her companion led her around the back of the car to the far side, which Jean interpreted as a maneuver to avoid being seen by the others. Under different circumstances, Jean probably would not have noticed this subtle little tactic. She climbed in the car, deliberately pulling herself in by grabbing the dashboard beneath the glove compartment. She was leaving fingerprints in places that her adversary might not think to wipe clean.

Talk was awkward as they drove toward the trails that lead to the eagles' nest. Jean spotted what she thought was a limpkin dabbling for snails on the margin of a slough. She asked the driver to stop a moment. This gave her the opportunity to get out and activate the concealed tape recorder as well as the larger one.

It also bought a little time for one of the deputies to locate her. Starting now, she had 45 minutes of recording time before the machines would click off. Would that be enough time? Would her companion hear the click?

The driver showed no interest in the limpkin—which was not the usual behavior of any member of the Sunday breakfast group—and left the engine running. The limpkin wasn't cooperative, so Jean had to get back to the car soon if her companion wasn't to suspect she was purposely stalling. As she got in, she muttered, "They are supposed to do their wailing on dark days like this, but not this fellow."

After they started up again, the driver uttered the first words that were tinged with hostility. "You don't need that thing now," indicating the tape recorder, "Why don't you turn it off?"

Jean agreed, "Good idea," and turned it off with a flourish, happy to preserve some tape.

The car was being driven fairly slowly. Jean had mixed feelings about that; it gave a little more catch-up time for the deputies, but it used up minutes on the mini. The two birders were silent until the driver said, "You don't seem your usual chatty self this morning, Jean. Any particular reason?"

She shrugged her little body and said, "No reason at all. I guess I didn't realize it." Then, as if to validate her interest in being "chatty," she pointed off to the right and said, "Look, a red-shouldered hawk at two o'clock. At least, I <u>think</u> it's a red-shouldered. Can we stop and make an identification?"

"Come on, Jean. You know it's a red-shouldered. Anyone would know that. Why are you so anxious to keep stopping all the time?"

She was beginning to show a little edginess. "I didn't realize I was. Let's get on to the eagles' nest."

"OK, forget I said anything." The car was slowing to enter West Road #2, the lane that led to the turnaround where Jean had seen Don's car and soon discovered Doris and him together.

They were silent until they reached the turnaround and got out of the car to begin their tramp. Her companion asked, "You've been to the nest before. See anything interesting?"

"Well, I had magnificent views of the eagles and their chicks from both approaches."

"Both approaches?" There was surprise in the voice, if not concern. "I thought the other way was impassable because it was never cleaned up after hurricane Andrew did his thing."

"Well, I got there," she said noncommitally. There was no edge in her voice now. Then she added, "I just wanted to see if anyone who wanted to could get there."

It was her first attempt to elicit comments that might have use on the tape. The other person glanced at Jean, but didn't take the bait. "See anything else of interest back there?"

"An osprey was hovering around."

"Nothing special about that," was the sour comment.

Jean looked at the other person but discerned no reaction to her feeler. She assessed her situation. The path they were on didn't just evolve; it appeared that

283

years ago it had been deliberately hacked out and graded. On their left was a cypress swamp dotted with ancient trees with their silver and black bark and numerous "knees" poking through the motionless onyx water. Occasionally, brambles of palmettos and sabal palms invaded the swamp; she recognized the trysting place of Don and Doris. The late spring rains had made the area much wetter than it was then.

On their right was a pinkish-brown saw grass prairie, and a little beyond it a large hardwood hammock of mahogany, live oak, and red-barked gumbo limbo trees. At its nearest point, the hammock was only about 75 feet from their path. It would afford a good cover for anyone assigned to protect Jean.

She tried to place herself to the left of the other person so that she would be shielded from the line of fire from the hammock. But her companion would have none of it, almost forcibly keeping Jean to the right side of the path. Seeds of suspicion have sprouted.

"Stay on the path, Jean. You don't want get into that muck, do you?"

Despite the somewhat sneering comment about the osprey moments ago, her companion brought up the subject again. "Did you see the osprey nest?"

"Yes I did." (She hadn't actually, but she would have to force the issue soon, and here was a chance.) "Aren't they amazing structures? I've seen some abandoned ones and you might find almost anything in there that catches their eyes." She was trying to sound very clinical, but then added, "Maybe a rag, a piece of fancy cloth, even a towel."

The other hiker only said, "Everybody knows that, Jean," but at the words "a piece of fancy cloth" Jean was quite aware of a sudden turn toward her and a tightening of facial muscles.

Clearly Jean was in better control than her adversary was. And clearly the other person didn't know how much Jean knew. How far should she go? Here was an opening to give an unmistakable signal that she knew that Max was killed in this area—that she had found a piece of his yarmulke and speculated that the rest of it was in the osprey's nest. But she was not ready to be that direct. She wanted to buy more time to be sure Rusty and company had found her. She took a furtive look at her watch; just a few minutes left on the mini's tape—if it were working.

They were beginning to draw away from the hammock out to the right and toward the one with the eagle's nest. The cypress swamp on their left was getting blacker, wetter, more foreboding. But to the right, across the saw grass, she could almost make out the the debris-littered road that she had struggled over when trying out the second path to the nest. She could glimpse what almost certainly were human forms making their way through the debris. She needed just a little more time.

Just then an anhinga, frightened by their approach, spiraled straight up from a young cypress where it was drying its wings. It screamed its alarm cry. Her companion flinched.

"I must record this," Jean whispered, simultaneously flipping on her recorder. She was trying to act as if they were on a routine bird walk.

"Oh no you don't," shouted her companion, pulling the instrument off of her shoulder, unsnapping the strap by force, much like a purse snatcher does, and flinging it into the black water.

Even at that perilous moment Jean was rational. She realized the instrument could be recovered later and its tape might have an identifiable voice on it although the words might not incriminate the speaker. But it could be important evidence if the tiny concealed recorder wasn't functioning or was also ripped from her.

Jean rubbed her neck where the strap gouged into it. "Why did you do that?" Jean asked plaintively. And then daringly, "You shouldn't let a bird's alarm call upset you so."

Her companion looked at her with hatred and snarled, "I don't know what you are talking about." But Jean knew that a message had been delivered and it had hit home.

She was emboldened to probe further. "Coming after me that morning was a foolish mistake. I didn't know it was you then. You were no more a suspect than anyone else. Your needless act cost a dear woman's life."

Believing that their talk was unrecorded, her adversary was less guarded. "You were ruining everything. Maybe you didn't know it was me, but you had gone too far. You seemed intent on clearing the Indian kid. Why? Everybody was satisfied that he did it, and that was that. He was free. He wasn't going to be indicted. Nobody was getting hurt. Then you got chummy with that idiot Torrance, and we found out about that kidnapping up north. I could see my perfect setup disintegrating. Besides, I…"

The thought trailed off, so Jean finished it. "Besides you knew you'd made some mistakes that I might find out about. Like leaving Max's yarmulke back here when you did whatever you did to him. Or leaving a paper trail when Beggs' house was sold. Or failing to remove the journal from Max's car."

"But Beggs took care of the journal." Then the voice took on a nasty mock prissiness. "Oh, you smug little busybody, you think you know so much. You don't, but what little you know, you shouldn't."

Jean was at a point of no return. She was either covered or she wasn't, but this was her chance to get more incriminating words on the little tape recorder.

She quickly reviewed a mental roster of possibilities and decided to go for broke. "You don't know how much I know and have told others." She wished for a moment that she wasn't bluffing and <u>had</u> called Rusty this morning with her latest news. "But one thing I don't know and never will and that's why you thought the information Max had about you was worth two lives."

"What information?" The other person was snarling now. "I don't know what you're talking about, and neither do you, so shut up."

"Don't I remember someone saying one morning that he hated cowbirds and cuckoos because they make a smaller birds do all the work and then take credit?"

In a mocking aside, her adversary addressed the swamp. "Has this little bluffer gone mad? What on earth has that got to do with anything?"

287

"Just this." Jean's voice was steady. "Max caught you claiming in print you saw birds you never saw and stealing his research data. Max did the work; you claimed the credit. He was the little bird who did the work; you were the cowbird who claimed the result. It happens in different academic disciplines—and at all kinds of prestigious institutions. It's lamentable but on the scale of crime, it's about a two. Murder's a ten."

Bill Long's demeanor changed from fierce arrogance to painful whimpering. "But it would have been so <u>humiliating</u> for me to be exposed." Emotions now out of control, he was sobbing, then recovered. "You don't really know me, Jean, and neither did Max. But you are wrong when you say two lives. It will be three."

Excited as Jean was to have this confession on the tape (if it was working), she knew she must venture a bluff if she had a chance to survive. "You would never get away with killing me. I've told too many people what I know. They'll have airtight proof against you."

The two were lurching along more slowly now, approaching the eagles' nest hammock. "Airtight proof, hell," the other said scornfully. "I knew you were trying to get me to say things on that tape recorder that would incriminate me; that's why I tore it off of you. You're smart, but not that smart. The tape is useless in that muck. But just to make sure, I'll retrieve it on my way back and destroy the tape. Then I'll rejoin that stupid little group of birders, just as I did the other time, and act worried when you don't return. I'll even lead the search for you." The once engaging face is contorted in indescribable ugliness that Jean never before had seen on a human.

Bill continued. "It'll be a piece of cake this time. I can drive my own car back. The other time I had to take a calculated risk and drive that scheming little weasel's car to the hammock where everybody thinks he disappeared. Of course, I knew where everyone was planning to go that morning, so I could plan a route where they wouldn't see me." He was spitting out words as if trying to get rid of a mouthful of venom.

"Better give yourself up. Ouch. You're hurting me!" Jean reacted as the 71-year-old's amazingly strong grip seized her left arm and his sharp nails dug into it. She was aware that his free left hand was groping for something, perhaps in his pocket.

Just then she heard the dreaded sound of the mini's tape wheels groaning and squealing. The grip on her arm tightened even more. A hideous voice sputtered, "What's that? Sounds like a…"

"Duck, Jean, Duck!" Rusty's strong voice screamed from the eagle's hammock, now close on the right. Bill sensed that Jean was in the line of fire and clutched her body to keep her there, a hostage and shield. She was aware that her captor's left hand had found what it was groping for and that his arm was being raised.

A single gunshot made a piercing racket. The bullet found a victim. Jean heard what she supposed was the sound of shattering bone followed by a hideous half-gasp, half-scream. She felt nothing; she was not hit. But Long was. Still gripping her, he staggered, fell, and pulled Jean down too. A short piece of lead pipe rolled a few inches away. It had dropped from his left hand, to be used to crash into Jean's skull.

Jean extricated herself from the grip and examined her adversary. She noticed that the bullet seemed to have entered the left shoulder area from the rear and exited the front.

From the rear? Pieces of information that were too startling for her brain to process seconds ago now were begging for explanations. How could the bullet come from behind, while Rusty's shouts, just a second before the gunshot, came from her right and front?

Joe Bob perhaps? She would have to work that mystery out later; for now she had her hands full trying to attend to Bill, who was writhing in pain and in the mortification of defeat.

She was aware that Rusty and Fred were sloshing through the saw grass toward them. Rusty shouted, asking if she was all right. She assured him that she was, but he and Fred had their pistols drawn as they approached. Their flushed faces were drenched with sweat, their pant legs and shoes sodden with water from the wet prairie, their bare forearms slashed by the sharp grasses.

Both men gasped as they recognized the murderer. Fred exclaimed "Oh no!" while Rusty merely scowled in contempt at the person, now whimpering like a wounded animal. Satisfied that there was no immediate danger, Rusty turned to Jean and extended his two large hands and placed them around her two upper arms. He pulled her to him, saying only, "Thank God."

Meanwhile Fred radioed to Joe Bob to send the ambulance that the ever thorough Rusty had standing by out at the road. He then dropped to his knees and joined Rusty in an effort to administer first aid. In time, they stanched the bleeding. Then they tried to quiet and care for the murderer.

The latter rose to one knee and, hunched over with hands on the firm path to provide a boost, implored, "Let me get up, please. Please." It was a plaintive voice, altogether different from the guttural one that had been snarling at Jean. Taken by surprise, Rusty and Fred acceded to this unexpected request. They raised up the spent, wounded body, serving as a pair of human crutches.

Suddenly, with a mighty final effort, Bill Long wrested himself from their grasp and plunged into two feet of black swamp water beside the path. Dripping with muck, he pulled himself up, placed his hands around his left thigh and tugged at it, freeing that leg from the resistance of the ooze, and moved it forward. He repeated this labored process once more, then flung his body into a deeper hole that had been hollowed out by alligators as a damp refuge in the dry season. He spoke some unintelligible words, but later the observers agreed they heard "Take care of Alma" among them. The blood of the reopened wound floated upward in an expanding dark red blob atop the black water.

The men plunged in behind him. Against the twin pulls of Bill's suicidal struggle and the mire, they managed to drag him back to the path. He became quiet. They tried to clean him up and calm him while they awaited the ambulance, which arrived at the turnaround quickly. The attendants ran down the path, then put the man's sodden, filthy body on a litter as he looked up at Jean.

One of the emergency technicians listening to Long's chest reported that he heard the wounded man whisper, "Jean, you were right."

The activity had been so feverish that neither Jean nor Rusty nor Fred had had a moment to consider where the saving bullet had came from. Jean assumed that her ears had deceived her and that one of the men had fired it. Inexperienced as she was with bullet wounds, she supposed she had confused the entrance and exit wounds. Not until the ambulance started off were they aware of another presence in the deep shade behind them. They turned around. It was Con, aka Consuela Martinez, world-class marksman, a small caliber pistol in her hand.

Jean exclaimed, "Con! You!" She choked. She could say no more.

"I was worried about you, Jean. That's why I asked you where you were going this morning at breakfast. Then I saw that awful man talking to you. He was watching me and the others, so I acted as if I was starting out on the way I said I would. Then I sneaked back and spied on you out on the parking lot from the ladies room window. It didn't look like you were headed to the swamp with the king rails that you had mentioned, so I decided to follow you."

The two women embraced, crying.

～ EPILOGUE ～

Despite the best efforts of Rusty and Fred Billie as well as quick and effective action of the emergency crew and the E.R. people, Bill Long died the next day in the hospital. Con's shot didn't kill him. A member of the team that tried to save the defeated man put it like this: "He died from the combination of the gunshot wound, near drowning in the alligator hole, and self-loathing."

Sandy Sanderson soon faced charges for appropriating his cousin's effects before Max was declared dead. With the news of Bill Long and the end of the conspiracy against Bobo, Sanderson became evasive and dispirited. A warrant was obtained to search Max's apartment, and it had been all but stripped of furnishings, artwork, and valuables. Rusty had no problem bringing Sandy in and getting him to admit that he had converted the items to cash.

Charges also were pending against Consuela for owning and firing an unregistered firearm. Rusty was busy talking to legal experts about tactics that would make it easy on her. Besides she had strong public opinion on her side. She became a media favorite when she coolly described her decision to follow when she saw Bill draw Jean aside. She sneaked to her car and got a gun out of the glove compartment.

"Even though you knew it was unregistered and you could get in big trouble if you used it?" a television reporter asked.

"Small price to pay," she replied, and the phrase became a banner headline in one of the Monday evening newspapers. Jean and Con were destined for a lifetime friendship.

Not so with Jean's first friend in the group, Doris Groot. Before she headed back to Oak City, Jean suggested a farewell lunch with Doris. Although Doris had been very affectionate before they left the cafe the last morning, she declined the invitation and was cool on the phone. Jean had never told anyone but Rusty and Joe Bob about the affair with Don or her reasoning that Doris had sent the phony post card from "Max." But she sensed that Doris felt Jean was responsible for the end of the romance and had also probably doped out her awkward attempt to divert attention from her lover with the post card. The most likely reason for Doris' coolness, however, wouldn't have occurred to Jean. It was that Doris was jealous of Con's new close friendship with Jean.

Don Purvis had confessed his affair with Doris to his wife and muttered unconvincingly to Rusty, "My priority now is to save my marriage." The word was that he was sending out his resume.

Don's other conquest, Paula, was another victim of the events. Rusty liked her and her work, but she had made too big a mistake to overlook. He had dismissed her for divulging confidential information without authorization. He gave her the most generous terms that the rules permitted. She immediately had found a fulltime position in a popular dress shop where she'd been working part-time and went to work Monday morning.

As to Jean, after Bill was taken away she gave in to pent up human emotion. She began to sob and shiver and was in a state of near collapse. There was talk about taking her to a hospital, but Rusty was concerned about the media finding her there and making a fuss. Instead, he arranged to have her sent in an unmarked car to his mother-in-law's comfortable house in a quiet Bonita Springs neighborhood.

The mother-in-law, Helen Everson, was a recently retired RN who knew just how to care for Jean. She was a tall, still pretty widow in her late fifties who had the air of authority that characterizes good nurses. Her former employer, a family physician, was called and prescribed conservative medications. Jean recovered quickly and wanted to go back to her trailer Sunday evening. That was out of the question, but they did agree that she could attend a controlled press conference, which was scheduled at a Naples hotel on Tuesday morning at 11:00.

With Jean sequestered, the media had gotten its stories from Rusty and Joe Bob as well as Consuela, Don, and Doris. But they craved to quiz the woman they'd described in heroic terms. For the occasion she had nothing to wear but the tramping clothes she'd worn that last Sunday. Rather than have someone try to fetch something suitable from the trailer, she became one of Paula's first patrons. Jean knew she would be the center of media attention that Bill Long's prominence brought. She had turned down a feeler from Good Morning America but rather liked the thought that some TV film might find its way to the homes of her Oak City students and they would learn that an owl had essentially saved her life. And maybe, perhaps unconsciously, she also wanted her special friend, Rusty Torrance, to remember her as more than a drab little nobody. For once she looked on her appearance as a positive opportunity.

Paula rose to the occasion and brought out a nicely tailored light blue size 2 petite cotton suit to Helen Everson's home. It fit Jean just right. She accented it with a silk scarf with an appropriate bird motif. To replace Jean's ever present bulky New Balance shoes, Paula found some bone-colored pumps with enough of a heel to make a difference. With the help of Paula and Helen, Jean managed to control her hair in a soft, fluffy wave.

At exactly 11:00 Tuesday morning Rusty entered the hotel's largest meeting room from a side door followed by Jean, Con, Don, Doris, and Joe Bob. The media people strained to get their first look at Jean, whispering to each other about the small woman. She, in turn, was taken aback by the number of journalists and cameras and lights. She never did get used to the competitive hand waving for attention, but on the whole, the media representatives were respectful of her recent ordeal.

Rusty went to the microphone and said. "Good morning, ladies and gentlemen. I believe most of you already know most of us, so I'll skip the introductions except to the lady who worked this complicated story out and then bravely confronted the killer. Jean McKay."

Jean strode confidently to the mike and smiled her broad smile. Apparently, the journalists were expecting a prepared statement and were quiet. After a few seconds, Jean simply said, "OK, fire away." She acknowledged a CNN reporter whose face was familiar to her.

The reporter wanted to know how Jean narrowed in on Long. She reviewed the first few weeks of gradually increasing suspicion that someone in the group knew something about Max Wein's disappearance. "I even entertained the notion of a conspiracy by all five—sorry Con, Doris, and Don."

In time she could find only one remote suggestion of a motive, the show of prosperity in the face of claimed poverty by Sanderson. "Bill Long never gave me a serious reason to suspect him for a long time. He was such an elegant gentleman; his polish masked his underhanded deeds. For instance, he directed the search to Panther Hammock (where Bill had driven Mr. Wein's car) and then volunteered himself and Sandy Sanderson to go there to look for clues. In doing so they obliterated any footprints Long had made a couple of hours earlier. For two years it was assumed that whatever happened, happened at Panther Hammock. No one had any reason to think otherwise until I found a piece of Wein's yarmulke several miles away in a desolate area."

Another reporter asked Jean, "I'm still not clear about a motive. What was it and how did you dope it out?"

Jean said, "I began to note a character flaw, you might call it, that possibly could lead to a motive. It was so unlikely that I could barely entertain it, even to myself, not to mention Sheriff Torrance. But as I reexamined my impressions of my friends I became struck with the idea that Bill Long was the most compulsive, intensely competitive bird lister I'd ever known. After a few Sundays, I noticed that he always had the longest list, that no one ever saw a bird that he also didn't claim to see, and he usually claimed to see one or two that nobody else had. So I began to question to myself whether he was always totally honest about his sightings."

"And was he?"

"Apparently not. As I became increasingly suspicious of that I began to think that somehow this could lead to a motive, outrageous though it seemed. After working up to be a top lawyer he couldn't stand being anything but a champion bird watcher. And when Max Wein caught him appropriating his records without credit, I guess Long also couldn't stand the thought of being publicly humiliated over such a relatively trivial thing as cheating on bird sightings if Wein exposed him. In fact, he said so Sunday morning."

Rusty added, "It's on the tape that Jean got. By the way, a psychiatrist who listened to the tape and tried to talk to Bill before he died said he believed the man was showing signs of being mad. The senseless murder of Annie Weeks substantiates that."

Jean sighed, paused a few seconds, then recovered and told them why she went to Great White Heron Key and found the ranger had good records of the separate visits of both Max and Long. Later when she found Wein's work in Bill's article, Jean surmised that Bill photocopied the ranger's copy of Max's research and put it into an article under his own name.

"Explain about the journal. Wasn't there something funny about the date?" This came from an AP reporter.

"The <u>Journal of Ornithology</u> dated July/August 1991 was listed on the inventory of items found in Max Wein's car. Since Wein had disappeared in March of that year, that date was impossible, so I assumed the secretary had simply typed the wrong date. Anyway, when I asked to see it, it was missing, whatever the date. If Wein thought it important enough to lock it up in a concealed compartment of his station wagon, I thought it could contain a clue. And since it was missing, my index of suspicion was raised even farther. Somehow, I had to see a copy."

Then Jean recounted how she sent for back issues of the year of the disappearance, 1991, and of 1990 on the assumption that the inventory contained the wrong date. She examined them all up through the issue that would have been current at the time of the disappearance. She could find nothing that would suggest why Wein would save it and lock it up.

"On a whim I decided to look at the issue that bore the date the typist had listed, even though it was <u>after</u> the date of the disappearance. There in the July/August 1991 issue was a scholarly article by G. Williamson Long Jr. claiming sightings of birds well out of their usual range—with carefully documented records, which of course were Wein's records."

"I still don't get how the future date got on the issue," the reporter persisted.

Jean explained: "It turned out that the secretary correctly typed the 'issue' date, but it wasn't an issue. It was a prepublication copy of a single article, not an 'issue.' The publisher sends copies of articles in advance to experts on the topic for their critiques and approval. I confirmed that by calling the editor Saturday night. Fortunately, he was home and recalled that Long's original draft was a general article and the editor had asked for more specific details. When Bill made extensive additions (Max's data), the editor recalled that they had sent the revised article to Max Wein as an expert on birds out of their usual territory. He said the details were still fairly vivid in his mind because he'd read of Wein's disappearance at about the same time and regretted not getting his reaction to the revisions.

"The editor also told me they have a high-tech typesetting system where the advance review copy already has the the name of the journal, issue date, and so forth, all made up on the page. That was the form of the revised article they sent Mr. Wein for approval and why the typist entered the future date of the article."

Jean was tiring a little, so Rusty took over while she drank some water. "On the tape that Jean got of Long's confession, Bill said, 'Beggs took care of the article.' We assume that Beggs showed Long the inventory and destroyed the article. For a price, of course."

"So Ed Beggs was heavily involved?" The question came from a Naples reporter who had covered the crime beat when Beggs was in office and was interested in angles that involved him.

Jean resumed, "I'm afraid so. Without any evidence, he targeted young Bobo Jumper as the prime suspect and apparently the birders bought it, pushed subtly by Sanderson and Long each for a different reason." With a wry smile she added, "At least I guess that's what happened. I wasn't there when they talked about it."

The media didn't catch the irony of her last remark, but Don Purvis did. "Jean is right," he chimed in. "We'd get together without Jean, especially recently, and discussed how to deal with what I called her probing. Long was relatively quiet in those sessions. But now I realize he would give a subtle nudge here and there and really was in control of us all along. Skills of a big time lawyer, I guess. If a killer ever had a good thing going for him, it was Bill. He didn't even have to push Beggs' idea that Bobo did it; he had Sanderson and the rest of us, especially me, to do it for him. All he had to do was sit back and gently fan the flames at the right moments. He stage-managed the whole thing."

Although Jean was still unhappy with Don, she appreciated what he said and looked back over her shoulder at him and smiled. Then she continued. "When I learned Beggs took off suddenly, I was even more sure that he was involved somehow. Just a few days ago we even talked about Bill theoretically as a person who could have bankrolled Beggs' reported lavish lifestyle in the Caribbean. That is exactly what happened."

"Bill probably discovered the money belt with the $4,500 in it when he tussled the little man's body about," Joe Bob added, glad to have the spotlight. "If the body was found, the missing belt would clinch the motive of robbery. Then when Beggs pointed his sights on Bobo, Bill reasoned that he would be home free if he could foist the bills on Bobo since their serial numbers were known. Beggs went along. Fortunately, Bobo didn't.

"Then there was his house."

"Yes," said Jean, "just last Friday I learned that Beggs sold his house one day after he offered it for sale and got top dollar," Jean explained. She recounted how she found the names of the buyers, Wilma and Dan Blakeley. She remembered that Wilma was Bill's daughter's name. Quite a coincidence. She found that the Blakeleys were absentee landlords, so she concluded that Bill had bought it for his daughter as an investment and that put a wad of legitimate money in Beggs' pocket.

"When Wein discovered Long had stolen his research, he must have confronted Long. Know anything about that?" asked a writer from Oak City who came down for the story.

Jean could only guess, but a receipt from a Holiday Inn for the night before was found in the victim's car. She surmised that he arranged a meeting with Bill there that Saturday night, at which time he confronted Bill.

"Mr. Wein may have threatened to call the editor and expose Bill if he didn't withdraw the article," she hypothesized.

"I suppose Bill may have appeased Max by telling him he would. That concession would have allowed him to approach Max on fairly amiable terms in the area of the remote eagle's nest that Sunday morning. Or maybe he sneaked up on him. We'll never know for sure."

Jean was gracious but visibly tiring. Rusty said, "Good place to stop," and brought the conference to a close.

* * *

In a few days things wound down. Jean finished her project and began packing. Soon she would be back in Oak City going over a lesson plan for a summer school session. She learned that the local outlets for the major networks as well the cable news channels carried at least snippets of the press conference. And, yes, many of her students saw her.

The night before she was to leave Joe Bob and his wife Marge invited Jean, the Torrances, Consuela and her son, and Bobo and his new bride, Carol, to his fraternal lodge for a farewell dinner. They gathered in the bar where Jean surprised the others by quizzing the bartender knowledgeably about beers and ordering a Sam Adams. Then the nine of them trooped into a small private room for dinner. Ten places were set. At the tenth Joe Bob had placed a stuffed owl.

ABOUT THE AUTHOR

Phillips Huston has published dozens of magazine articles and editorials, mostly on medical and business subjects. He has written a successful business book and was the founding editor of three journals. As an avocation, he has had a lifelong interest in birding and has also been published in a birding journal.

In *Alarm Cry* he has married his knowledge of birding with his writing skills to produce a mystery novel set in the swamps and forests that surround Naples, Florida, where he lives. He is a trail guide and lecturer at the Conservancy of Southwest Florida museum in Naples.

Huston is a native of Indianapolis and an English literature graduate of Princeton University where he served on the news board of the *Daily Princetonian.*

Printed in the United States
1455400001B/175-255

9 781410 731647